The Jefferson Files

- the expanded edition

by Martin Herman

194 Rodney Press

The Jefferson Files – *the expanded edition*
...A WILL JAMES MYSTERY
Copyright ©2015, 2016 Martin Herman
ISBN: 978-1-945211-00-3 PRINT
Library of Congress Number: 2016905028
First printing: February, 2015
Second printing: August, 2015
Third printing: May, 2016 (*the expanded edition*)
Fourth printing: August, 2016 (*the expanded edition*)
Fifth printing: January, 2017 (*the expanded edition*)
Sixth printing: June, 2017 (*the expanded edition*)
Printed in the United States of America
Published and Distributed by:

194 Rodney Press

521 Simsbury Road, Bloomfield, CT 06002

"The Jefferson Files" by Martin Herman

It is 1806; a powerful and criminal secret society has almost complete control over many of the elected officials, international finance, and commerce in the young nation. Its leaders arrange for a dissident to be brutally murdered and left floating in the Potomac River so that the body surfaces within clear site of Thomas Jefferson's White House.

This criminal act is intended to send a message to the President and all those around him: 'the society's power should know no limit – elected officials – including the president – must acknowledge and support us, allow us to do whatever we want, when and wherever we choose, or suffer the consequences'.

Almost two hundred years later, after discovering a hidden diary written by someone who lived in the White House during that time, a small group of college students and a world class computer hacker learn all there is to know about this particular crime... the identity of the victim and what, if anything, Jefferson did about it? They also learn all about the secret society.

By digging into this two hundred year old crime the students attract the attention of the modern day version of the secret society. The current leader threatens the student's very existence - but rather than retreat, the students decide to fight back.

- *the expanded edition*

In this expanded edition the author added about 10% more copy than in the first printed version in order to expand and advance the story line while further developing some of the characters. These additions are in response to the massive amount of reader correspondence received since the novel was first published in February, 2015.

Dedication

To Jessica Weitz, a remarkable and accomplished young woman whose very first breath gave me the title that means the most to me – "Dad". I wish I had been as good as she is at harmonizing the needs and responsibilities of a family with the often excessive demands of a professional career.

To Aimee Herman-Durica, who cares so very much for the exploited, oppressed, and rejected people around her and matches her concerns with her words and deeds each and every day, and who edited this manuscript with the understanding of a writer and the love of a daughter.

To Lora Chan, who encouraged me to publish this manuscript and whose intelligence, basic honesty, support, and counsel are traits which I grow to appreciate more with every passing day.

To Jonathan Weitz, an intelligent and thoughtful young man who is wise beyond his years and the kind of father/ role model I wish I had when I was growing up.

To Barry Gray, New York radio personality during the 1950's and 1960's, whose late night conversations with politicians helped turn me into the political news junkie I am to this day.

PART ONE

Chapter 1
Sunday 12 January, 1806,
Washington City, District of Columbia –

Pre-dawn during the middle of January in almost any east coast city can be filled with all sorts of intimidating sights, sounds, and unexplained comings and goings; most of which seem to be far less troublesome in the light of day. On this specific night, in America's newly designated capital situated far from major population centers, it all seems to be far more menacing for Horace Freeman. On the best of nights the shadows radiating from the many lanterns as they sway in the wind barely illuminate the unfinished walkways much less the hazards surrounding each of the massive construction sites. Most days Horace can easily deal with the darkness and visualize the hope and potential greatness this *work in progress* represents... but not today.

Horace was Thomas Jefferson's body man. Although both Horace and his wife, Becky, were officially registered as slaves, Horace was generally able to come and go as though he were a free man. He usually walked proudly through the new streets, tall and dignified, giving little notice to the few people still up and around or the stray animals foraging for warmth and food. He related the sights and smells of the new construction with the hopes that many had for the young nation. Although always deep in the background, he was proud in the knowledge that he held a front row seat to history. These walks provided an easy separation from his full and active day while providing him a little time to think through the events of the day and allow him enough time to shape them into interesting little stories he could share with Becky when he returned to their room.

In good weather or bad, Horace felt safe along the makeshift streets that surrounded the new nation's President's house. Shortly after he and Becky were brought here from Monticello, Horace began this nightly ritual. After the President retired for the night Horace would take one last look around, making certain that everything was in its place. He then methodically selected and gathered the President's clothing for the next morning, and quietly slipped out through the side door of the President's mansion. Becky referred to this as Horace's soothing time.

The length of the walk, and even the route changed ever so slightly from day to day. How long he would stay out on any given night depended mostly on the anticipated demands facing him the next day. With a clear view of the sky, he felt free to stare up and converse with God: to say a nightly prayer of thanks for all he and Becky had, most of which was the love for each other, and the faith and trust of his master, Thomas Jefferson.

Ultimately, Horace returned to the small space he and his wife shared in the basement of the President's mansion by the Potomac.

On the rare occasion when the walk and fresh air did not act as calming agents, just knowing that he would be returning to his darling Becky was enough to rev up his spirits and bring the day to a peaceful close.

Tonight, making his way through the second heavy snowstorm of the New Year, Horace was deeper in thought than usual. The cold winter air with fresh snow beating against his face or even the thought of Becky's waiting arms could not take his mind off of the events of *this* day.

*****

When he was in the mansion, President Jefferson spent as much time as he could inside the drafty room on the southwest corner of the first floor. He often worked on multiple projects at the same time. The President opted to keep this room entirely for himself as his office and personal library. Here he could quietly work or reflect on the problems facing the new nation as well as his personal concerns about his farm and home in Virginia. He would look out the window at the new War department building or towards Alexandria, Virginia, just beyond the flowing waters of the Potomac, or just think. He ended most days reading. During the cold winters what little warmth there was in the room came from the well-used fireplace on the East wall.

During most days, this time of year, bright sunlight streamed through the tall window on the side of the building. The President kept his pet mocking bird, Dick, in an ornate cage suspended by the tall window. The bird was often let out of the cage to fly freely around the room. Jefferson trained the bird to ride on his shoulder.

Heavy tables filled the majority of the space within the room. Each table had assorted books and documents and objects pertaining to a specific project or current interest of the versatile leader. It was not unusual for him to move from one table to the next and back again, numerous times during the day.

Although this was a strange place for the leader of the new nation to spend so much of his time, it was his favorite part of the house. No one dared disturb him while he was within its walls. The rest of the household understood that he would re-enter their world when he wanted to – and not a minute sooner. Very few people other than the President's children and grandchildren and Horace, whose regular place was on a tall stool just inside the main door, were ever permitted inside this room. Martha, the President's eldest daughter, was the first to refer to it as *"the sanctuary"*, and the name stuck.

*****

It was a particular source of pride for Horace that he was the only non-family member permitted free access into this room. Even during confidential discussions, Horace was always within clear sight of the President. Conversations were open and free around him, never hushed because of his presence. Horace was trusted by all.

Horace could anticipate most of the President's needs and more often than not was able to anticipate Jefferson's need even before it was expressed.

*****

Thomas Jefferson had a knack for filling his days with a wide variety of subjects and visitors. Each visitor was expected to come to the point quickly and stay on message. When he felt it was time to move on to the next topic or for the visitor to leave he would nod to Horace who promptly stood and brought the visitor's coat as a sign that anything left unsaid would have to wait for another time.

This day was different, very different. One single meeting with the same three visitors lasted from very early in the morning until well past midnight.

John Breckinridge, former senator from Virginia, now Jefferson's Attorney General and close personal friend and confidant, arrived just before dawn. He quickly jumped from his carriage and went to the front door, pounding on the door until a sleepy servant responded.

As soon as the door opened Breckinridge pushed through and demanded to see the President. Sensing the seriousness of the request, yet fearful of disturbing the man of the house after he had gone to bed, the door servant woke Horace instead. Horace quickly dressed and went to meet the early visitor.

When Breckinridge saw Horace, the usually soft-spoken Virginian spoke in hushed tones, "Horace, I must see him straight away. Wake him for me *now*."

"May I take your coat and offer you something hot to chase the chill away?"

"No, Horace. Nothing for me, just tell him I am here and it is essential that we speak."

"But he is still asleep, General, can't it wait, sir?"

"No, I must see him now. Please, do as I ask without further delay."

"But Mr. John, he just went to bed. He will be up in a few hours..."

Raising his voice, Breckinridge grabbed Horace's arm, "Horace, wake him. Wake him now!"

Horace knocked lightly on the President's bed chamber door and without waiting for a response slowly turned the door knob and entered the room. He walked over to the President and barely touched his arm as he whispered, "Mr. Tom."

The President rolled over. Horace tried again, "Mr. Tom, please wake up. Attorney General Breckinridge is here and he says it is of utmost importance that he sees you."

The President leaned on his elbow and looked towards the window. "I've just gone to bed. What is he doing here now?"

"I do not know, Sir, but I have never seen him so stressed as this ever before. He says it is of the greatest importance."

"Horace, just tell him to return later in the day. It is even more important for me to try to get back to sleep."

"He says it is very important, Sir. And he emphasized, *very*."

The President sat up on the edge of the bed, rubbing his eyes, "Horace, God help you both if this is not 'life or death' important. Bring him here if it is so important."

"Here, to your bed chamber?"

"Yes, Horace, right here. The quicker I find out what is on his mind the quicker I can get back to sleep – or at least try to get back to sleep."

"Yes, Sir."

Horace placed the President's robe at the foot of the bed and left the room, quickly returning with the early morning visitor. Breckinridge was still wearing his overcoat and boots as he pushed ahead of Horace. "We need to speak, Tom."

"So speak. You have already brought the nighttime chill and fresh snow into my bedchamber. Just tell me what is so important that it couldn't wait for a more civilized time."

Horace stood frozen at the door as Breckinridge leaned over and whispered into the President's ear. Even in the dimly lit room Horace could see anger building on the President's face.

Breckinridge stepped back and waited for a response.

Staring past his visitor, in a hoarse whisper, the President said, "Give me a moment to get dressed." Then, in a more forceful voice he turned to Horace, "Please help this messenger of doom and gloom off with his snow covered coat and wet boots and bring him some hot tea." Almost as an afterthought he added, "Take him to the sanctuary. No need to wake everyone else in the house. I will be along shortly."

By the time Horace returned with a fresh pot of tea the two men were already deep in discussion. He filled each cup, added a new log to the roaring fireplace, and took his place by the door.

"We should have exposed him and that band of scoundrels a long time ago, Tom."

The President sat quietly with his hands in front of his face. He abruptly stood and began to pace in front of the fireplace. He walked towards one of the tables, began moving some of the documents around, then in a fit of temper grabbed the edge of the table and banged both hands against the top until they ached.

"Send for the Speaker of the House," he yelled, "and that devil reincarnate, Philthrow. If they have to be dragged out of their warm beds, do it and do it NOW!"

Within an hour, the two men had joined the President and Breckinridge in the sanctuary. As usual, Horace maintained his place on his tall stool by the closed door. Given the subject matter he was hoping that he would be sent away, but it seems that was not likely to happen.

James Philthrow, unofficial aid to Jefferson's former Vice President, Aaron Burr, and full time influence peddler – or as the President referred to him, the 'one man corruption ring', did most of the talking. The President and Breckinridge asked questions from time to time – anger and obvious disgust growing on each of their faces. The Speaker seemed to have little to say; looked relieved that the spotlight was on someone else.

Horace could hardly believe what he was hearing – this was not good, not good at all, he kept thinking.

Shortly before midnight, Horace watched as the three visitors left. There was none of the usual small talk about the weather or anything else. Each man quietly put on his own overcoat, not waiting for a servant to assist, as was the custom. Then, each walked silently to their own waiting carriage and left.

*****

Regardless of the hour, Becky always waited up for Horace to return from his nightly walks. Together for more than 40 years, the bond between them seemed to get stronger with each passing year.

"Let me help you off with your wet shoes, Horace," she said when he returned from his walk, "How about a hot cup of cocoa?"

"No cocoa tonight, dear. I just want to take my bath and go straight to sleep."

"Want company?"

"No dear, not tonight. Go to bed, Becky, I'll join you soon."

"Is there anything wrong, Horace?"

"No, dear, I just want to think something through, nothing to be concerned about, everything is good. Everything is good."

Horace gave Becky a hug, holding her so close that she could feel his heart pounding. He held her tightly for what seemed like a very long time. Then he released his grip, gave her a kiss on her forehead and went to take his bath.

Becky looked around the now empty room and sighed, "Everything is good, indeed." She shook her head slowly from side to side, "Oh my poor Horace, why are you hurting so badly this night?"

She moved over to their bed and sat quietly on the edge,

eyes fixed on the door, her hands on her lap, waiting anxiously for him to return.

*****

Horace took an extra long bath. He was hoping that Becky would already be asleep when he quietly returned to their room. He should have known better.

"Feeling refreshed, dear?"

Startled, surprised to see her still awake and sitting on the edge of the bed, he whispered, "Why are you still up?"

"I was waiting for you, my love. Are you feeling refreshed?" She asked.

"Much." He said.

"Then do you feel better about talking to me now?" She asked.

He smiled nervously, "It has been a very long day, Becky. Let's talk in the morning."

"Now Horace, I know you so well and I know that this is not at all like you. Something is deeply troubling you tonight, my darling."

Horace joined her on the edge of the bed and leaned over to gently kiss her cheek. "It has just been a very long day. Please leave it at that."

She cradled his face in her hands and said, "Now, look me in the eye, Horace Freeman. Something is weighing heavy on you tonight. I can feel it. Please, lighten this load by talking to me so we can both go to sleep."

He stood up and slowly walked towards the small window just below the ceiling.

The accumulated snow outside blocked much of his view. His eyes fixed upon one of the shapes closest to the thick window. He began to speak slowly, "Becky, this is not something that I dare to speak about."

"Not even to me?"

"Not even to you."

Becky stood and walked over to him, "Horace, my darling, I have never seen you like this. Are you... are you in any trouble?"

"No, Becky," he smiled weakly. "It is not about me."

She reached for his hand. "Horace, you're trembling. Is it Mr. Tom? Is he all right?"

Knowing how persistent she could be, especially if she believed that something was wrong, he held her close.

She put her arms around him and spoke slowly, "Share the weight of this burden with me, Horace. Please."

He looked at her then turned his head away and gazed down at the floor. Becky gently moved his hand up to her lips.

"Horace Freeman, I love you with all my heart. There is never going to be anything that can or would change that. Talk to me."

Gently cradling her face in his hands, he whispered, "Becky, I wish with everything that is holy to me that I had never heard what was spoken in this house today. Just knowing what I now know is more frightening than anything you can possibly imagine."

"What could be so horrifying for you?"

Slowly, almost mechanically, he began sharing the events of the day with his partner of four decades. As he spoke, her eyes widened until he thought they would pop out of their sockets. When he was all done he leaned closer, bringing his lips to her ear. "I hope that I will not be sorry that I brought you into this dirty, dirty mess, Becky. Only God knows where this will end."

"Poor Mr. Tom," she murmured. "What will he do?"

"I don't know. I fear that whatever he does he will become knotted in with something that can soil his good name for many years to come. Becky, you must promise me, in the Lord's name that you will not tell a living soul what I have shared with you this night."

"But surely it will all soon be known by everyone anyway. Won't it, Horace?"

"I don't know if it will or not."

"No one, not even Mr. Tom could keep this a secret for very long."

"Just tell me that you will not share this with anyone."

"Don't you trust me after all of these years?" she said with a weak smile.

"Becky, this is very different. Very different from anything we have ever spoken about before. You must never utter a single word about this to anyone. Not a word. Do you understand?"

"I understand."

"You must say the words, Becky, please."

He was frightening her; she had never seen him this agitated. "I promise I will never tell another human being. As

God is my witness, I promise." She crossed her heart and pressed her fingers tightly against her lips. "Now, try to sleep, you have to get up in just a few hours and you will need all of the rest you can get for the new day ahead."

He held her close and whispered in her ear, "I love you, Becky."

"And I love you, my darling. Now try to rest your body and your mind and go to sleep."

Horace kissed Becky and then walked around to his side of the bed and got under the covers. He leaned in, gave Becky one more kiss, and then turned over, tightly wrapping the cover around him.

Staring into the darkness, he was feeling guilty for having sworn her to secrecy. From his unique vantage point he regularly saw the President at his best and his worst. He was often reminded of his father's response when Horace told him he was chosen to accompany the new President to Washington. "Just remember, Horace, no man is a God, the best of all men are still merely human and capable of being both very good and very bad. Now you will be able to see up close every wart on this man's soul. You will soon understand why no man is a hero to his valet."

Each night as he cuddled next to Becky he would tell her about everything that happened during the day. She always listened quietly as he described the President's comings and goings, interrupting only occasionally to ask for more details as the stories ranged from human frailties to important matters of state for the still fragile republic.

Horace always felt secure in sharing these events with Becky. She never gave him reason to doubt that whatever news and happenings he shared with her would stay within their four walls. To the best of his knowledge she never repeated a single word to anyone. But then again, never before had they talked about such potentially explosive information as he shared with her this evening. He closed his eyes, thinking to himself: of course Becky can be trusted. More than anyone else in the world, Becky can be trusted, shame on me for doubting her.

Neither Horace nor Becky nor the master of this house slept very much this night or for many nights to come.

*****

Horace's remorse would have quickly turned to fear if he had known that Becky kept a personal diary. On its pages, she regularly recorded the events of her day, including the contents of their late night discussions.

In one form or another she kept the diary since she was a young girl and just continued the practice in her adult years. The events of the past fifty or so years now filled numerous bundles of individual pieces of paper. Each bundle neatly tied on all four sides with thin red hair ribbons.

Becky stored them in her special hiding place, the hollowed out compartment of a cabinet that her father had built for her when she turned ten years of age. Her father was an experienced carpenter. He had been brought to Monticello to build various pieces of furniture and shelving to hold Thomas Jefferson's massive collection of books. Although the cabinet he built for Becky was made from scraps and odd pieces of wood left over from his work for Jefferson, it was sturdy and to Becky, it was a treasure in itself.

It was rare in that time for the child of a slave to be taught to read and write, and even more rare for a female – slave or free. In exchange for his unique carpentry skills, Becky's father arranged for a local minister to secretly teach his youngest daughter to read and write. Becky was an eager student and by the time she was seven she could read the bible from cover to cover. Fearful that she would be labeled a witch for these abilities, both the minister and her father warned her not to ever let anyone know she could read or write. "Never tell nobody you can do this," her father warned, "Never!" Early in their marriage she thought of telling Horace but never did.

The day her father gave her the cabinet he showed her the secret compartment. "This will make my gift to you even more special," he whispered. "a secret compartment for your very own treasures." He showed her how to gain access to the compartment by twisting a portion of the upper molding to the left while pressing the side with her other hand. To the best of her knowledge, no one else ever knew about this private hiding place or about her diary and any of its contents.

Chapter 2
Monday, September 9, 1985,
Brooklyn, New York –

Max Barnes was not like most of the other kids on the block in either his appearance or his interests. He was shorter than most of the other kids in his neighborhood, overweight, and lacked many of the usual child-like notions usually held by most other kids his age. While the others talked about sports and as they grew older, girls, he talked about current affairs, and as he grew older, even more current affairs. Most of the other kids on his block had many heroes to idolize and daydream about but from the time he was nine years old and had been introduced to early American History in Mrs. Abondola's 4.1, 4th grade class in Brooklyn's P.S.16, he had only one hero: Thomas Jefferson.

Two powerful themes greeted all who entered Mrs. Abondola's classroom – an overabundance of freshly cut flowers and a wide variety of *things Jeffersonian.*

The building that housed P.S. 16 on Wilson and Lee Avenue in the Williamsburg section of Brooklyn had a long and proud past. Its brick front covered an old wooden structure that served as a makeshift hospital during the American Civil War, more than a hundred years earlier. As a result, there was a musty old smell almost everywhere in the building; almost everywhere *except* in Mrs. Abondola's classroom. Thanks to her husband's popular florist shop further down on Lee Avenue, there were vases upon vases filled daily with fresh roses and wherever flowers were not, pictures and artifacts of and about Thomas Jefferson were. From the time she had achieved tenure in the New York School System, Mrs. Abondola's entire career was little more than a constant tribute to her lifelong passion: the appreciation of and for Thomas Jefferson. She found ways to weave his name and very being into everything she taught. Literature was based upon *his* favorite books... geography centered on *his* travels. For each subject there was a Thomas Jefferson aspect to be considered. The study of Thomas Jefferson was the foundation and key reference point for every lesson plan she had prepared for more years than she cared to remember. It filled her with patriotic pride and fed her intellectual curiosity - and because it did - it was expected to do the same for her students. During her long teaching career few things gave her as much personal pleasure as bringing Jefferson to life for each term's new group of students.

"A brilliant mind," was how she usually began the first day of the school year, emphasizing Jefferson's range of interests and skills. "A clear thinker, *the* man for his time, no, make that *the man for all* times. Smarter than all of the rest of our historic figures put together, pure genius this fellow, pure genius!" A dramatic pause as she walked amid the desks, eyes gleaming, staring at each of them and none of them, almost as if in a trance. "We haven't seen his measure since and it is unlikely we ever will again."

Mark James, a tall thin boy sitting behind Max, leaned forward and whispered, "My sister warned me about this. She had Abondola when she was in the fourth grade and from what she told me, this is the same thing she tells every class, so *boring*. I bet she's gonna crack the chalk in half just from how excited she is."

Abondola glared at Mark, then slowly walked to the front of the room and continued. "He was a brilliant legal and legislative mind. Remember students, there were few if any precedents for what he and his band of free thinkers were contemplating. Freedom? Liberty? Independence? They could have all been hung as traitors to the King. These were difficult times and thank God there was a Thomas

Jefferson around to make such a difference for us all."

She went to the blackboard, dramatically grabbed a piece of chalk and with a flourish began to make a list. The chalk snapped in half under the pressure. "Forgive me people, my emotions..."

Mark leaned forward again, "What a crock! See, I told you about the chalk, didn't I? Didn't I?"

Abondola slowly turned in Mark's direction. "One more peep from the high grass and some little mood breaker is going to wish he were somewhere else."

Returning her attention to the blackboard, she continued with even more emphasis than before, creating a list of Jefferson's many interests. "You might be surprised to learn that he is credited with bringing French fries and ice cream to America, as a result of his years of diplomatic service in France." She paused, staring around the classroom, then added, "A resourceful, you might say, self taught architect, he designed the University of Virginia; a deep scientific mind, he invented the plow and brought the dumb waiter to the White House; an accomplished musician, he loved to sing and played a mean violin; an accomplished linguist, he could speak three languages by the time he was your age and learned 3 more plus more than a dozen Native American dialects later in his life." She paused, took a deep breath and continued. "He was a gardener, responsible for growing more than two-hundred and fifty different vegetables – fifteen types of peas alone - plus about one-hundred and seventy different fruits in and around his home, Monticello; but..."

There was a long dramatic pause as she stared directly at the boy now sitting at full attention behind Max. "As a writer he was without equal. His words, today, are every bit as moving and inspiring as they were when first put to parchment."

Mark quickly scribbled a note and passed it on to Max, it said, *He so loved the world that he gave us his only begotten quill.*

Abondola walked to Mark's side and snatched up the note. She read it quickly, rolled it into a ball and dropped it on Mark's desk. Moving just behind him she put both hands firmly on his shoulder. "It is a safe bet that his words will live on for centuries yet to come. I refer of course to the words of Thomas Jefferson," she paused, then focusing her glare directly at Mark she slowly continued, "and not the empty vessels which are those who are destined to remain in the peanut gallery of empty space for eternity."

She moved swiftly to the front of the room and leaned against the edge of her desk. With her eyes tightly closed she said in a loud whisper, "it was at a White House dinner honoring Nobel Prize winners that President John Fitzgerald Kennedy said, 'I think this is the most extraordinary collection of talent, of human knowledge, that has ever been gathered at the White House-with the possible exception of when Thomas Jefferson dined alone'"

Yes, she had given this same speech so many times before but what made it fresh for her was the student's reactions and personal hope that it would nurture an interest and respect for American history in general and this specific 'founding father' in particular. Each new class was a fresh opportunity to spark a new group of young minds. Perhaps this was the underlining reason she became a teacher. It certainly was the driving force for continuing to be one.

"Have you any idea how many other countries have modeled their ideals against his Declaration of Independence? You would all do well to study the smallest detail of this great man's life and fashion your dreams after this giant among men."

A girl in the front of the class raised her hand and when

Abondola pointed to her she said, "So much has already been written about President Jefferson. Is it really possible that anything new could still be found?"

"Yes, much has been written by and about him. But it will be up to you and your generation and the many generations to come to continue to look for more. Never assume that all which can be learned has been learned – not about Mr. Jefferson, not about anything or anyone else. Keep an open mind and continue to seek more knowledge. That is *your* challenge."

*****

As the class moved towards the cafeteria, Mark whispered into Max's ear, "Big deal, he was just a human being, not some God. So he had a lot of hobbies. Who cares anyway?"

Max smiled at Mark, "Yes, he was just a man. But his story has lasted for almost two hundred years. Don't you think that's cool?"

"Oh, Max, give me a break. Just because she has a crush on him doesn't mean *we* have to."

"Yeah, I know." Max said, hoping it would help change the subject. Although he didn't fully realize it at the time, Max was hooked.

*****

From that time on, Max searched out and absorbed all that he could about the life and times of Jefferson. During a summer vacation his parents took him and his older sister to visit Monticello, Jefferson's home. At one point the tour went into the space Jefferson designed as both a bedroom and a work room separated by an alcove style bed, a unique design that permitted Jefferson to get into bed from his bed chamber and roll out the other side of the bed into his private study. Max could hardly breathe from the excitement he felt just by being in the same space Jefferson occupied almost two centuries before.

"Quick, touch the books," his sister whispered. "See if you can feel his spirit."

"I can't," he responded. "It's bad enough that we and so many other strangers are invading his personal living space and staring at his belongings. We're just lucky to be here."

"Don't be such a jerk," she responded. "We're paying homage to him. I bet he would be flattered."

"I don't think so. He'd probably be wondering how come we don't have anything better to do with our time."

Max returned to Monticello many times after that vacation, especially during his college years. This single human being continued to intrigue him more with each visit.

Max was definitely hooked.

Chapter 3
Thursday, October 2, 1997,
Washington, D.C. –

For his senior year at American University, Max shared an old brownstone with six other students. After a quick walk through, he chose the semi-finished attic for his bedroom. No one had a problem with that; after all, it was the smallest of all the possible living areas with no closet space and a low slanted ceiling making it impossible for anyone to stand erect in more than a third of the space. It had a musty smell and promised to be drafty and damp in the cold months and hot and stuffy in the warmer months. But he knew it would be perfect for him. It offered him total privacy from the rest of the house and the rusty fire escape attached to the only window in the room provided an airy space to read and study or just think. When the weather permitted, he could drop the rickety metal fire escape down so that he could come and go as he needed.

*****

There was never a question in Max's mind as to the subject matter for his college thesis. In fact, the title was firmly in place while he was still in junior high school – *'The unknown chapter in Thomas Jefferson's life'*. He was committed to discover new ground, previously unknown interests, relationships, pleasures, problems. No tired, old, previously reported facts would do!

Sitting in the cramped space among piles of clothing, notes and reference materials, he had been at his computer for hours without writing a single word worth saving. *Writer's block on steroids*, he thought to himself.

It seemed like such a good idea at first, an original concept about one of the most written about figures in history. In preparation he read and cross-checked every biography he could find against other biographies of Jefferson as well as available books by and about members of his immediate family, friends, and contemporaries. There had to be something previous writers missed. He dug through everything written during the time; family documents, public records, at the very least he hoped to uncover a human interest tidbit or possibly unearth something of new historic value. But at every turn he seemed to hit a brick wall. He was beginning to think that he must have been out of his mind to go down this path, to think that anything – large or small – could possibly have been missed by generations of gifted historians during almost two centuries. But admitting defeat was not an option – at least not yet.

*****

Monday, October 13, 1997,
Washington, D.C. – 10:15 A.M.

Sam Nobal ran a new and used book store just off campus. Max was a regular and probably knew Sam's inventory as well as anyone, including Sam.

As Max entered the store Sam flashed a broad smile and yelled, "Hi Max, still writer blocked?"

"Does this look like the face of a man with a completed thesis, Sam?"

"Max, Max, what are you killing yourself for? You probably have enough stuff to write a dozen books on old Tom. Why make it so tough on yourself?"

"There has got to be a new hook, Sam. I know it is there, all I have to do is find it."

"Look Max, he probably wrote tens of thousands of letters, a lot of which are still around today. For hundreds of years more people have written about this guy than ate a corned beef sandwich at Katz's Deli. You're smart and you've been dedicated. You gave it your all... isn't it time to just move on?"

"You got to believe, Sam. It is there. This is just a temporary road block. I'll find something, I know I will." *Or die trying*, he thought.

Sam smiled, "The Pennsylvania Dutch were right, 'we grow too soon old and too late smart'."

Sam walked over to Max and gently put his hand on Max's shoulder, "O.K. so you hit a temporary wall; I got a suggestion. When I get stuck mentally what works for me is to do whatever I can to at least temporarily replace the problem with 'mind candy'."

"Mind candy?", Max asked, "What's mind candy?"

"It's probably different for each person, but for me, I open the newspaper to the sports pages and read and re-read every statistic, every number, every word, and every article, in the section."

Max laughed, "But you aren't even a sports fan, Sam."

"That is the whole point. At times like that I don't want substance, I want distraction. I want to fill my consciousness with anything but steak and potatoes. That is what 'mind candy' is. After fifteen or twenty minutes of such boring drivel I can usually go back to thinking about my problem with a really clear head. It usually works for me."

"Mind candy?" Max mused, "Why not? Nothing else seems to be working for me. Do you have any sports pages from the 1800's?"

Sam gave a hearty laugh. "I have back copies of newspapers – nothing from the 1800's – but it's all the same in sports anyway. Someone played and won, someone else played and lost, and a day later no one remembers or cares who won or lost. Go, take a look for yourself."

"Sam, you are one great friend," Max yelled as he walked back to the storeroom, then under his breath, "but a lousy housekeeper."

"I heard that!" Sam yelled back.

There were bundles on top of bundles of newspapers thrown into a corner of the back room. Knowing Sam as well as he did, Max realized that the only way these piles would ever get organized would be by students like him. It was Max who organized the Jefferson era books into a meaningful section.

"I don't understand how the fire department lets you get away with this, Sam. How can you store potentially price-less historic documents like this?"

Sam walked into the area and glared at Max. "Excuse me, Mr. College Man. Maybe you should go shop at one of the fancy reading room stores uptown. I imagine their vintage newspaper section is neat as a pin. That is, of course, as-suming they have any newspapers older than yesterday."

"Yeah, yeah, sorry for hurting your feelings, Sam, but you must admit that this is no way to store rare and valuable papers. Where did you get all of these? The cover dates are almost prehistoric yet most of them look brand new. Are they reprints?"

"No, they are not reprints. They are the real McCoy. Last month, just before they moved the newspaper office to the suburbs they called me to see if I wanted their old morgue. I had available space, so I said yes."

"You call a pile in a corner of a storeroom, mixed in with who knows what else, to be 'available space'? Bet they didn't store them in a great big pile like so much dirty laundry."

"Now, aren't we the opinionated ones?"

Max pulled one of the papers out of the top bundle, "I'll bet these have been kept in a climate control room. They look like they were just printed today."

"Maybe they could afford climate controlled rooms, but sure as shooting, I can't."

"So, you're just going to let these historic gems turn yellow and age?"

"Listen Max, I don't have access to their kinds of money. If it bothers you so much just write me a check and I will run out this minute and contract for a climate control annex to be built. I'll even name it after you – 'the undergraduate smarty pants room'."

"Don't get so huffy. It's just that these really belong in a college library. They're in pristine condition now but left like this it can't be long before they turn to kindling."

"Max, Max, if the college library or any library for that matter, wanted these papers do you really think they would have wound up here? You can't believe that I was the first one they called. It was probably me or a dumpster. Now, stop pontificating and start reading or you will never get past your own title page."

Max began picking through the piles, "Some of these are decades old. Here's one from 1956. Mind if I take a few back to my room?"

"Would it be too cranky of me to ask you to buy them first?"

"How much?"

"What's the cover price?"

"Three cents."

"Okay, you're the college man. How much would three cents in 1956 be worth today?"

"How about a buck each?" Max said.

"Two minutes ago they were priceless gems, and now they're worth less than the price of a cup of coffee? You have some hidden agenda about keeping me poverty stricken?"

"I'm even more poverty stricken than you, Sam, how about twenty bucks for these few papers?"

"Sold!"

Max tucked them under his arm and walked towards the front door. "Put it on my tab."

Sam smiled, moving his glasses down from his forehead as he reached for his ledger. He added $20 under a long list of previous numbers. He closed the book and thought to himself, *I'll never get rich from you, Mr. College Man, but you do make my days interesting.*

Chapter 4
Monday, October 13, 1997,
Washington, D.C. – 1:25 P.M.

Max made himself comfortable on his fire escape. He mumbled to himself, "A reheated cup of coffee, a day old bagel, and a forty year old newspaper. What more could anyone want in life?"

As he turned the pages, his eye focused on a series of high-lighted feature boxes, 'Lead story 50 years ago today'; Lead story 100 years ago today'; and Lead story 150 years ago today'. His gaze centered around the third box as he read it aloud:

Lead story 150 years ago today...

20th CRIME
AND THE YEAR IS
ONLY 10 DAYS OLD!

Friday, January 10, 1806, Capital

Mr. Illia Sharpell, age 31, was found dead this morning floating along the Eastern edge of the Potomac River.

His body was discovered at approximately 6 o'clock by a passing citizen. The Auxiliary Watch Captain promises an investigation and full report shortly.

Mr. Sharpell worked for the Speaker of the House as his Chief Stenographer.He regularly attended the Church of the Christian Brotherhood. He is survived by his Mother, Mrs. Megan Sharpell of Alexandria & his twin sisters, Mrs. Lamar Anderson and Miss Estelle Sharpell, both currently reside in the district.

Poor guy, Max thought, an unknown civil servant in a dead end job. Probably the only time he ever got his name in a newspaper and he couldn't even see if they spelled his name right. I wonder how he wound up in the river that morning.

Max carried his empty coffee cup and the newspaper back into his room. Maybe it was a suicide. Alone and lonely, 31 years old, probably no wife or kids, or they would have referenced them in the article. Mr. Sharpell, Chief Stenographer to the Speaker of the House of Representatives, your untimely death has just become my 'mind candy'. I just have to know the rest of the story.

He dialed information and got the phone number for the local newspaper and dialed the number.

"Hi, I'm a student at the American University School of Government and I was reading a back issue of your paper. How far back does your microfilm library go?"

"How many dates are you looking for?"

"I'd like to review 10 or 12 different days following a particular story. How can I arrange that?"

"I'll have to transfer you to back issues, sir, one moment."

There was a long delay and then, "Back issues, how can I help you?"

"Yes, I'm a student at the American University School of Government and I am researching a story from 1806."

The voice on the other end of the line sounded overworked and rushed. "Okay, you must mean 1906; we don't have issues stored from that far back..."

"Hey, I know what I mean and what I mean is 1806!"

The line went dead. Max stared at the phone. "You hung up on me?"

Max redialed. "Give me back issues, please."

Another long delay and then, "Back issues, how may I help you?"

"You can help me most by not hanging up on me again. I'm researching a death from 1806. I would like access to whatever you have from January and possibly February of 1806."

"Don't you have anything better to do with your time than to play practical jokes like this?"

"Hey, I'm not playing a practical joke here and I don't appreciate your attitude, either, and another thing..." The phone went dead. *I don't believe this*, thought Max. *He hung up on me again.*

Max walked towards the door. Poking his head into the stairwell he called out, "Hey, Gloria, I need a little help up here."

Of the seven graduate students sharing the small brownstone, Gloria Salizar was the only female and the one that all of the others turned to when help of any kind was needed. She could be counted on to dish out hearty servings of attitude but eventually she found a way to get them what they needed.

"I'm busy, Max."

"Come on, Gloria. I have a project here that is right up your alley."

"You'll just have to take a number and wait your turn."

"Oh, Gloria, you know you're going to help me, I know

you're going to help me, can't we cut to the chase? At least come up and hear what I need."

Max could hear her mumbling as she walked the flight of stairs up to his attic room. "If I wanted to deal with little babies all the time I would have started a day care center," she screamed as she entered his room. "You have exactly one minute to get and keep my interest, and the clock started when I took the first step up."

"Okay, don't ask me why but I'm researching someone's death. I need back issues of the newspaper and they keep hanging up on me."

"Do you have a phone number?"

"Yes."

She held her hand out, tapping one foot, further making a show of her disdain by staring in the opposite direction. She looked down on the paper, and mumbled under her breath, "Just admit it, sometimes the best *man* for the job is a *woman*." Without waiting for a response from Max she reached for the phone. As she dialed, she looked back at Max and said, "What is this worth to you?"

"Assuming you can get this done," he quickly responded, "you will get my undying admiration."

"And your admiration will come with your cleaning the bathroom the next time it is my turn?"

"Come on, Gloria, it is just a phone call."

"It's ringing!"

"Okay, you're covered. I'll clean the bathroom the next time it is your turn."

"Quick, give me the dates you need."

"I'm looking for the two or three week period, beginning on January 10, 1806."

She slammed the receiver down. "Are you out of your mind? 18 - 0 what?"

He showed her the newspaper.

"If it did exist, and it probably doesn't", she said, "You need a library, not a newspaper office. Tell me why, in this modern day, you feel the need to rummage through such old newspapers."

Max brought her up to date and then handed her the paper pointing out the article.

"Whatever, O.K., I can solve this for you but it will cost you two turns covering my bathroom duties and if you complain I'll double it to four or walk away and leave you to your own devices."

He knew how futile it would be to argue with her and quickly gave in. "It's a deal."

She ran downstairs and quickly returned with a dog-eared copy of the D.C. phone book. "Is there a pencil and clean piece of paper in this mess of yours?"

He picked up and smoothed out a crumpled sheet of paper from around the waste paper basket and handed it to her with a pencil. "Here, Mother dear."

"I can do without your sarcasm, Max." She leafed through the phone book, wrote a number on the paper and again reached for the telephone.

"Washington Historical Society, how can I direct your call?"

"Head librarian, please."

Several rings and then a male voice said, "Mike Fenster, how can I help you?"

"White House calling, the President's chief speechwriter needs hard copies of all available local news reports from the District from early January, 1806 through end of February, the same year. Also, print a hard copy of any data you have on a Mr. Illia Sharpell who served as an aid to the then Speaker of the House. We need this information pronto! I will be dispatching a special messenger to pick up this information in half an hour sharp. Make sure it is ready and waiting for the messenger the second – and I mean the very second he gets there. Now, whom shall I have the messenger ask for when he arrives?"

"Did you say 1806?"

"Yes, 1806."

"Who is this again?"

"Look, I don't have all day here and you are wasting valuable time. The messenger will be there in half an hour and I would not keep him waiting if I were you."

As Gloria hung up the phone Max gave a loud scream. "Gloria Salizar, you are terrific!"

"Yeah, yeah, just run over there before they catch their breath and call the White House back for confirmation."

*****

Later that evening, Max was back in his room looking through the copies of documents he had picked up from the Washington Historical Society. He yawned loud enough to wake the dead as he looked at his watch, "Almost three o'clock in the morning. Wow!" He stretched his arms towards the ceiling and then reached for his alarm clock. A little more than three hours and this little baby is going to screech me back to consciousness. I guess some sleep is better than no sleep, he thought.

He stood up, banging his head against the ceiling. Closing his desk light he plopped onto his bed. Soon the room was filled with the sounds of his heavy breathing and a series of light breezes coming through the open window.

Chapter 5
Tuesday, October 14, 1997,
Washington, D.C. – 6:00 A.M.

The sharp sound of the alarm was particularly piercing this morning. Max squinted as he slammed his hand down on the snooze alarm button. Ten more minutes, he lazily thought. The world will just have to get along without me for ten more minutes.

As he turned over, his eyes wandered around the room. Still not fully awake and not sure what he had just seen, he reached for his glasses and stared over at the small work-space he had been using as a desk.

He flung the covers off and jumped out of bed, slamming his head against the ceiling. Rubbing his head with both hands he looked around the room with shock and disbelief. His computer was on the floor and the rest of his room looked like a hurricane had been there and gone. "What the hell is going on here?" he yelled.

He wandered through the debris, still rubbing his head, moving towards the door. He stood for a moment at the head of the stairway and then yelled, "Hey, which one of you trashed my room?"

The first response came from Steve Berman, always the first one up. Berman rushed towards the foot of the stairway and in a loud whisper he said, "Hold it down up there, it's only six o'clock in the morning, how about a little neighborly consideration?"

"Neighborly consideration my rear end, come see what one of your 'neighbors' has done to my room."

"Shhhhhhh!"

"Don't shhhhhhh me! I'm telling you that someone has trashed my room and I am not going to take this lying down."

Berman walked up the stairway and when he reached the room took a long look around, "You weren't kidding, were you?"

"When I find out who did this I intend to hand them their heads, and I am not kidding about that either."

"When did this happen?"

"It must have happened sometime during the night, although there really wasn't too much 'night' for anyone to do this. I was up until about three A.M. and it wasn't like this when I went to sleep, I assure you."

"So you were asleep when this happened?"

"So it seems."

"How could anyone sleep through something like this?"

"Forget about my sleeping habits, I just want to know who did this and why."

"Hey, are you accusing one of us for this mess?"

"I don't think we can blame it on a caravan of traveling gypsies!"

"What makes you think it was one of us?"

"Now let's see. I don't think it happened by itself," he said sarcastically. "And the one door that leads into and out of this house is always locked tighter than a drum each night, Gloria sees to that!"

"Maybe whoever did this came in through your fire escape," Berman suggested.

"Don't be ridiculous," Max screamed. "Who would come in here from the outside just to trash my room? And if someone did - say to rob something - they would have grabbed my computer, not smash it against the floor."

"Calm down. I will go downstairs and check the door and all the windows."

As Berman left, Max sat on the edge of his bed shaking his head in disbelief. Soon Berman returned with Gloria close behind. "What have you gotten yourself into now, Max?" she asked.

"Look around Gloria," Max shouted. "I was in bed when this happened."

Gloria started to move things into piles, "The one day a week I have late classes and can get a little extra sleep and you have to wake me by screaming like a drunken banshee."

"Well, excuse me Gloria; I guess it is my entire fault that someone decided to turn this room upside down?"

Berman returned, shaking his head, "The front door is still double locked Max, and from what I can see none of the windows have been disturbed. Everyone else is still sound asleep. Whoever did this had to have come in through your fire escape."

Showing a bit more concern Gloria said, "Who could have possibly wanted to do this to you, Max?"

"I have no idea." Max said, shaking his head slowly from side to side.

"Is anything missing?" Gloria asked.

"Hard to say, there certainly can't be anything of value missing. I don't own anything of value except my computer and it's right over there, smashed to smithereens."

"A real mystery, Max." Berman said.

Gloria punched Berman's arm. "That's easy for you to say, Mr. big and muscle bound football hero! But the possibility of someone sneaking around my home in the middle of the night is very disturbing to me."

Max tenderly picked up his laptop and set it on the desk, "Whoever did this is lucky that he or she or *they* bypassed your room, Gloria. I would bet my tuition loans that if they came even close to you they would be floating face down along the Potomac River, just like good old Illia Sharpell."

"What is an Illia Sharpell?" Berman asked.

Max started scrambling through the mess on the floor. "It's gone!" he yelled. "It's gone!"

"What's gone?" Gloria asked.

"All of the stuff I had about Illia Sharpell. It's all gone."

Gloria asked, "Is that all that is missing?"

"It seems so, makes no sense, but that seems to be all that was taken."

Berman's eyes wandered and fixed upon the mirror on the small bureau, "What is that on your mirror?"

All three bent down to avoid hitting their heads as they walked towards the bureau; taped to the mirror was a large index card. Printed in red ink were the words, "WE WILL LIVE FREE – OOTAP."

Chapter 6
Tuesday, October 14, 1997,
Washington, D.C. – 8:05 A.M.

From time to time the seven roommates held house meetings. They set up the rules when they first moved in. Any one of the seven could request a house meeting, for any reason. Once called, the others were required to attend. Up until now, only Ferde Batista had ever called a meeting. Ferde was a second generation Cuban-American. He called the house meeting to ask the others to join him in a peaceful protest against the school's plan to permit a pro-Castro speaker to address an undergraduate assembly.

Today's meeting would be the first one called since the contentious Castro debate and Max wasn't quite sure if anyone would show up, but they all did, including Bruce Fields, the only roommate who tried slipping out on the pro-Castro meeting.

Max got right to the point, "By now you all are aware that someone trashed my room. I'm calmer now and would like to have a civilized conversation to determine who did it and why. If that person or those persons prefer to remain anonymous it is O.K. with me as long as that person or those persons arrange to have my computer repaired or replaced. No questions asked. I would like the missing documents back too but I will settle for my computer to be brought back to life or replaced."

Gloria interrupted, "And you think it is one or more of us?"

"I would prefer not to think that."

Gloria stood up placing her hands on her hips, "What would you prefer to think, Max?" accenting the word would.

"Look Gloria, I WOULD have preferred it if this never happened at all, but it DID happen, and so NOW my preference is for something like this to never happen again. Got my drift?"

Bruce Fields spoke up. "It couldn't have been me; I spent the night in the study hall. There were plenty of other people there who will testify that I was there all night."

Gloria stared at Fields and said, "Once again, the non-team player is heard from."

All eyes turned towards Ferde who just stared straight ahead.

Fields responded, "Look Gloria, I don't think any of us would do such a thing either. All I said was that I was nowhere near the house last night and could prove it."

Allan Design interrupted, "O.K. Max, let's be logical here. There is no way that one of us did this thing. It must have been an outsider and it is most likely that they came and went by way of your fire escape. Steve checked the door and windows as soon as you made him aware of the incident and they were locked. Now, if one of us did this don't you think we would have been smart enough to leave some way open so it would at least LOOK like an outside job?"

Steve moved forward, "That makes sense to me."

"Look," Max finally said, "I am the victim here, not any of you, just me, and I find this whole thing unnerving."

Gloria sat down and said, "Let's recap. The only thing missing is a bunch of old newspapers and the file you were accumulating on this Illia guy. Between you and me, we did make a lot of calls about him and maybe someone didn't like our digging into it. Why don't you just go back to Sam's store and pick up the rest of the newspapers. I'm sure each of us will be willing to pitch in and look for some follow up to the story."

"Good idea," Ferde said, "Good idea."

"Today is my heaviest day," Max responded. "I won't be able to get to Sam's store until the end of the day."

"So it will wait until the end of the day," Gloria said. "Those newspapers sat for decades; another day won't make any difference. Let's agree to meet here as a group, sometime late this afternoon or early evening."

"Now, since you called the meeting, you need to move that we are adjourned."

"And what am I supposed to use for a computer in the meantime?"

Mark James was Max's friend since fourth grade and also lived in the house. He was the brownstone's computer wizard and had been quiet up to this point. "It really isn't our problem but you are my friend and in a spirit of joint support," Mark said, "I can pull the hard drive out of the broken computer and put it in the backup computer my dad gave me. I'll look over what's left of yours to see if I can replace the screen and fix whatever else may be out of whack."

"Thank you, Mark", Max said, "All right, I move that the meeting is now adjourned until later today."

"I second the motion." Gloria quickly said.

"This meeting is officially adjourned."

Chapter 7
Tuesday, October 14, 1997,
Washington, D.C. – 3:17 P.M.

The day seemed to drag for Max. He couldn't get the ransacking of his room out of his thoughts. He barely functioned all day, moving almost mechanically from class to class, constantly looking at his watch. He tried to will the day to end so that he could get over to Sam's store.

The moment his last class broke he was the first one out of the door and ran most of the way to Sam's store.

Large sheets of plywood covered the front windows. Tacked to the front door was a hand-lettered sign:

WE ARE OPEN FOR BUSINESS
PLEASE COME IN

Max opened the door and looked around. It was like a tornado had hit. Shelving units were turned over; books and loose papers seemed to be scattered everywhere. He walked carefully around a pile of broken glass while calling out for Sam. Looking a bit more bedraggled than usual, Sam waived to Max from the rear of the store.

"What happened, Sam?"

"I guess some of the kids thought last night was already mischief night and left me a Halloween mess to clean up."

"This is terrible, Sam. How long will it take to get up and running again?"

"They broke the window and tossed some shelves, but nothing I can't fix."

"Any idea who could have done this?"

"Not a clue."

"Did you call the police?"

"No, Max, they have real problems to deal with, this is just a little mischief."

"How can you be so blasé about this?"

"Thank you for your concern, but it's just part of doing business in a college town. I prefer to think that it was just a random act of vandalism, nothing more or less."

"Sam, your face is ashen white. What is really going on here?"

"Well, I have to admit that when I first arrived this morning and saw all of the broken glass and spilled shelves I was a bit frightened. It reminded me of the Nazi book burnings in Germany before the war." Sam gave a huge sigh, "But now that I have had time to think about it, it is probably just what I said, a random act of vandalism."

"Are you at least insured for the damage?"

"No, Max, you can't insure a place like this. Even though it has provided a fair living for me over the years, on paper the inventory has little insurable value. Hey, you said it yourself; it is a fire waiting to happen."

"So, what are you going to do?"

"I called for a glazier to repair the window. Assuming he ever shows up I'll have a new window in place before I close tonight. Meanwhile, I'll put the books back on the shelves. Things will return to normal and life will go on."

"And if the glazier doesn't come before you close?"

"Then I'll sleep here tonight. It isn't like I've never done *that* before."

"This isn't at all like you, Sam. Where is your outrage?"

"It wouldn't help."

"It wouldn't hurt, either."

They both smiled.

"And what if they come back?" Max asked.

"Max, Max, it was a once in a blue moon thing. I don't have any enemies. I'm sure the next time they want to raise a little hell they'll find a better place to do it."

"Was anything destroyed or taken?"

"It might come as a shock to you but there isn't anything here worth stealing. They did a lot of damage but nothing that can't be reversed."

"So, they didn't take anything?"

"Funny," Sam paused and then added, "They *did* take something."

"What?"

"Remember that old batch of newspapers you looked at the last time you were here?"

"They took the newspapers?"

"Yeah, every last one of them; strange, isn't it?"

"Yes, Sam, it is."

Max put his hand on Sam's shoulder, "Would you like me to stay with you until the glazier gets here?"

"No, don't worry. The jerks that did this won't be back. I'm sure of that."

"Okay, but promise me that you will call me if you need anything or even if you just want to talk to someone."

They walked towards the door when something on the counter caught Max's eye, "What is that, Sam?"

"Oh, just some dumb note they seemed to have left behind."

They both stared at a large index card. Printed in red ink were the words, "WE WILL LIVE FREE – OOTAP."

As Sam reached for the card, Max breathed a heavy sigh.

Chapter 8
Tuesday, October 14, 1997,
Washington, D.C. – 3:42 P.M.

Max waited in front of the house until Gloria came home. He put his fingers to his lips and then pointed down the street. Instinctively, she followed him to the bus stop on the corner. They stood quietly until the bus creaked to a stop along the curb.

Max paid for the two of them and led Gloria to the back seat. There was only one other passenger on the bus.

Max waited for the bus to pull out, looked through the rear window and then moved closer to Gloria. "Either the house is being bugged or one of our roommates is trying to drive me crazy."

"Please, Max, don't get paranoid on me."

"I went to Sam's store today after classes."

"So, that was the plan wasn't it?"

"Someone broke into his store before he opened for the day."

"You're kidding."

"No, Gloria, I am not kidding. And it gets even stranger. Sam thinks that the only thing missing is the rest of those old newspapers. Out of his entire inventory, that was all that was missing!"

"Is he sure?"

"He seemed to be. The very same newspapers we all agreed I would pick up today."

"That's unbelievable. Is there any way this could have been just a coincidence?"

"Come on Gloria, you know the answer to that."

"Well, it could be a coincidence."

"The coincidences don't stop with the newspapers. Someone left a large index card on his counter with the words, 'WE WILL LIVE FREE – OOTAP' on it with a red marker."

"Isn't that the same thing someone put on your bureau mirror?"

"Yes, do you still think it was a coincidence?"

"What can this all mean, Max?"

"I wish I knew."

They both sat still for a while, then Gloria broke the silence, "Look, if there is one common denominator to describe the five guys we share that house with it is that none of those dorks could ever think something like this up by themselves and the second common denominator is that no two of them would even think of teaming up with anyone else in order to plan such a prank. They just don't have the imagination, or the nerve, or the team spirit, for something like this. Individually or collectively they are also just too self absorbed. I, on the other hand, am very capable of such a creative prank." Before he could respond, she quickly added, "But I swear that I did not have anything to do with it."

"I never thought you did. I certainly wouldn't be talking about this with you now if I thought you were involved. But somehow, the two break-ins are connected and I can't for the life of me figure out how or why." Max said.

"You must go to the police, Max."

"And tell them what? Someone stole a few bundles of old newspapers and I think it has something to do with a death that took place almost two hundred years ago? They would laugh me out into the street."

"What about the campus police?"

"Don't be ridiculous. You yourself refer to them as keystone Cop *wanna-bees*. They wouldn't have a clue what to do, and even if they did, all I could tell them is what I would tell the *real police*. As useless as the campus police are, even they would laugh me out of their office with a story like this."

"You can't fight this alone."

"I know, I know."

"I'm not any more experienced in this kind of thing than you, Max, but is there anything I can do to help?"

"On my way home I was thinking and yes, you might be able to help."

"What do you want me to do?"

"Remember the security geek who used to follow you around like a love sick puppy dog?"

"Sidney?"

"Yeah."

"We went out once, Max, and it was the longest forty minutes of my life. He is such a dork."

"Would you be willing to ask him for some help?"

"Oh, Max. It took so long to shake him the last time; I don't want to go through that again."

"You always said that he was good at what he did. He could sweep through the house in a flash without raising any suspicions."

"Come on Max, I'll do anything but don't make me call Sidney."

"You don't have to marry the guy, just get him to do this one thing."

"That's easy for you to say; *you* never had to sit with him while secretly praying that some giant bird would lift you or him up and carry either one away."

"Gloria, I am really scared about this. You offered to help; well here is how you can help. Maybe I am just being paranoid, but I must know for sure."

"Yeah, but Sidney, it would be like bringing a bigger scary thing in to get rid of another scary thing. Sure, the other scary thing would almost certainly be done away with, but then you're stuck with the bigger scary thing."

They sat quietly; he staring ahead, she looking out of the window. Then Gloria turned to face Max and put her arm around him, "Okay, I'll call Sidney."

Max smiled broadly, "Thank you. But don't do it from the house."

"Why not call from the house?"

"Now Gloria, if the house is bugged we would only be tipping them off."

"Okay, okay, not from the house!"

As they stood to get off the bus, Max turned to Gloria and asked, "What will this cost me?"

She punched his arm, "Drop dead, Max! What kind of person do you think I am?"

"Look, you are doing me a very large favor here. I don't mind cleaning the bathroom for the rest of your life in exchange for this."

"Some things don't have a price, Max. This is one of those things."

He reached over and gave her a big hug. She pushed him away, "Don't get mushy on me. I'll call Sidney from the phone booth at school tonight."

"I can't thank you enough, Gloria."

"Don't thank me until we find out if Sidney will or even can do this. Somehow, I don't think he is sitting by the phone waiting for my call. You may not have noticed but I am not always the easiest person to be with."

"Yeah, I have noticed."

They both laughed.

*****

It was almost 8:30 in the evening before they returned to the house. Four of their five roommates were waiting in front of the house. "Where have you two been?" Steve demanded. "After what happened last night, we were really worried about you."

Gloria waived him off, "Don't get possessive here. Max and I were just picking out furniture. We've decided to end the pretense and get married."

"Not so funny, Gloria," Steve insisted. "We all agreed to meet here hours ago; we've been sitting on this stoop worried that something was terribly wrong. If you two decided to go it alone you should have given us the courtesy of a heads up call. I don't think that is asking so much."

Max moved between them. "I am sorry, guys. It was my fault."

"Well, where are the newspapers? Let's get started," Alan broke in.

"There aren't any newspapers. Someone broke into Sam's store last night and stole them," Gloria said.

"That's a strange coincidence," Steve said.

Gloria quickly responded, "We aren't so sure that it was a coincidence."

Max grabbed her arm and gave it a squeeze as he talked over her, "I think it is just a coincidence. Just two freak acts of vandalism, probably nothing more than that."

"Well, what do you want to do now, Max?" Steve asked.

"Not much we can do. Sam thinks it was just a group of kids out to do some mischief, nothing of value missing from either Sam's break-in or mine and no real damage to either place."

"What about your computer?"

"Yeah, there is my computer."

Mark James, spoke up. "I checked it over after the meeting this morning. It will need a lot of work but I should be able to get it working by morning with a few replacement parts. Meanwhile just use the one I loaned you this morning."

"Thanks, Mark," Max said. "That would be great. All I want to do now is put this whole thing behind me and get on with my life."

"You think the same kids did both break-ins?"

"Who knows? Hey, I'm sorry if I blew this thing out of all proportion. Let's just forget about it and move on. I was the one who called the house meeting; let me officially close the matter." Max said.

The others seemed relieved that they were now free to get on with their own priorities. Gloria watched as they all filtered back into the house. After they closed the door she ripped a page out of her binder and wrote, "Either they are all great actors or they really did not know about the break in of Sam's store until you mentioned it. What do you think?"

Max nodded his head in agreement.

*****

Neither Max nor Gloria noticed the powder blue mini-van with dark tinted glass, parked about halfway up the block. The driver turned to speak to a heavy set man in the back of the van. "You think that's the end of that, P.H.?"

"I don't know, Myron. Let's give it a bit more time before we jump to any conclusions."

"Whatever you say, P. H., whatever you say."

Chapter 9
Thursday, October 16, 1997,
Washington, D.C. – 6:15 A.M.

Every morning Max's alarm jarred him awake at 6 A.M.

When he first moved into the house he kept the oversized wind up alarm clock at the other end of the room to insure that he would have to get out of bed quickly, if only to stop the irritating noise before it woke the others. But the combination of the screeching alarm along with the loud thumping noises he made by jumping out of bed and running to the other side of the room woke most of his housemates anyway. To keep peace in the brownstone he moved the clock closer to the side of his bed.

Most mornings he pushed the snooze alarm button several times to get additional 5 minute increments of sleep, but ultimately, he succumbed to the inevitable and rolled out of bed. Within minutes of getting out of bed he was dressed, had connected his oversized earphones to his mini recorder, positioned the earphones onto his head, and after exiting the house through his fire escape, he was soon out on the street to begin his morning run. He never really enjoyed the exercise part of the run and judging from the looks of misery on the faces of most other runners he was convinced that no one really enjoyed running. He was convinced that an extra twenty or thirty minutes in a warm bed was much more civilized and might even be better for the body but that was not to be. There were benefits though, the fresh morning air almost always cleared his head and prepared him for whatever the new day held in store.

His usual routine was to leisurely jog from the house to Hadley Park, just outside of campus, up to the huge Willow tree in the center of the park. After circling the tree two times he would run back towards the house at a somewhat faster pace.

This morning, when the alarm went off at six A.M., he slowly got out of bed, dressed, and with his headphones firmly set against his ears, left the house. After the break in, he nailed his window shut from the inside and started using the main door to come and go from the house.

As usual, he was listening to classical music with the sound so high that anyone passing him could hear the sounds coming from his earphones.

There weren't many people coming or going at this hour. He seemed to be oblivious to the powder-blue minivan with dark tinted glass windows and Maryland license plates, moving along at a snail's pace several hundred yards behind him. The van continued to inch along as he entered Hadley Park. When he circled the huge tree he came within a few feet of the mini-van which had just jumped the curb and screeched to a halt in front of him. Both front doors swung open and two men, each in their early to mid thirties, ran towards him. Without saying a word, each of the men grabbed one of Max's arms and roughly pulled him towards the van.

As they neared the van the side door slowly rolled open, revealing a heavy set man seated in a huge swivel chair. Behind the man, Max could see several small television screens with an electronic panel of some kind.

The man gave Max a toothy smile, then in a strong southern accent said, "I don't know, for the life of me, why people jog. They always look like they are in excruciating pain."

"Maybe you should try it. It would do wonders for your love handles." Max said nervously.

The two men tightened their hold on Max but the man in the van waived his hand at them, "Easy boys. Let's not damage the goods." Then looking at Max he said, "I do not know very much about you, young man, but from the little I do know, I suggest that a battle of wits between you and me would show that you are only half prepared."

"Look, if this is a holdup, all I can say is that you have really picked the wrong guy."

"It is not a hold up, Max."

"You know my name?"

The man in the van smiled and said, "Yes, Max, we know your name."

"Well, the police are all over this park. If you and your goons don't let me go I am going to scream for help."

The man in the van gave out a hearty laugh, "Please Max, we both know that there isn't a policeman for miles in any direction at this hour. But have no fear; my associates will let you go whenever I tell them to let you go."

"What is this all about?"

"It's about two kinds of people, Max. Good, solid, patriotic Americans and their opposites, or as I choose to label them, traitors. My associates and I believe that every person is one," a long pause, "or the other. There is no in between." He moved forward in his chair and pointed his finger at Max. "Which of these are you, Max? Are you a patriot who loves and honors this wonderful, God fearing country of ours, or are you a traitor who would love nothing more than to smudge the good people in our glorious past and bring dishonor to our beloved country and the true patriots who fought to keep it free each and every day of their lives? Which one describes you best? Hmmmmmmmmm?"

The man in the van moved his finger to tap a pin on his lapel. It was a replica of the American flag. Max watched as the sunlight bounced off of the man's massive gold colored pinky ring. On its face were three raised initials, P, I, H. Each letter was outlined with what looked like sparkling gems of some kind.

"Look, if I want a civics lesson I'll call you. Meanwhile, if I were you, I would let me go, now."

"But you are not me, Max. That is becoming clearer each moment we spend together. Just remember this", he paused slightly, "the past is always best left alone. To dig into that which does not concern you is folly, at best, and could be life threatening, at worst."

"Are you threatening me?" Max asked, his legs beginning to shake.

The man's mood quickly turned from easygoing to unpleasant. He waived his hand in the air and barked, "I think this young man has taken quite enough of our time and attention. Let him go."

Max asked, "Were you the ones who broke into my room?"

"I thought you were anxious to end this conversation Max."

Max mustered up all of the strength he could. "I don't want any of you to bother me or my roommates again or I will go straight to the police. Do you understand me? I think you will find them to have very little tolerance for such forceful civic lessons."

"But you *will* see us again, Max. You can count on that. And as far as the police are concerned, you might find them to be far more understanding of our version of events than yours. We have many friends who believe as we believe.

I suggest to you that they don't have much tolerance for non-patriots, either."

The man in the van moved forward and quickly swung the door shut. The two younger men got into the front of the van, slammed the doors behind them, the driver gunned the motor, and they all sped away.

Max squinted to read the license plate as the van quickly drove away. Most of the license plate was covered with mud. All he could make out were the first two letters, 'O', 'O', and the last digit, the number '1'. He kept repeating those characters to himself during the run back to the house.

*****

When Max reached the house, he went straight to Gloria's room. He gently tapped the back of his hand on her door and entered the room. She was still asleep. He covered her mouth with one hand and shook her awake with the other as he whispered into her ear, "Don't be afraid, and don't say anything when I remove my hand from your mouth. I must talk to you but not here. Quickly get dressed and meet me at the library."

He slowly removed his hand and she nodded her head acknowledging that she understood.

He stood up and walked towards the door, then moved back towards her and whispered, "Please make certain that you are not followed." She was barely awake but knew from the look in his eyes that the only choice she had was to nod her head in acknowledgement.

Max went up to his room and quickly traded his running clothes for a pair of jeans and a warm pullover. He grabbed some books and notes and ran in the opposite direction of the library, ducking into alleys and up the wrong way on one way streets. When he felt sure that no one could be following, he jumped onto a bus that circled the campus. By the time he reached the library Gloria was already there.

"What is this all about Max?"

"This 'Illia thing' is getting weirder and weirder. Three CIA types jumped me while I was on my morning run."

"This isn't funny anymore, Max."

"This was *never* funny, Gloria, least of all to me."

"Well, what are you going to do?"

"I don't know what I can do. But, what I do know is that I feel a little like Alice in Wonderland, things are getting curiouser and curiouser and I am scared out of my wits."

"O.K., calm down, just tell me what you do know and let's see if we can find some way to make sense out of it."

Chapter 10
**Wednesday, February 8, 1995,
Brooklyn, New York – 11:00 A.M.**

Although most antique dealers genuinely enjoy dealing with the people as they browse through the shelves
searching for items which remind them of their actual or
imagined past; some of these merchants also welcome
the periods when they are the only human being in their
store. During such pockets of isolation they fill the time
with personal or business correspondence or reach out to
acquire additional inventories, or do research on items
already in stock, or catch up on their reading, or just day
dream. For a portion of these urban archeologists, any
and all negatives applied to these quiet periods are more
than made up for by being around the items in their store
– so many of which represent positive reminders of *their
own* past. But, the greatest of all times for them come
when they are permitted to rummage through someone's
dark and dusty attic or basement in hopes of salvaging
a rare find or unique example of simpler times; seeking
hidden treasures which had been considered ordinary a
generation or more before but whose value has grown
disproportionately over the years merely because it can
now spark someone's happier memories.

Most of these professionals wouldn't trade their jobs for
anything.

Albert Froog was definitely *not* one of those dealers. In
fact, he regularly told anyone who would listen how much
he despised this line of work... how his mother and grandmother had conspired to entrap him into this dead end
life as a caretaker of *'yesteryear's garbage'*. Albert Froog
was brought into the business kicking and screaming.
No, he definitely was not in it for the sense of discovery

or the satisfaction of saving something from extinction –
believing that he had no way out he was now in it strictly
for the money.

'Better Times Remembered', a small antique store was first
started by Evelyn Zaleson, Froog's maternal grandmother.
Less than three hours after hearing about the vacant store
at 70 Lee Avenue in the Williamsburg section of Brooklyn,
she signed a three year lease and began her proud career
as an antique dealer.

During the busy weeks prior to her grand opening, while
she was building inventory and getting the empty space
ready for her new business, she visited with many of the
other shopkeepers within a two block area. She had a
warm and friendly way about her which turned many of
the neighboring retailers into powerful supporters of her
new business.

Nancy Myerson, who ran the bakery directly across the
street, and Moisha Rubens from the hardware store down
the block were the first merchants to begin talking about
the new shop of old treasures and its friendly and informa-
tive owner to their customers. Milton Kahn, who operated
the drugstore diagonally across from the new store, actually enclosed one of Evelyn's promotional flyers with every
prescription he filled. Soon after opening for business the
little store became a regular stop for local shoppers. The
business prospered and so, when the store next door became vacant, she convinced both of the landlords to knock
the connecting wall down, doubling her space.

Evelyn loved being around people and they instantly
sensed her genuine commitment to making anyone who
entered her store feel as if she woke up that morning with
only one purpose, to take care of *them*.

When she died, she left her only child, Elizabeth Morgan

Froog, Albert's mother, several million dollars worth of AT&T stock, some local real estate, and her most prized possession, the antique store. Elizabeth inherited her mother's love for the business. She described her new position as the protector of priceless reminders of simpler, more glorious days.

As a small boy, Froog constantly complained about the business, especially the many hours his mother spent in it. Over dinner she would try to share the experiences of her day only to be bombarded by Froog's negative jabs – "How can you spend so much time in that stuffy old fire trap and deal with that even stuffier clientele?" "Who needs all of those dirty, rusty things?" Regardless of where any given conversation might have begun, it usually ended with, "Can't we just get rid of that undersized garbage can."

Inwardly, he knew his mother would never abandon his grandmother's pride and joy. Eventually he accepted that one day it would be handed down to him, as the only child of Elizabeth and Manny Froog, and spent most of his waking moments thinking how best to do away with the store when that day finally came. He dreaded the thought of being trapped there for the rest of his life. Unfortunately for Froog, his mother's will contained the very same clause, word for word, that was in his grandmother's will:

> *The inheritor must personally operate the business known as "Better Times Remembered" at 70 Lee Avenue, Brooklyn, New York. Others may be hired to assist but the inheritor must be physically in the store during every minute of its operation to insure proper care of the inventory and respectfully serve each and every guest in the store; regardless of how much they purchase, even if they choose to make no purchase at all.*

> *The store may not be sold or permanently closed*

for any reason other than official condemnation of the property. (If condemnation occurs then another location must be established within walking distance of the existing space and be ready for business within two weeks from the time operations in the original location ended). If the business itself fails to generate sufficient operating profits of its own then monies are to be transferred from the balance of the estate. As long as there is as much as $1.00, (one dollar), remaining in the overall estate, these are to be binding conditions. Should this clause be legally tested or if the store is not personally operated by the inheritor then the balance of any stock and all remaining funds, less $1.00, (one dollar), is to be turned over to the Salvation Army. The inheritor is to be paid the remaining $1.00 (one dollar), and not a penny more.

When the family lawyer read the terms of the will to Albert he almost exploded. "She knew I hated this business." Albert complained to the lawyer, "There must be a way to break this will."

The lawyer, who never liked Albert, matter-of-factly told him, "If you fight it you will lose everything but $1.00. The terms are quite clear and binding. I know this to be true because I wrote this will."

"Well, she may be able to hang that pathetic little dump around my neck but she can't make me like it."

The will also specified that the store must be opened for business every day but Saturday from 10:00 A.M. sharp until 5:00 P.M. It may close for lunch - at any time of the inheritor's choosing - during the day. Albert kept coming back to the phrase, *any time of the inheritor's choosing*. It didn't take too long for the devious Albert Froog to work this to his advantage. He had a huge sign made for the front window:

NEW STORE HOURS
OPEN <u>EVERY</u> DAY
SUNDAY THROUGH FRIDAY
OPEN: 10:00 A.M.
CLOSED: 5:00 P.M.
CLOSED FOR LUNCH
10:01 A.M. – 4:59 P.M.
CLOSED SATURDAY

He showed the sign to his mother's lawyer. The lawyer delayed his response as long as he could and then told Albert, "it definitely does not meet the spirit of your mother's will, but legally, it meets the conditions."

Albert gave a hearty laugh and that was that!

*****

Tuesday, May 7, 1996, Baltimore,
Maryland – 8:03 A.M.

As his mother's health began to suffer, so did the business's profitability. By the time he inherited the store it was little more than a financial drain and a tax loss against the rest of the estate. He made up his mind that if he had to be tied down to it he was going to find a way to make it profitable or at least be more than just a tax loss. He was one of the first antique dealers to effectively use the internet to buy and sell merchandise. It was on the internet that he first learned about the attic full of belongings for sale in Baltimore, Maryland. It sounded like the kind of merchandise he could turn quickly and at a good profit.

A lawyer was responsible for the sale of the merchandise. This was usually a bad sign for him. Albert preferred to deal with owners or better yet, grieving relatives. They rarely knew the true value of their property, enabling him to underbid. Lawyers, on the other hand, shared his lack of emotion. They too were only in it for the money.

He had developed a successful process when negotiating such purchases. First he would quickly review the lot, come up with a net resale value of the pieces he could turn quickly; then he would base his bid for the entire lot on between ten and fifteen percent of the amount he believed he could get for the few prominent pieces. Sometimes it worked, sometimes he had to go a bit higher, but generally his *formula* resulted in a successful buy, huge profits, and quick turnover. As he walked through the attic storage area in the old Baltimore home he started the first stage of his process while belittling the overall value of the lot.

"I don't know", he would say, scratching his head, "so much of this is quite lovely and in acceptable condition but frankly, quite worthless to the customers with whom I deal," he mumbled in the general direction of the lawyer handling the sale. "But, I'm here already; I guess I should at least make an offer as long as you understand that we are talking about low value goods. What are you looking to get for the lot?"

The lawyer smiled, "Please, Mr. Froog, let's not play games with each other. This is not my first day at the rodeo and I surmise it isn't your first day either. Let's do this my way, just tell me what you are willing to pay and I will either thank you and take your cash or money order or I will wish you a good day and wait for the next dealer to make a more serious offer. There *are* other dealers, you know?"

"Come on; be reasonable, you know we aren't dealing with priceless valuables here."

"Then I guess you have wasted your time. Shall I see you out?"

While they were haggling, a man in his early forties joined them. He shook the lawyer's hand and smiled at Albert.

The lawyer greeted the young man with a broad smile, "Morning Fred, this is Mr. Froog from New York. He was just telling me that he had no interest in buying your mother's valuable belongings..."

"Wait a minute, I never said that."

"Look guys, my sister and I just want to empty the house so it can be sold as quickly as possible. What is your best offer, Mr. Froog?"

Albert saw this as a good sign and pounced on it. He had already estimated that he could quickly turn a pair of lamps in the far corner of the room for several thousand dollars.

"I can give you $200 or maximum $215 but I would want to leave the few pieces of furniture. Frankly, it would cost me that and more to just ship it back to my shop."

"That is just an insult," the lawyer quickly cut in. "Let's just call another dealer, Fred."

"That does seem rather low, Mr. Froog," the young man said.

"I hate arguing. O.K., my partner will kill me but I'll make it $500, but I can't go any higher," Albert said.

"Forget it," the lawyer shouted.

Froog feared that he would lose the lamps and knowing that there were at least five or eight thousand dollars more to be made from several other interesting pieces in the dusty attic he quickly cut in. "My partner will wonder if I have completely lost my mind, but I'm here already. Okay, $725, but that is it!"

"Make it a thousand and you have a deal," the young man countered.

"Whooooooweee," Albert groaned and after a deep sigh he said, "I can't believe that I am doing this, but it's a deal, a thousand dollars."

"Sold," the younger man said, over the objections of his lawyer. "But you will just have to take it all. The room must be emptied, so if you choose to drop the furniture off along the way at some thrift center that is completely up to you and fine with me."

"But the freight charges, at least help me with the freight charges," Albert begged.

"Take off a hundred dollars for the freight," the young man offered, "but that's it. Take it or leave it."

Albert couldn't resist trying to drive an even better deal, "How about $750 in cash, and I will pay for the freight."

"How about $900?" The younger man asked.

"That's it," the lawyer jumped in. "Fred, if I were to let you accept such a low ball offer I would be unworthy of your mother's trust in me."

"Thank you for your concern but he is here and Stephanie and I just want all of this to be gone." The younger man said.

"Can I at least leave those heavy pieces of furniture and that broken down cabinet? They look like they weigh a ton..."

The lawyer grabbed his client's arm, "You are just giving this away. I know you can get more than $900 for these treasures."

Worried that the lawyer might change his client's mind, Albert quickly counted out nine one hundred dollar bills and motioned to the two waiting moving men to begin moving the pieces into their truck.

"You are making a terrible mistake." The lawyer whispered loudly in the young man's ear.

"You drive a hard bargain, sir." Froog said, "You must be very successful in your line of work. I'm just a simple antique dealer. What do I know?"

The lawyer glared at Albert.

*****

Monday, May 13, 1996, Brooklyn, New York – 11:10 A.M.

Almost a week later, the truck pulled up to Froog's small store in Brooklyn.

"You will have to help us with some of the heavier pieces," the driver demanded. This is one heavy load. What is it made of, lead?" the driver laughed.

The last piece on the truck was a small wooden cabinet. It took the driver, his helper and Albert all of their combined energies just to move the piece to the edge of the truck. They started to lift it and it proved too unmanageable for them. "I'm losing it," the driver yelled. "Look out, it's gonna fall."

Before the other two men could react the piece slipped off the truck and onto the ground, breaking into numerous splintered pieces. "Gee, I'm really sorry, but it was so heavy."

"Well, I will just have to deduct the cost of this valuable cabinet from your bill," Albert howled, as he quietly thought to himself that the deduction could cover much of what he paid for the entire lot plus the freight costs to get it to his store.

"Hey," the driver's assistant yelled, "It looks like the piece wasn't emptied, look at all of the stuff that was left inside."

The driver looked down at what appeared to be numerous blocks of yellowed paper among the broken boards. "You know the rules, Mister; furniture must be emptied of all contents prior to shipping. If you failed to empty it then we are not responsible for any resulting damage. It's all there in the original set of documents."

Albert jumped down from the truck to examine the damage. "Not so quick, you aren't off the hook yet," he yelled. "Looks like some papers were stuffed in the backboard. Probably just packing materials, couldn't even have added that much weight and I had no way of knowing it was even in there."

"You'll have to take it up with my dispatcher, but if you don't pay for the delivery according to my paperwork it all goes back. That's the law."

"Fine! Fine! Meanwhile just help me get all of these valuable treasures off the street and into my shop. Clearly you have no idea how irreplaceable these artifacts are."

*****

After the truck drove off, Albert took a closer look at the damaged piece. "It will be easier to get rid of this junk now that it is in pieces. At least they didn't damage the lamps."

He gathered the various packs of papers that had fallen out of the cabinet and tossed them into a garbage can along with the broken remains of the cabinet. He assumed the papers were just packing materials or worthless insulation, although he did stop to wonder why a cabinet would need insulation of any kind. He then went on to review the more interesting pieces of the lot.

He carefully unwrapped and inspected the lamps. These

are really nice, he thought. They are going to fetch a pretty price once I clean them up. He started to check them out using various reference works. If I could source and date these beauties they might bring in an even better price than I initially thought.

There were no factory marks but from the extensive gold leafing, overall design, and hardware he knew they would fetch a pretty penny. O.K., he thought to himself, if I can't match it to a premium manufacturer, perhaps I can tie it to a specific artist or craftsman. It would definitely help if I could pinpoint a place or even a date of manufacture. He went back to the garbage pail and dumped the contents out onto the floor. Maybe the packing papers will give me a clue to a time or place.

He took a closer look at the items that initially fell out of the cabinet. They seemed to be packages of individual papers, each package tied on all four sides with faded pink or very light red colored ribbons. Water damage over the years caused some of the packages to form solid blocks of paper. He looked around the room for a clean empty box and began sorting through the small bundles of paper. He accumulated about a dozen packs that were in better condition than the rest and tossed them into the box and carried it to his backroom office.

He set the individual packages on his desk and as he picked up a package, the ribbon almost disintegrated in his hands, setting free a number of individual papers. He shuffled through the pages. Instead of newsprint, which he expected, he found small written notes, each individual character beautifully formed. At first glance they looked like part of a journal but after a while he felt confident that he was reading correspondence, mostly, to the same person, Virginia; all from the same person, Becky.

Each entry seemed to cover thoughts for an individual day.

Some entries were just a few words while others went on for pages. He began reading:

> *Virginia, 9 August, '79*
> *Daddy is much weaker today and seems to be suffering so much. Please Lord; watch over this good and caring man.*
> *-Becky*
>
> *Virginia, 10 August, 79*
> *All we can do now is pray for Daddy's soul while we make him as comfortable as possible. The end seems near...*
> *-Becky*

"Now, why would this be used as packing materials?" He wondered aloud. Picking up another bundle he twisted the ribbon until it snapped. So what do we have here, old journals or letters? He began reading from the new batch:

> *Virginia, 23 September, '79*
> *Today we put Daddy to rest. God rest his soul. Miss Martha asked to be able to say her own goodbye and the Governor gave his permission. Daddy was always happy to see Miss Martha. Miss Martha spoke about how he taught her how to ride and always made sure she got the sweetest tempered horse in the stable.*
>
> *She said that she will never forget him. No one who ever knew him could possibly ever forget him. I know that I will never forget him, or her, for her kindnesses during this painful time in my life.*
> *-Becky*

He was beginning to get bored with these papers. He picked up another batch and snapped the ribbons.

> *Washington City, 16 January, '06*
> *Horace is so deeply troubled by the President's problem.*
>
> *Surely it can't be long before the secret is out and*

someone is made to pay for Illia Sharpell's murder. He was indeed a terrible man but killing is a sin and either in this life or the next, someone must be made to pay for it.

It was written in the good book, an eye for an eye, a death for a death.
-Becky

This was the only page that was legible in this batch. He read it again. "So Virginia isn't a 'who' it is a place. I know where Virginia is but where the hell is Washington City? It could be anywhere." All he could read from a fragment of another page in this group was:

Early in the morning Horace left for Monticello.

"There's a 'Monticello' in upstate New York," he said to himself. "Yeah, the Catskills has a Monticello. Maybe they have a Washington City up there too. Good, we are closing in on a location for these lamps, he thought.

He pushed his chair back and lit a cigar. As he leaned back in his chair, blowing smoke circles in the air, he put both hands behind his head and thought aloud, "these papers cover the better part of a hundred years, from early 1900 to at least the late 1970's. They involve a Governor and a President, of something. This Becky broad sure got around. He reached over for the first paper he read and compared it with the last one. Strange though, he thought, her handwriting didn't seem to change over the years. I thought everyone's handwriting gets shaky as they age. She had to be in her eighties when she wrote this last note, maybe even her nineties.

He reached for another batch. The top page was almost completely smeared but for the last two lines on the page.

...so evil that he would blackmail the mighty Speaker of the House. Illia Sharpell will surely burn in hell.

A President, of something; a Speaker of the House, those aren't small change positions... this maybe even be about a real Governor... his mind was racing now, "either this old bag had a mighty powerful imagination, or this could be even more valuable than the lamps", he screamed at the top of his lungs.

He went back to the garbage area and picked up the remaining batches of papers, regardless of condition. This time he handled them with much more care. He placed them on the desk alongside the others. He cleared a space on the work table behind his desk and began organizing the batches – as best he could – by date. Froog had no way of knowing how truthful the contents were, but what was 'true' never mattered very much to him anyway. He regularly made up 'back stories' about the antiques he sold. The stronger the story the more he could get for the item. And in the end, he not only made up most stories using a phony source but then added a seal of legitimacy by personally authenticated it. "Who's gonna prove me wrong? The original owner is long gone most times," he would brag to other dealers. Staring at the piles of loose papers he said, "If these are even 'close' to being true they could be worth hundreds, no, thousands, maybe even millions of dollars to some crazy collector. Some days I love this business!"

He placed a call to the lawyer who handled the Baltimore sale. When the lawyer came to the phone Albert said, "Hi! Remember me? I'm Albert Froog, the New York dealer, I purchased –"

The lawyer quickly cut him off in mid-sentence, "A deal is a deal, Mr. Froog. No returns no complaints. This transaction is done and done."

Albert laughed, nervously, "Nothing like that, sir. I am not calling to undo the deal, a deal is a deal, yes, a deal is a deal. It is a belief I fully live by and have always followed."

"Well then, why are you calling?"

"I just wanted to ask you a few questions."

"You will have to be brief; I am due in court within the hour. What is it that you want to know?"

"Was your client the original owner of the goods I purchased?"

"Sorry, Mr. Froog, I can't help you there. I just don't know the answer to that question."

"Could you tell me how old your client was when she died?"

"She was just shy of 60, Mr. Froog."

"And when, exactly did she die?"

"We lost her earlier this year."

"Was she from a prominent family?"

"Strange question, what do you mean by prominent?"

"Was she or any member of her family in what we might call public life or politics?"

"I don't believe so."

"I was hoping to put a date on some of the items in the lot, to help me sell them. Can you help me do that?"

"Not really. I'm afraid your guess is as good as mine. Now, I don't want to be rude, Mr. Froog, but if there isn't anything else I really must get on my way."

"Wait."

"Yes, Mr. Froog, I'm still here."

"Had Becky's father been sick for a long time before he died?"

"Becky? Becky who?"

"Wasn't that the name of your client?"

"No, it wasn't. My client's name was Alma Cereen. I thought you knew that. It was in the original notice I placed to advertise the sale of the lot. Well, as I said, I don't want to be rude but I really must go now."

Albert slowly put the phone back on its cradle. "I should have picked up on that, these couldn't have been his client's notes, she wasn't even alive in 1900. So who was Becky?"

Over the next few days Froog carefully arranged the legible pages in what he thought was their chronological order. More than half of the sheets were either partially or entirely lost due to water damage and the ravages of time. As he read from the remaining pages he thought he had pieced together a story of political intrigue and possibly even criminal activity involving local or state politicians from 'somewhere' in this country. He was now convinced that properly positioned to the right buyer, this part of the lot could be worth a fortune, and if so, it would add even more value to the remaining pieces from the Baltimore lot.

Albert scanned each page into his computer. He cross referenced names and places and selected key details. Since he assumed '00 was 1900 he actually put them in reverse sequence and settled on a dateline that he thought was early January, 1900 through late August, 1984. He concluded that this timeline would have made the writer, 'Becky', the better part of a hundred years old when she either died or stopped writing. The handwriting never aged, which made no sense to him, but then again, it didn't have to make sense, it only had to make money. He was confident that he could create a story into something that would make him money and plenty of it. His primary focus was now centered on finding out who was involved, the more prominent the names, the better for him.

Each time he thought about a selling price for this hidden treasure his mental asking price added a zero, or two. If all else failed he was more than willing to invent names that was the part of being an antique dealer that satisfied him the most, "All the better to fleece the sheep!"

He drafted a short description of his 'find' and placed it on the internet and waited for a response. He had almost given up hope of hearing from anyone when he received Mark James's e-mail.

Chapter 11
Wednesday, October 15, 1997,
Washington, D.C.–

Mark James wasn't *just* the best computer wizard within the brownstone; he was lovingly trained to be 'the' computer wizard's computer wizard. His father, Will James, had been the first juvenile ever to be tried and convicted for computer hacking. He was found guilty of breaking into the Defense Threat Reduction Agency server, a prime asset of a sub agency of the Department of Defense. This department was charged with reducing threats to the U.S. and its allies from nuclear, biological, chemical, conventional and special weapons. James claimed that he was just playing around, trying to see what he could do and was more surprised than the government when he finally succeeded. The backdoor he created gave him access to sensitive emails, official employee usernames and passwords.

He had mixed emotions about accessing the Department of Defense servers. His first reaction was that he had outfoxed the best, but that quickly turned to concern. He was bright enough to realize that if he could do it then so could real enemies of the country. He anonymously sent a letter to the Secretary of Defense in the Pentagon, in which he detailed the vulnerabilities of their systems. He suggested changes they could make to improve their system's security. Several weeks after sending the letter he went back into their system only to find that nothing had changed. They had clearly chosen to ignore his suggestions and failed to even make any changes of their own. It was as easy to hack into their system now as it had been the previous time. He wondered, could it be that they just didn't care?

He sent another letter, this time much stronger and more detailed. He waited another few weeks and still was able to move in and out of their system as freely as before. Well, he thought to himself, maybe they just need a louder wake up call. He infected their files with a virus, changed some of their commands and copied sensitive employee passwords and usernames. He read and selected a series of files that had been marked confidential and sent them all, anonymously, to the Washington Post.

His involvement might never have been traced back to him had he not been so brazen as to send the Secretary of State's personal security code to one of the underground newspapers. This brought his activities to the personal attention of the United States Attorney General who created a special task force led by no less than the Director of the FBI. They swooped down on the underground newspaper with a vengeance. It didn't take too long before the editor of the newspaper gave them James' name and address.

If he had been an adult at the time, he would most likely have been sentenced to at least ten years in a Federal prison. But he was only 16 and considered a juvenile. The court banned him from recreational computer use and gave him a six-month sentence under house arrest with probation. He wound up serving most of his sentence in a juvenile prison facility anyway for violation of parole.

The government never stopped watching him. He, every member of his immediate family and it seemed like anyone he ever knew was followed around the clock and repeatedly brought in for questioning. To the authorities, he was a threat to the nation's security; to the underground 'hacking' community he became a super hero.

Under his father's watchful eye, Mark grew to be every bit as capable and devious with a computer keyboard. Mark also copied his father's rebellious nature in other ways. He kept pretty much to himself, trusted few others than his closest friends and immediate relatives, and accepted as his personal responsibility the task of thumbing his nose at authority as often as possible.

At school he avoided all social functions and although he could easily have excelled he chose instead to maintain a low profile. Few fellow students even knew his name, and he liked it that way. As a true act of rebellion he decided that he would not take any of the final exams. When he realized that not taking finals meant that he would get automatic failing marks he decided to *bend* his self-imposed rebellion. Thumbing your nose at society was one thing, not graduating or getting a diploma was quite another. He tapped into the school's computer system and gave himself barely passing grades on all of the final exams. He could have given himself any grade he wanted – and probably deserved much higher ones than those he plugged in for himself - but all he wanted was to graduate. It was enough for him to know that he could have scored well in the exams had he chosen to take them. He reasoned that the marks, in and of themselves, were of no value in the greater scheme of things. Knowledge was the prize and he absorbed all of the knowledge they had to offer.

It was no secret within the brownstone that he had a huge crush on Gloria. He hung on her every word. In fact, it was something she said to him in passing that ultimately led them all to the Becky Freeman diaries.

The day Max's room was trashed Gloria was in a worse mood than usual. "Can you believe his nerve," she said to Mark. "He just assumed that one of us had nothing better to do between the hours of three and six in the morning than to turn his closet of a room upside down."

It was rare for her to talk to him about anything and so Mark was grateful for the opening. "I'm sure he would never suspect you, Gloria," he told her.

"Yeah, yeah, whatever, but the reality is that someone did trash his room. If none of us did it then who did? It didn't happen by itself."

Mark said, "He could have just stumbled around in his sleep. His room is so small that it wouldn't have taken much to create such a mess."

"I don't know," she responded. "He never walked in his sleep before that we know of. I just don't know," she began to smile. "Maybe Thomas Jefferson came back from the dead to try to get Max to finally leave him alone." They both laughed.

Mark, trying to comfort her, said, "You know, Gloria, if there is someone from the outside trying to do bad things in this house maybe you should let us watch over you and protect you. You know, I wouldn't mind -"

She patted his arm, "That's sweet, Mark, you're okay, really okay, but I'll be fine. No one is going to send me floating down the Potomac like poor old Illia Sharpell."

"What is that?"

"What is what?"

"What is an Illia Shapnal?"

"Illia Sharpell, it's some person. Anyway, according to Max, he was a stenographer for the Speaker of the House."

"A male stenographer, that's unusual. Tell me more."

"It was in something Max found in the newspaper. According to the article this Illia guy was found floating in the Potomac."

"I don't remember reading about that."

Gloria gave out a hearty laugh, "There is no way you could have read about it; I bet you only read current newspapers. For some reason the self defined Jeffersonian authority upstairs prefers century old newspapers. And he calls me weird."

"Century old newspapers," Mark said. "That is certainly different."

"Well maybe not century old, but definitely older than the ones 'normal' people read. Seems his friend Sam introduced him to these back issues and one of those papers reported about this Illia guy getting his ticket punched. I don't know what about that got Max's interest, but it did."

"An old crime, hmmmmmm." Mark mused.

"Hey, don't you get weird on me too." Gloria shot back.

"Well, you do have to admit that it is somewhat intriguing." Mark said.

"Oh, give me a break!" Gloria said.

"And the dead guy was Illia Shapnal?" Mark asked.

"Not Shapnal. *Sharpell.*" She corrected.

"Illia Sharpell, funny sounding name." Mark said.

"Yeah, real funny," she said, sarcastically.

*****

Later that night, in the school library, Mark James began 'noodling', as he called it, on the school computer. He entered a series of search words, typing each in both upper and lower case combinations. Then he entered Illia Sharpell. When nothing surfaced, he used an old trick his father taught him. He typed in a series of letters the British intelligence agency came up with during the war to break codes. He then combined the results with 'Speaker of the House', 'Thomas Jefferson', and 'Potomac'. The screen filled up with lines of what looked like gibberish. He began to work through each line and then the screen seemed to come to life. "Bingo!" he yelled in excitement to the glares of the others in the room. He ran back to the house and up to Gloria's room.

Disappointed that Gloria was not there, he went further up the rickety stairway to Max's room and knocked on the door.

"Whoever it is, just go away!" Max yelled.

"Okay by me, Max," Mark said. "I just thought you were interested in this Sharpell guy."

Max jumped up quickly, hitting his head so hard he could see stars, "Wait, wait."

He quickly opened the door and put his hand against Mark's mouth and whispered in his ear, "Don't say another word."

Still, with his hand tightly against Mark's mouth he led him into the bathroom, closed and locked the door, and with one hand still tightly held against Mark's mouth he turned all of the water faucets on full speed and kept flushing the toilet. "I'm going to take my hand away from your mouth," Max whispered into Mark's ear. "And when I do, I don't want you to say a word. Do you understand me?"

Mark slowly nodded his head up and down but when Max removed his hand Mark screamed, "Are you completely out of your mind?"

"Shhhhhhhhhhh!"

"Don't shhhhhhhhh me, Max. I think you have finally gone over the edge!" Max covered his mouth again, this time he brought his face close to Mark's and said, "Do not say a word. DO... YOU... UNDERSTAND... ME?"

Then in a more pleading tone Max said, "Listen, Mark, I promise I will explain fully, just do not speak until we are away from the house. Just trust me for the little time it will take us to walk down the street. Okay?"

Again, Mark nodded up and down.

Max led Mark out of the door and towards the corner bus stop. When the bus arrived he gently pushed Mark towards the open door. "Get on the bus, Mark."

"I will not."

"Mark, get on the bus."

"You're acting like a crazy man, Max. I am not moving another inch until you explain what is going on here."

"Please, Mark. I promise to clear this up. Just not out here, please get on the bus."

The bus driver yelled, "On or off boys. I have a schedule to maintain."

"Please, Mark, get on the bus. Use your head, what can I possibly do to you on a public bus?"

"Don't tell me what to do, Max. You're being irrational and scaring the hell out of me."

"Hey, if anyone should understand what I am going through right now it is you! Get on the goddamn bus and I promise you a story that will make your father's experience with the Feds look like a walk in the park."

"What the hell does this have to do with my father's experiences? And just for the record, old pal, I don't appreciate your throwing that in my face – now or ever."

The bus driver pressed his horn, giving it a long and loud blast. "I do *not* want to have to tell you boys again. I have a schedule to keep. Either get on the bus or clear the doorway. Do one or the other, your choice, but make that choice *now*."

Max moved closer to Mark and whispered, "If you will get on this bus I will answer any question you might have." Hesitantly, Mark climbed the few steps onto the bus. "Okay," he said, "but this better be good."

Max stuffed the necessary coins into the fair box for both of them and gestured for Mark to take a seat in the back of the nearly empty bus.

When the bus pulled away from the curb Mark turned to Max and said, "This better be good, Max, real... damn... good!"

Max looked around the bus and took a long look out of the back window, and then with his face inches away from Mark's he slowly began, "There are some very scary people after me."

Mark groaned, "That's it? That is why you practically suffocated me?"

"I'm not kidding around here, Mark; this is very, very heavy stuff. And I may inadvertently have gotten everyone else in the house involved and I am truly frightened about what might come of that."

"Just come to the point, Max. Why did you try to suffocate me and why are we on this bus?"

"Just tell me what you know about Illia Sharpell."

"Hell no! First tell me why you tried to suffocate me and why we are on this bus?" Mark's voice was getting louder and the driver and other passengers were beginning to stare at them.

"Mark, I am only going to say this one more time, what do you know about Illia Sharpell?"

Mark looked carefully into Max's eyes, "Okay, I'll tell you. He was a little blackmailer."

"How do you know that?" Max asked.

"It was all on the internet. I know a whole lot about him." Mark said.

"Did you use the computer in the house?" Max asked.

"No, I was in the school library and tapped into the Dean's private line like I always do."

"Don't use any of the lines in the house." Max broke in.

"Why not?" Mark asked.

"They are all bugged." Max said.

Mark began to laugh, "Hey, I am the house conspiracy nut, what are you trying to do, take away my claim to fame? Who could possibly want to bug our lines?"

"I don't know. But I do know that we are being bugged."

"Hey, if we were being bugged, I would certainly know before you would."

"Well, this time you missed it and I can tell you that we are being bugged – every room – every one of us – every line."

"How can you be so sure?"

"Because I had a security expert sweep the house. He went through every room with his gear."

"You allowed someone to wander around my room without my permission?"

"Yes. I'm sorry Mark, but I just had to know for sure."

"You had no right."

"Calm down."

"It was a rotten thing to do!"

"Don't be a jerk. Be honest, if you were in my shoes, wouldn't you have done the same thing?"

"That's beside the point. How do you think the rest of the guys will react to the news that you invaded their privacy? Do you think that what you did is any different from what the people who trashed your room did?"

"First of all, you cannot tell the other guys. It will only get them deeper into whatever this is. Second of all, it is already done, move on."

"That's really easy for you to say. My family has been spied on since I can remember. This is really hard for me to listen to and just move on."

"Okay, whatever you feel, you feel. I can't change that now. Just tell me what you know about Illia Sharpell."

Mark stood up, "Go to hell, Max."

Max pulled him back onto the seat. "Listen Mark, I have already been grabbed and threatened by three C.I.A. types. Somehow I have entered a nightmare through a one-way mirror and I am asking for your help."

"Hey, I don't have to do anything. I'm a suspect, remember?"

Max took a deep breath, "You know, Mark, for a very bright guy, sometimes you can be a real baby."

Mark put his hand on Max's arm. "You win. Just tell me about the C.I.A."

"Well, I don't know for certain that they are C.I.A. All I do know is that they followed me on my run this morning and roughed me up a little. They tried to scare me and were successful at it."

"Did they flash their badges?" Mark asked.

"No, they didn't." Max said.

"Hey," Mark yelled back, "*if* they were C.I.A. you'd know it. These guys like flashing their creds."

"Well, they didn't 'flash creds' this morning, but it sure made me feel that they had the power to crush me and no one would ever make them pay a price for it. You have no idea how that felt."

"I have no idea? I have no idea? My family knows all too well about the 'shove now, apologize later bunch'. So you think whoever broke into your room and Sam's store also bugged our house?"

"It's the only way this thing seems to fit together."

"A real goddamn mystery."

"Yeah. So tell me what you learned about Illia Sharpell."

"I told you, he was a blackmailer."

"How do you know"?

"His name popped up when I inquired on the internet."

"Maybe you should tell me from the beginning."

"I put out a search using various phonetic versions of his name. I found a message posted by an antiques dealer in New York. Seems this dealer was trying to evaluate a couple of boxes of old diaries written by some rich old lady between 1900 and 1980. He put her name and various other names that appeared in the diaries onto the internet in hopes of attracting someone who knew more about any or all of the people named in her diaries. He told me that my response was the only one he got after almost a year of trying."

"1980? You're certain that the outside date was 1980?"

"That is what he posted."

"But Illia Sharpell supposedly died in 1806. I can't believe that the newspaper would get the date wrong. Why would his name show up in diaries written so long after his death? It must be another Illia Sharpell."

"Come on, Max, we aren't talking about a very common name here."

"And this lady mentioned knowing Illia Sharpell?" Max asked.

"I didn't get to read all of her diaries but according to the portions put on the internet, one of the names mentioned in her diaries was Illia Sharpell. From what I did read this Illia guy was no sweetheart either, seems he tried to blackmail one or more famous politician..."

"Did she mention the details of his death?" Max interrupted.

"Yeah, she said that he was murdered and left floating on the Potomac."

"That is exactly what was in the initial newspaper article. It would just be too much of a coincidence for your Illia and my Illia not to be one and the same" Max thought for a while, "What was the lady's name?"

"Becky something."

*****

Max and Mark walked slowly, back from the bus stop.

"I may now know as much as you do about this Illia person," Mark said, "and I still can't figure out why anyone would give two shakes about him. And I can't figure out who or why anyone would feel it was necessary to bug our house because of him."

Mark stopped walking and grabbed Max's arm. "So what are you going to do next?"

Max said, "The only thing that is important now is to keep whatever we know about this antique dealer to ourselves. We also need to find a safe place to work this out because the house is definitely not safe anymore. And finally, we need to keep the circle of those who do know about this to a relatively small few. The more people we get involved the larger the chance for harm to come down on all of us."

"So I am no longer a suspect?"

"Come on, Mark. Don't start all of that again."

Mark smiled, "At least are you now satisfied that none of the guys in the house are involved?"

"Yes, I am," Max quickly responded, "But I sure would like to see all of the 'Becky letters' up close."

Mark patted Max on the back, "No problem, dude!"

"You're planning to go to the antiques dealer and ask for a copy?"

"Well, not exactly. I don't think this guy is going to let anyone see all of those letters up close without some assurances that it will lead to a sale, and I mean a big sale. This guy is convinced that he is holding the find of the century."

"So then how exactly can you help?"

"When I e-mailed the antiques dealer he told me that he scanned all of the legible portions into his hard disk so that he could cross reference the details."

"So?"

"So? What do you mean, so? You know that there isn't a computer made that I can't glide in and out of at will."

"You're good, Mark, but are you good enough to access someone's personal computer without their knowing it?"

"Mr. Non Believer, it makes no difference if it is personal or public or protected or tucked into his underwear, the minute he signed onto the web to respond to my e-mail I had him and everything on his computer – even most files he thinks he erased years ago."

"I'd hate to cheat this guy out of some fair payment," Max said.

"I wouldn't worry about this guy," Mark said. "It only took one e-mail exchange to realize that his picture must be in the dictionary under the word, 'sleaze'."

"Okay, when can you do this?"

Mark smiled broadly, "As soon as we get back to the house."

"No, don't use any of the lines in the house, they are all tapped."

"Then I'll do it in the library. I'll go there after dinner."

"Can you be certain that it won't be traceable back to you?"

"No sweat! I can bounce it back and forth until it gets dizzy. It will never be connected to me."

"How can you be so sure? More importantly, if *you* can do this how can you be so certain that no one else can reverse what you did to its source?"

"I didn't say no one else can; I know that my father could."

"And if he could why can't anyone else?"

"Of course it is possible, just not very probable. At any rate, these aren't government secrets here, let's not be paranoid."

"Hopefully, it is not government secrets," Max said softly.

Mark tried to lighten the mood, "If you want, I can print it on rice paper so that you can swallow the evidence if they rush the house."

"We may not know what this is but we do know that it is not a joke, Mark."

As they approached the brownstone Max grabbed Mark's arm and said, "Please Mark, not a word to anyone."

"Not even Gloria?"

"We'll tell Gloria, but not in or near the house. Remember, it's bugged."

"You can trust me, Max."

The powder blue mini-van was parked along the curb, several hundred feet up the street. The driver turned back to face the man rocking back and forth in the rear of the van. "Did you hear that, P.H.?"

"Yes, Myron, I heard every word."

"How do you think he found our bugs?"

"He's a very smart young man, Myron, maybe a little too smart for his own good."

"You want us to put a tail on everyone in the house?"

"That won't be necessary. Just follow Mr. Barnes, no need to take extra risks. Eventually everything will find its way back to Mr. Barnes and through him we will learn whatever he knows or thinks he knows."

"Should we pull the bugs?"

The man thought for a moment then said, "No, we can't risk going back in again. Just leave them." He slid the side door open and stepped out of the van. He stretched his hands up in the air and walked around to the driver's window. "I'm going back to New Jersey. You stay here until you are relieved. I want to be notified the minute he moves in any direction. Understood?"

"Understood."

"The very minute."

"I understand, P.H. I understand."

Chapter 12
Monday, 13, January, 1806,
Washington City, District of Columbia – 12:13 A.M.

The President tried to sleep after his visitors left. Try as he might, sleep would not come. George Washington himself had cautioned that eventually they would have to confront the OOTAP councils; it was only a matter of time. Well, that time had finally come and like it or not, the grownups in the room could no longer look the other way.

Dawn was beginning to break; Jefferson spent the better part of the night staring up at the ceiling.

Because he knew right from wrong he realized that his first act upon learning about the crime should have been to demand the arrest and conviction of those involved; regardless of what other questions such arrests might set off. Each minute that passed tied him closer to the ones who actually did the deed. Because he was a practical person he knew that this crime put into question everything his government claimed to stand for. Because he was a politician, he had concerns as to how this would redefine his place in history; and because he was trained in the law, he understood all too well that the law alone might not insure that justice would ever be served, regardless of what he did or did not do.

What was absolutely certain was that time was not on his side.

He decided to return to Monticello for what he hoped would be a less contaminated atmosphere, to allow him to think about what to do and how best to do it. Monticello, surrounded by the natural beauty of the Virginia countryside and within the isolation of his precious gardens offered a far better environment to think this through. He yearned to leave this drafty shell of a residence in the newly designated capital district that was little more than a "work in progress". After all, Monticello was home, Monticello was forever, this was barely a temporary place of shelter.

His personal staff and servants traveled ahead in order to prepare Monticello for his return. As usual, Horace traveled with the President. Both men felt relieved to be leaving Washington, especially at this time. On his many journeys between Monticello and the President's Mansion in Washington, D.C., Thomas Jefferson usually traveled the same route, although he did not always stop in the same inns along the way. The journey usually took four days and three nights. He arrived at Monticello early Friday morning, the 17th of January.

$$*****$$

Tuesday, 21 January, 1806,
Monticello, Virginia – 9:25 A.M.

Other than Horace, few others saw very much of Jefferson after he returned to Monticello. During the daylight hours he wandered aimlessly around his precious gardens. At night he sat quietly by the roaring fireplace in his study, often just staring into the flames. He made it clear that he wanted to be left alone. From time to time he sat at his writing table. Horace was always within clear sight.

Julien, his French chef, prepared all of Jefferson's favorite dishes but he didn't have much of an appetite and barely touched his food.

By the end of the third day he sent for John Breckinridge.

$$*****$$

Friday, 24, January, 1806,
Monticello, Virginia – 1:10 P.M.

Jefferson and Breckinridge shared a common love for the law and they often spent hours arguing its finer points. In these discussions it wasn't unusual for both men to switch debating positions several times, going back and forth in order to insure that all aspects of a law would be considered.

"It's not mathematics, John," Jefferson would say, "it isn't always white and black, there is plenty of gray in the law and that is the way it must be if the law is to be responsive to the inevitable variables of life."

"And so the high judges of the Supreme Court will always be the last word," Breckinridge would argue, prompting Jefferson's belief that judges were no better or worse than any other citizen, "Judges are as honest as other men and not more so. As with others they have the same passions for party, for power, and the privilege of their corps. To consider the judges as the ultimate arbiters of all constitutional questions is a very dangerous doctrine indeed."

Meeting now in Monticello, individually deeply troubled, collectively uncertain about what to do next, there was only one position as their discussions covered practical reality. "We both know enough about the law to know that this matter can't be brushed aside, John," Jefferson said. "Even if we wanted to brush it aside, the high offices held by those who did this argue for you and me to be even stricter in our adherence to the letter and spirit of the law."

"I know that all too well, Tom, in fact in the eyes of the law you and I are already deeply involved - accomplices after the fact – because we didn't go immediately to the people as soon as we heard the dirty details. But, we couldn't have, Tom, and you know it."

Jefferson quickly responded, "What I do know is that to do or say nothing is indeed to become part of it and the longer we wait the harder it will be to argue our virtuousness."

"We could choose to take Philthrow at his word and believe that this was nothing more than an accident," Breckinridge said.

"Oh, John, stop it! At least let us be completely honest among ourselves. This is no ordinary crime and these are no ordinary criminals. They were sending me a message. More than just a man died that morning, when life left his body so did any possibility to further ignore that reprehensible bunch at OOTAP."

"Even you cannot stop OOTAP, Tom. Others have tried and failed. There may have been a time when we could have, should have snuffed them out, but that boat has left the harbor. They are now just too powerful for anyone to stop. You know it; I know it, and worse of all they know that we know it! Time has made them almost invincible."

Jefferson sat with his hands clenched, "No John, not time, it is we who have made them almost invincible. We did it and we can, no, we must, undo it."

"I'm just another voice in the wilderness," Breckinridge argued. "You are a sitting President of the United States and if they get an inkling that you are ready to hold them to task they might be able to bring you and your entire administration down."

"You are not just another voice, John. You are the Attorney General of these United States. You are the people's lawyer."

"I realize that full well, Tom. Maybe it is best for us to bring the opposition into our thought process," Breckinridge said.

"You are assuming that they do not already know!" Jefferson responded.

"I'd wager my last coin that they do not know." Breckinridge said, "Most of them already wish Aaron Burr a slow and painful death. If they knew that his OOTAP played any part in this awful thing – especially if they could involve you in it as well - they would already have been melting the tar and gathering the feathers."

"What makes you think that they aren't just waiting for the best possible moment so that they *can* include us or at least me in the tarring and feathering?" Jefferson asked.

"They are not that patient, Tom."

"Since returning to Monticello I have been drafting a letter to the people," Jefferson said. "Here, read it and give me your comments."

Breckinridge took the document from Jefferson's outstretched hand while reaching into his pocket for his magnifying glass. He leaned closer to the fireplace for more light and began reading.

Breckinridge set the document down on the side table and looked up towards Jefferson, "This is the beginning of a letter of resignation, isn't it?"

"I asked for your comments," Jefferson said.

"It is out of the question that you should resign. That is my comment," Breckinridge said.

"That is not your decision to make," Jefferson said.

"I will not stand still and allow you and your presidency to become the latest victims of OOTAP," Breckinridge said.

"John, as much as I respect and honor your opinion, this is

not a decision for you to make."

"Look Tom, even if you resign you will still have to explain the delay of responding. This will affect not only everything you do from this time forward but will tarnish everything you have ever done before. If you thought the libelous comments hurled at you during the election were bad just think of what the other side would do with this kind of ammunition. Your enemies would have a field day with this and most of your 'so called friends' would quickly disown you."

"I am aware of all that. I am also aware that each new day this announcement of mine sits makes any 'indignation' on my part look like little more than self serving bluffery."

"Why have you waited so long, Tom?" Breckinridge asked, "All day during that long and tedious Sunday I expected you to grab the two of them by the scruff of their necks and pitch them out of the window. It wasn't at all like you to just sit there and listen to their justifications and claims of patriotism and the 'need to stick together for the good of the country' and the rest of their self justifying claptrap."

"We did not know then that they personally played any part in the murder of that man."

"Oh, Tom", Breckinridge sighed, "You couldn't possibly have believed that they were innocent bystanders. There isn't and never has been anything innocent about them or their entire bunch. They have always used fear and anything else that could to cloud the facts that they were just murderers, thieves, and power hungry scavengers with the single minded interest of feathering their own nests. And now, their power and personal fortunes may have made them virtually untouchable."

"We did not know, *for certain*, that they personally played any part in the murder of that man." Jefferson broke in.

They both sat quietly for a while then Jefferson heaved a sigh, "Okay, let's just say I had a moral responsibility to hear them out." Jefferson said.

"What do these scoundrels know about moral responsibility?"

"Would you have me damn them without fully thinking this through? Then I would be no better than they." Jefferson stood up and walked closer to the fireplace, rubbing his hands together for warmth. "All I know," he finally said, "Is that we are quickly losing any separation we might have been able to claim from this awful mess by our silence. The reality is that the clock began ticking for us on Sunday and it has been ticking louder each and every minute since."

"Oh Tom, not everything in life is so cut and dry. We don't even know for certain that they told us everything."

"John, as I said before, at least among ourselves we must be completely honest. Since before the revolution we have ignored the evils of this group, while they were targeting the 'redcoats' it was convenient to look away and pretend that they were helping the cause, when in actuality they were no better than the forces we were fighting. We had a common hatred for the powers in place and excused the excesses of this band of extremists. They knew how to build upon our fears and our willingness to look away, while we, in fact, got into the mud with them. The ends justified the means. And so, at the end of the day are we really any better than those we fought?"

"Would you have preferred the King to have further enslaved us, Tom?"

"I would have preferred to win in such a way as to be able to hold our heads up high by showing that our priorities were correct, not that two wrongs make a right!"

"What is past is past."

"Perhaps it is time to create a new past," Jefferson said. "Perhaps OOTAP's solutions should be even less acceptable to an honorable people than the King's were. We have danced with the devil, old friend, the time has come to bid him goodnight."

"Tom, I relished the struggle with our foes who crossed the ocean to suppress us. This fight I do not relish. I am not even so sure that we can win a new struggle, especially with an adversary that has proven themselves to be more devious and calculating then the mighty King of England with all of his forces."

The two men stared into the raging fireplace. Jefferson finally broke the silence, "God protect us from these haters and fear mongers and extremists," he looked into Breckinridge's eyes. "We are being tested, John. I just hope we are up to it."

"God help us all if we are not," Breckinridge whispered.

God help us all if we are not, Horace thought to himself.

Chapter 13
Tuesday, March 1, 1774,
Boston, Massachusetts – 9:25 A.M.

The Organization Of True American Patriots, or OOTAP as it quickly became known throughout the colonies, started innocently in the cluttered backroom of Melsh's Tavern, alongside the Boston docks.

Megan Melsh inherited the tavern after her father's death and ran it with the help of her Uncle Gus. Megan's father had been beaten and left to die following an argument with several British soldiers. It was believed to be about an unpaid bar tab. Realizing that she would never be permitted to refuse service to the British, Megan secretly set aside the backroom for those she labeled 'True American Patriots'. This became known as the TAP Room.

The 'TAP Room' slowly became the haven for a handful of dockworkers that drank and played cards into the early hours while they cursed the British. On Fridays, the few small tables had to be stored away in order to make room for Megan's 'steadies', the 20-25 men who filed in, paychecks in hand, ready to drink their troubles away, along with it their family's food and rent money.

Spurred on by Megan, whose hatred towards anything and anyone British grew stronger with each passing day, the discussions generally turned meaner as the night went on. From time to time, Megan's Uncle Gus Sheit, joined the drinkers. Although he made his fortune selling arms and liquor to anyone with the price of the goods, including the British, he resented the occupying force and silently cursed them with every penny he was forced to pay in taxes to the Crown.

By late 1774, Gus, Megan and her new husband, Frank Sharpell, helped channel the Friday night 'pay check brigade' into weekly underground attacks against everything and anything British. They moved quickly from harmless graffiti to ever stronger acts of vandalism. When smearing windows with raw sewage no longer satisfied their hatred they moved on to placing small explosives besides British camps, followed by larger explosives, and finally, murder.

Their first victim was a British sailor who caught Megan and four of her cohorts setting an explosive charge near a banker's home. Gus convinced them that the banker was a British sympathizer. They overpowered the sailor and in the middle of the struggle Megan pulled out a knife and stabbed the sailor. She persuaded those with her at the time to help her drag the dead body to the edge of the river. She helped them strip the sailor from the waist up and using her knife, carved the words, 'WE WILL LIVE FREE - OOTAP', on his back.

From that moment on, OOTAP became a force to be feared.

The British Governor posted a huge reward for information leading to the arrest and execution of the 'new band of criminals' behind the 'cowardly acts being conducted against honest and law abiding citizens of the Crown'. His proclamation had a reverse effect: it turned Megan's group into anonymous heroes among the colonists.

Made even more brazen by their apparent ability to attack at will and fade into the darkness, Megan and her Uncle began fanning out to start similar groups as far south as Virginia. Each new member was sworn to secrecy and supplied with training, arms and explosives, courtesy of the 'TAP Room'. 'WE WILL LIVE FREE - OOTAP' became their battle cry. It was scrawled on public buildings and carved onto the backs of their growing number of victims throughout the colonies.

In early 1775, a nineteen year old Aaron Burr became a regular at the TAP Room. He often joined the conversations and showed a strong ability to organize small groups of men into underground fighting teams. It is believed that Burr's involvement with OOTAP was the reason George Washington, then Commander-in-Chief of the Continental Army, refused to give Burr a commission. It was also thought, but never proven that some members of the First Continental Congress also belonged to local OOTAP councils or, at the very least, were OOTAP sympathizers. No official attempts were ever made by the colonists or their leaders to bring members of OOTAP to justice.

When Megan was in her fifth month of pregnancy, the British captured her husband. He was caught with a quantity of explosives and was dragged to jail. Although beaten and questioned for hours on end all he would say was "we will live free." This only increased the anger of his captors and he was beaten until all signs of life spilled out of him. His limp body was hung in front of the town meeting hall as a warning to others. The British never got him to confess or could even link him to OOTAP but it was just assumed that he was a member of that band of terrorists.

A little more than four months later, Megan gave birth to her son, Illia.

Chapter 14
Wednesday, November 5, 1997,
Washington, D.C. – 5:15 A.M.

Mark gently knocked on Max's bedroom door. He waited a few minutes and then turned the handle and slowly entered the room. Max was sleeping soundly. Mark walked towards the bed and gently shook Max's shoulder. Trying a couple more times he finally leaned forward and whispered into Max's ear, "Max, wake up!"

Max jumped up and quickly looked around as he reached for his glasses, "Mark? Is that you?"

Mark put his finger to his lips and then pointed towards the door and then down to the floor.

Max slowly got out of bed, brushed his hair back with both hands and put his shoes on. He had fallen asleep in his clothes. He quickly changed his shirt and smoothed his pant legs with the palms of his hands. Neither man spoke as they tiptoed down to the bathroom.

After turning the faucets on full speed and flushing the toilet, Max spoke in a barely audible whisper, "Did you get it?"

"I did, I did," Mark answered with excitement in his voice. He pulled a computer disk out of his breast pocket and held it towards Max. "It is all here – or at least the ones that made it through decades of hiding in that cabinet, The Becky Diaries!"

"Did you read them?"

"I read enough to know that we have some interesting stuff here, very, very interesting stuff."

"How soon can we see a hard copy?"

"From the little I did read I am not so sure you want a hard copy to exist."

"Why?"

"If this is true and not some old lady's pipe dream, we have the story of a century here. I can now understand why some people are ready to crush you to keep it under wraps for another hundred years. Politicians are named, crimes are detailed, this is *really* hot stuff!"

"How does Illia Sharpell figure in to it?"

"He may actually have been the hero of the story before he became the murderee. He was tapped to lead a group of conspirators and it seems as if he was trying to get them to reform."

"Oh my God," Max sat down slowly on the edge of the tub, "You don't say."

"Exactly."

"Oh my God."

"So, 'Mr. soon to be joint-Pulitzer Prize winner', what do we do next?" Mark asked.

"First, I would like to see everything that is on this disk but if it is everything you say, we will have to be even more careful from here on out."

"Here, take it."

"Is this your only copy?"

"Yeah, I thought the fewer copies floating around, the better."

"We need to make an insurance copy or two. Hide it where

it can be easily retrieved – if necessary – to save our butts, but not so accessible that it can fall into the wrong hands. And any hands but ours will be the wrong hands."

Mark thought for a bit, and then said, "I am sure that I can come up with a few good hiding places."

"This is really going to be dangerous, Mark. You need to think hard and long if you still want to be part of it. Gloria too will have to reconsider her involvement. But that is for later. For now, let's get Gloria up and make plans for getting to the 'Sundae Funnies' later today."

"Gee, Max, this is too exciting to walk away from."

"Not exciting, Mark, dangerous; this is no game and the guys on the other side of this seem to be playing for keeps. I don't think I am being overly dramatic to say that our lives could be on the line."

"Neh, bullies are easy to fool. That I know," Mark emphasized each word. Then he smiled and added, "Hey, Max, if they were all that good you would already be dead."

"Isn't that reassuring?" Max mumbled.

Chapter 15
Wednesday, November 5, 1997,
Washington, D.C. – 12:42 P.M

Max brought Gloria up to date and suggested they meet at the 'Sundae Funnies', the campus ice cream parlor and hang out. During her freshman year, Gloria worked part-time as an ice cream dipper and became good friends with the owner's daughter. Gloria had her friend arrange for a table to be set up in the little-used basement storage room. She told her friend that she needed some quiet space to work with her study group. Max got there first and was soon joined by Mark and Gloria.

After they were all seated Max said, "First, in the interest of honest and open disclosure, I asked Sidney to check this space out and he did, at least as of half an hour ago, it was clean."

"Holy cow, not Sidney, again!" Gloria screeched.

Max put his hands up, "Hey, this is quickly becoming a 'David and Goliath' scenario, Gloria, and we don't even have a slingshot."

"And how can you be sure that Sidney won't *accidently* tell anyone?"

"I told him I was planning a surprise party for you and would let him come to the party if and only if he makes certain that you or anyone who might come in contact with you never learns about the party before it happens. He knows that if you knew of such a thing you would never show up. It was a calculated risk and I think it worked."

Gloria glared back at Max, she started to complain. Mark put his hand on her arm, leaned closer and whispered,

"Priorities, Gloria. Let's just keep our heads here – I have read the Becky diaries - this is gazillions of times more serious than any of us could have ever imagined. We need to reduce any and every risk."

Max quickly took control. "O.K., the space is bug free, a given, at least for the moment."

Mark broke in, "Maybe that is a given for the moment – but I don't think we should assume it will stay that way for ever and so I suggest we come up with at least one, preferably more, alternate meeting sights and a code to help us communicate between ourselves as to which is best for any given future meeting."

"Good idea," Max said, "Gloria, you grew up around here, any suggestions?"

"I would think that any location can be bugged if these guys are as plugged in as we think, but there is a place near campus that would be a more challenging place to bug," Gloria said. "My father's embalming room at his funeral home."

"Your father owns a funeral home?" Both men asked almost in a single voice.

"Yeah, he owns a funeral home, so what," Gloria asked.

"What else don't we know about you?" Mark asked.

Gloria blushed, "I never said that he didn't."

"You never said that he did!"

"It never came up before. But it is very secluded and almost impossible for anyone other than the family to access."

"Where is it and how would we gain access to it?" Max asked.

Gloria smiled. "It is just outside of town. My father reno-
vated a really old building that he later learned had been
part of the free slave route 'underground railroad' decades
earlier. Growing up it was fun rummaging around. I kept
finding new passageways and all kinds of secret hiding
places in and around the building. I used a couple of the
secret exits to get into and out of the house whenever I
didn't want my parents to know I was going out. It has a
maze of underground tunnels – one of which leads to the
center of town just under the old courthouse."

"Wow," Mark said, "where were you when my family was
being chased by the Feds? I think I really do love you, Gloria Salizar."

"Cut it out, and don't get any ideas – either of you," she
said.

Max thought for a while. "Mark, you and your family lived
in D.C. for a short while during your Dad's trial with the
Feds, right? Did your parents ever come up with safe places of their own?"

"Nothing like Gloria's, but after we left Brooklyn we felt
like this was a really hostile place and when we first got
here my dad and his lawyer used a local movie theater as
a safe place to talk about his case. It is an old art house
that was donated to the college as a tax loss. My dad felt
relatively safe there because few if any other movie goers
were ever around, especially during the week. Most days
the movie house was operated by a really small unsuper-
vised staff – usually just a few college kids who spent most
of their time doing homework because there was so little
else for them to do. I went there with him a few times and
he would whisper under the soundtrack. My father wasn't
even sure if we needed to whisper; we never used the same
seats and he didn't think that such a large space could be
effectively bugged. Although, he did suggest that each seat

could have been wired, I thought he was just being a little paranoid."

"Okay, so here at the 'Sundae Funnies' will always be the 'cool place'; let's refer to the funeral home as 'the still place'; the tunnel, 'the long place'; and the theater," Max seemed to be at a loss.

Gloria said, "The dull place!"

They all laughed.

"O.K., let's get down to the reason for getting together today," Max said. "We need to do a few things to make absolutely certain that we aren't going down the rabbit hole chasing some old lady's imagination gone wild. Then, and only then, we will have to take the risk of making a hard copy of these *Becky diaries,* even if we destroy them soon thereafter, working with hard copies may be the quickest way to put them in real time order. It is clear that the antique dealer mixed them up and we need to establish a timeline that can be independently verified. Have you come up with any names that can be cross checked?"

"Hold on to your hat," Mark said. "The name Thomas Jefferson is mentioned a number of times."

"Get out!" Gloria screamed.

"*The* Thomas Jefferson," Max asked.

"*The* Thomas Jefferson," Mark answered. "This Becky woman refers to Jefferson specifically, and his home in Monticello, many different times. If we accept the dates to be 1800's and not 1900's – as I now believe the antique dealer did in error - then it is possible that we are smack damn in Jefferson's timeline. Really sounds like it could be legit."

"I sure hope no one is playing with me here," Max said.

"The break-in of your room quickly followed by the one in Sam's store, bugs in the walls, toughies following you to the park, a blue van taking up permanent residence on our block – that's no college prank, Max." Gloria said.

Max gave out a long sigh. "This is crazy. Then you think that there is some connection between *the* Thomas Jefferson and the 'Illia' stuff?"

"Who knows? What I do know is that there are plenty of loose ends and the only common ties seem to be the Becky diary, the article on Illia Sharpell, and the reality of the blue van bullies." Mark said.

"O.K., so what do we do now?" Gloria asked.

"We need to check this out very carefully," Max said.

"O.K.," Mark said, "but with who and how and when? Who do we know that can be a trusted and a dependable check and balance for something as potentially hot as this?"

"You and I may know the best single source on anything to do with Thomas Jefferson – our fourth grade teacher – Mrs. Abondola," Max said.

"Mrs., *'I love Thomas Jefferson and so should you'*, herself," Mark laughed.

"Your fourth grade teacher?" Gloria laughed, "How will you ever find her?"

"I've kept in touch, somewhat, over the years. Last few Christmases I got cards from her; she is currently living up North."

"Mrs. Abondola!" Mark repeated, almost in a trance, "And you kept in touch with her? She must be several hundred years old by now."

"Don't be so judgmental, Mark." Max said

"Well, if she was your fourth grade teacher she really must be old." Gloria said, "And if she is really old, what makes you think she would want to get involved? This might not lead to a happy ending for old Tom Jefferson and you did tell us that she idolized him." Gloria said.

"That is a good question and the only way to find out is to look her in the eye and ask her straight out," Max responded. "It is worth a try and I could pay her a visit to find out for sure."

"With finals coming up, the earliest you could even begin to track her down could be weeks away – can we delay this for that long," Mark asked.

"I might need your help on that, Mark. You would have to get into the college's system and mark me present, even during the tests if I don't get back in time to take the actual finals. If the blue van guys know anything about me they know that I wouldn't risk getting thrown out of school by missing finals. It might be the perfect cover."

Mark smiled, "Even the purest succumb to a little crafty cheating, huh?"

"I'm not looking for A+'s, just a bit better than a passing grade. You know I would do at least that well if I took the finals."

"Okay, move on," Gloria said.

"Mark, you will also need to make one or more copies of the disk and hide it somewhere safe nearby as 'get out of jail cards' if needed."

"I have been thinking about that," Mark said, "how about

mixing it in with disks at Sam's store. They already tossed his store and we have not given them any reason to go back."

"Maybe, let me think it through a bit. Sam has already suffered enough from this and I have to think through how much more involvement he can reasonably handle. Meanwhile, let's all continue to think about other places where a duplicate disk could be quickly and safely stored. It needs to be easily accessible at a minute's notice – any time of the day or night and completely out of the blue van's reach."

Gloria and Mark nodded in agreement.

"Speaking of the blue van," Max continued, "we need to find out who the blue van brigade *really* is and how plugged in they may be; any suggestions?"

Mark spoke up first, "This is a job for my Dad. We don't have an awful lot to go on and he has a unique talent for taking little nothing bits and pieces and finding the glue that binds them."

"How would you communicate with him? We can't both disappear from campus and you would have to do this in person, wouldn't you?"

"Maybe, maybe not, my Dad and I have always had ways to communicate with each other that no one has yet been able to catch."

"As far as you know!" Gloria said.

"Okay, as far as I know." Mark responded.

"It's the best we have. Go for it." Max said. "But, make it clear to him that this is no lark; he could be opening himself up to people who could be even worse than the Feds."

"He's a big boy, and I think he misses the intrigue of years past."

Max slammed his hand, face down onto the table, "Safety first, don't give these guys any reason to think we are better dead than alive!"

Mark put his hand on top of Max's, "Agreed, and to quote the blue van brigade, 'we will live free!' "

Gloria smiled, "And this Lady makes it three." Gloria said, as she slammed her hand on top of Mark's.

Chapter 16
Wednesday, November 5, 1997,
Washington, D.C. – 7:35 P.M

Later that evening, Max stood in the entry hall of the town-house, directly under the ceiling light fixture where Sidney found one of the listening devices. Doing his best to imitate Ferde's accent he loudly proclaimed, "To hell with all of you guys, I'm going for a walk."

Max put on one of Ferde's jackets and a cap that hid most of his face and noisily left the brownstone. He saw the blue van out of the corner of his eye and slowly walked towards the park. He slid into an alley and waited to see if he was being followed. About 20 minutes later he moved on towards the bus station and bought a one way ticket to New York City. Shortly after 3:00 A.M. his bus arrived at the New York Port Authority building. He walked over to a small hotel and checked in for the night. He paid cash and registered under the name Jeff Thomas.

*****

Thursday, November 6, 1997,
New York City – 6:00 A.M

After a couple of hours of restless sleep, Max's internal alarm clock woke him promptly at 6:00 A.M. He showered; checked out of the hotel; stopped in a coffee shop for a quick breakfast and hailed a cab to Brighton Beach.

He stopped the cab about 7 blocks and two avenues from the address he had on the last postcard he had received from Mrs. Abondola. He paid the fare in cash and added a large tip. He waited for the taxi to drive out of sight and then, slipping into an alleyway, he removed his hat, the crumpled red hairpiece he wore during the taxi ride, peeled away the fake facial hair he had applied earlier in the morning, and put on his glasses. He walked towards the Sunrise Assisted Living Center, a huge red bricked building with a dark green awning. Looking straight ahead, he walked past the entrance and continued on towards the end of the street. Max then leaned against a street sign for a while, occasionally looking around to see if he had been followed. The scene around him looked quite normal, nothing seemed to be out of the ordinary or in any way suspicious, but just in case, he walked completely around the block, once again passing the red brick building. At the corner he stooped down to retie his shoe laces. Took one more look around and then walked back towards the entrance at 2211 Emmons Avenue and quickly ducked inside.

At the receptionist's desk he asked for Mrs. Anna Feldstein.

"Is she expecting you?" the receptionist asked.

"No, please tell her a former pupil is here and just wanted to pay his respects."

"And your name is?"

"I'd kind of like that to be a surprise."

The receptionist smiled, "I guess that would be okay. She doesn't get very many visitors."

Max had not shared the fact that Mrs. Abondola had remarried about seven years after her husband died. He felt that by keeping that bit of information and her new married name and exact location to himself he might further insulate Mark, Gloria and even Mrs. Abondola from the 'blue van bullies' and any of their possible sympathizers.

About ten minutes later a tall elderly man walked into the reception area. He walked towards Max, "Are you here to see Mrs. Feldstein?"

"Yes, may I visit with her?"

"Of course, she just finished breakfast and is in the atrium. I'll show you to her."

Although they had been keeping in touch over the years Max was surprised to see how frail she now looked. She was sitting alone, in a wheel chair with a book on her lap.

"Good morning," he said as he bent down, extending his hand.

"I'm sorry, they did not tell me your name," she said, haltingly.

"It's Max, Mrs. Aboldola, Max Barnes," he said softly, "I'm kind of undercover," he smiled. "Do you remember me?"

She stared up at him, seemed to be deep in thought and then a broad smile lit up her face and she said, "Of course I remember you, possibly my best student."

"I'll bet you say that to all of your former students," Max teased.

"Actually, I do. But in this case it happens to be true. I remember how open you were to learning. You had so much intellectual curiosity, even at the early age of a fourth grader. You seemed to soak it all up; it was such pleasures witnessing your growth. Every teacher feels a sense of authorship when young minds in their classes explore and expand. Believe me, it doesn't happen often enough and so when it does happen it is something you never forget. Yes, I do remember, you were bright and a lot antsier than your sister."

"You really do remember me," Max smiled.

"I'm far too old to lie. Rather, too old to remember any lie I might make up. So that leaves me to be truthful or say nothing at all." She stared into his eyes for what seemed to him to be an eternity, and then whispered, "What's this 'undercover' stuff all about?"

"A long story," he smiled, "I'll tell you all about it. Can we speak outside? It may be November on the calendar but with the sun out this morning it is quite nice."

She slowly removed her glasses and carefully put them in her pocket. "You know," she said, "that may be the best offer I will have today."

"And the day has just barely begun," he answered, as he rolled her chair towards the open-air atrium in the rear courtyard.

"Now, what is all this mystery about," she said as he sat beside her.

"I am working on my thesis about Thomas Jefferson and thought of you."

"Well, well, well," she said proudly. How about that? Someone actually heard my clarion call."

"I wondered what your advice would be if my research led to some things that might have been missed by earlier historians," he paused, then added, "although Mr. Jefferson was indeed a great man, he was also human, perhaps very human, and I wanted your opinion on how history might best be served if I wrote about what might be considered his human weaknesses," he stared into her eyes, not sure what her response would be.

"Now Max, it is true that I have always held our third President in the highest regard, but I attach more importance to recording a true and honest history. If what you have uncovered can help future generations gain a new insight into the actions of a leader, and that would be true of *any* leader, then you owe it to history to report it. But you also owe it to history to first check and recheck any *new* information so as to insure accuracy beyond a reasonable doubt. Yes, if it proves out, I would say you must add it to the record." She now spoke slower and with the authority he remembered as a pupil in her class so many years before, "Just remember, if the person is no longer around and no longer able to defend him or herself from this new information, then history can only be served if it is truly relevant to history and passes the, '*is this more than just idle gossip*' test."

Max thought for a while and then said, "Hypothetically, if you knew that, Mr. Jefferson, was somehow involved in a crime, would you add that to the historical record?"

She stared up at him, "A crime?"

"A crime," he repeated.

"Would it have been considered a crime in his day?"

"Hypothetically, let's say, yes."

"Would the penalty for the crime be exactly the same back then as it might be if it happened today?"

"Yes, there is no question about that," he said, quickly adding, "if it hypothetically happened at all, of course."

"Of course," she repeated.

She began cleaning her glasses with a tissue. He could almost hear the wheels spinning in her head as she quietly considered his comments. She motioned for him to sit closer. "If," she stressed each word, "if, there was unimpeachable proof that a crime was committed and that he was clearly involved, yes, I would add it to the historical record."

"Now the big question, would you be willing to help authenticate if in fact Mr. Jefferson committed such a crime?"

"Me, personally?"

"You, personally."

"Oh, come now, I'm not a historian, I'm no longer even a teacher, I can't think of anyone who would care what conclusions I did or did not come to, after all, I'm just an old lady sitting in the November sun."

"Oh come on, yourself, Mrs. Abondola, first of all, I care. Second of all, once a teacher always a teacher. Third, I can't think of anyone else who revered Mr. Jefferson as much as you did and probably still do. If all of what I have discovered turns out to be just some 'pipe dream', who better than you to figure it out?"

She gave a hearty laugh, "Touché, now enough of this ambiguity. Tell me what you came here to tell me."

Slowly, he shared all that he had experienced and learned since the early morning break-in of his room. He shared what he knew about the Becky diaries and stressed what he could not yet confirm.

"And you came here, on this 'secret mission', to ask me to – do what?"

"I came here half hoping that all of this was just a lot of hooey. The other half of me knew that if this was factual and somehow missed by generations of historians, then you above all others could help me to prove it."

"All right, you have my interest."

Max leaned closer. "I must also tell you that if this is all factual, by becoming involved you might be putting yourself in deep personal danger."

"Oh, Max! I'm an old lady in a wheel chair. I have had a long and rewarding life. I can't think of a bigger waste of time than to worry about what might happen to me. Let's just try to solve this mystery of yours."

Max looked around as he reached into his pocket and took out a small pad and pen. "Let's begin with the newspaper piece that seems to have started this journey. Does the name Illia Sharpell mean anything to you?"

"Illia Sharpell", she repeated, "no, I don't think so."

"In his obituary they mention his mother Megan Sharpell and his sisters Mrs. Lamar Anderson and a Miss Estelle Sharpell."

"No, none of those names ring any bells," she stopped in mid sentence and grabbed his hand. "Wait a minute, did you say Megan Sharpell?"

"Yes, do you recognize the name?"

"There was a Megan Sharpell who was active against the British just before the War for Independence from the British. Seems she and her father, no, her Uncle, yes, that's it, her Uncle, ran a small inn or hotel or was it a tavern along the Boston docks. Now what was his name?" She sat quietly for a while, "Uncle... Uncle... now, what was his name?" She seemed to be deep in thought and then yelled out, "Sheit, that's it, Gus Sheit – I can't remember the father's name but her Uncle was Gus Sheit. He and her father ran guns out of, oh, what was it called?"

Max asked, "Could it have been Melsh's tavern?"

"That's it, Melsh's Tavern," she said excitedly, "Melsh's Tavern, somewhere by the Boston dockyards." Her words were coming quicker now. "The British killed the father and the Uncle and Megan continued the business. There were many small groups of citizens scheming against the British occupiers during that time in our history but the Sheit brothers were particularly effective. They were also very bad men. They worked all sides; whoever paid the most got the guns and anything else they might want, legal or otherwise. There was a book about them that I read a very long time ago. It was out of print even then; it must be extinct by now."

"Can you remember the name or author?"

"It had the name of the tavern in the title, I think. Anyway, seems there was a disagreement about a bar bill − of all things. The Crown claimed that the father tried to cheat a British sailor or soldier; the father claimed the British fighting man was trying to get out from paying for a night of drinking. A knife appeared − in the book the author claimed it was the British boy's knife. In the struggle the father died. The book was written by a grandson or great grandson of Sheit. He tried to make a case that the old man was a patriot just defending himself but from everything I have read about that period in our history it is more than likely that the sailor or soldier killed him in self defense. The British fighters were no angels but the officials knew how important it was to keep the local merchants on their side as much as possible − especially known arms dealers like the Sheit brothers − the powers that be would never have covered up such a murder if it meant alienating such important locals. If one of their own was to blame they would have served him up without blinking, especially some low level recruit. What is interesting, as I remember, is that according to the author of that book, Megan used her father's death to spark an underground movement. It was all laid out in that book. Funny though, I tried to research it further and nothing about them or their movement was in any other book or article that I could find at the time, and I really searched high and low to learn more about this."

"If you can come up with the name of the book it might be helpful to fill in some of the blanks," Max urged.

"I found it in a used book store thirty five or forty years ago. It intrigued me then but I forgot all about it until you brought the name up. You know, I think the title was something like, 'One man's battle against the British Empire' or 'The Melsh's Tavern Patriots'. She rubbed her forehead, "I can see the cover so clearly in my mind – it was bright red, white and blue lettering, really tacky looking, even for the day. What was the name?"

Seeing how upset she was getting because of her failing memory Max patted her shoulder and cautioned, "Don't trouble with that now, it will come."

"She dropped her hand to her lap, looked up towards him and gave him a broad smile, "I got it! It was the 'Organization of True American Patriots', that's it."

"OOTAP," Max smiled.

"What did you say?" She asked.

"OOTAP," Max said again, "OOTAP, Organization of True American Patriots, OOTAP, that's what they wrote on my dresser and again on the counter of Sam's book store: We will live free, OOTAP."

"Yes," she said, "that was their battle cry, '*we will live free*'."

"So maybe this is all factual," he mused.

"Now, Max," she quickly said, "even if all of this *is* factual, and we really do not know that for certain – not yet, but even if it is true... even if you can prove each and every aspect of it to be true, it is still a long stretch to connect any of it to Mr. Jefferson."

"Maybe so," Max said slowly, "maybe so."

Chapter 17
Saturday, November 8, 1997,
Washington, D.C. – 9:15 A.M

Some years back Mark's Dad made up a game the father called *'it's only gibberish without a book of rules'*. He knew that the Feds were never going to stop hounding him and planned for the times when he might want to keep out of sight. The *'it's only gibberish without a book of rules'* game was created so that he could stay in touch with his wife and children without tipping off anyone who might be watching them. He chose Mark to be the one to receive his messages because he believed that Mark would be the very last person the Feds would expect to be a possible contact person.

Over the years the father and son teamed up to perfect the *game*. They established intricate codes that could be left in public spaces – as seemingly innocent graffiti – as well as within lost animal notices they would staple to telephone poles along the route Mark took to and from school.

The ultimate improvement was a system they came up with to write cryptic notes on seemingly innocent travel post cards – *messages that were hidden, in plain sight,* in the message section as well as the to and from address sections of the post cards and even under postage stamps. The father knew that this would drive the Feds crazy... the Fed had to know he was sending coded messages on these cards but how was he doing it? Mark wondered why his father would knowingly poke and prod the Feds in this way, "This is just going to make them mad. Why would we want to do that, Dad?" Mark asked his father.

"Just play it out, son." His father responded. "Even the Feds do not have endless resources. They are going to *want to* watch me like a hawk, but I assure you, they do have bigger fish to fry. So at some point, they will just have to pick and choose how best to proceed. I want to make them angry because angry people make mistakes. I think we have come up with a random system which may well be impossible to break, especially if we keep changing some of the elements, and we *will* keep changing some of the elements. IF we make them angry enough they will devote a disproportionate amount of their assets and man hours to breaking the code and I think that would be good news for us because try as they will, I do not believe they will ever break this code."

"Unless and until they do break the code." Mark responded.

His father smiled broadly, "Unless *or* until they *do* break the code." He repeated, then after a very long pause, "But they won't."

*****

Mark bought a picture postcard of a night time scene of Washington, D.C.; he addressed it to his father. In the message section he wrote:

> *I am now all about viewing fireworks, drinking pink lady's, and thinking about old times.*
> *Love,*
> *Znak*

Under the postage stamp he wrote: *mi je potrebna vaša pomoć*

*****

Translation of the postcard Mark sent to his Dad:

> *I am all about, (I have volunteered) viewing fire-*

works, (potentially hazardous) drinking pink lady's,
(possible political conspiracy) and thinking about
old times (something you went through long ago).
Love,
Znak (Mark – in Serbian)

Under the postage stamp he wrote: *mi je potrebna vaša pomoć* (Serbian: I need your help)

*****

Four days later on November 12, Mark received a picture postcard with a view from the Lincoln Memorial, Washington, D.C. It was addressed to Mark. In the message section it read:

> *Glad to know that your priorities are straight.*
> *If I was your age I would want to do the*
> *same things... even though they say some*
> *things never change, all of that now seems*
> *to be out of your system and so I don't.*
> *Love and hugs,*
> *The old man*

Under the postage stamp he wrote: *početka reći sudija*

*****

Translation of the response postcard Mark received from his Dad:

> *Glad to know that your priorities are straight.*
> *(Stick to basic survival measures) If I was your*
> *age (Don't take any risks I didn't) I would want to*
> *do the same things (Remember how tough it was*
> *for the family) ... even though they say some things*
> *never change, (They may still be watching me... the*
> *atmosphere is still dangerous) all that now seems*
> *to be out of your system (I don't think you are un-*
> *der Fed surveillance anymore) and so I don't. (Be*
> *careful).*

Love and Hugs (What ever it is – I'll be there for you,)
The old man

Under the postage stamp he wrote: *početka reći sudija* (Serbian: go tell the judge – meaning, post a more detailed message at the courthouse.)

*****

The next morning Mark got up earlier and went to the town courthouse and stapled the following message on the public notices board:

GRADUATE STUDENT
AVAILABLE
FOR PERSONAL TUTORING
I CAN PREPARE YOU
FOR YOUR COLLEGE FINALS
LIMITED AVAILABILITY –
FIRST COME, FIRST SERVED

On the bottom of the notice Mark added a series of tear off strips with his name and phone number on each strip. (However, the last 4 digits of the phone number on the tear off strips did not match Mark's current phone number. It was an exact match for the last four digits of the home phone number from his youth.

*****

Translation of the notice Mark posted in the old courthouse:

GRADUATE STUDENT
(YOUR SON IN COLLEGE)
AVAILABLE
(HAS IMMEDIATE SITUATION)
FOR PERSONAL TUTORING
(IN NEED OF HELP)
I CAN PREPARE YOU

(WE NEED TO SPEAK)
FOR
(LOCATION #4 –
THE OLD ART THEATER)
YOUR COLLEGE FINALS
(THIS COMING WEEK)
LIMITED AVAILABILITY –
(I CAN'T SPEAK HERE IN MORE DETAIL)
FIRST COME,
(I'LL GET THERE FOR THE START OF THE MOVIE)
FIRST SERVED
(I'LL BRING THE POPCORN)

By referencing the phone number of the home where he grew up, Mark was signaling that old methods might once again prove to be successful in handling this problem.

*****

Two days later Mark received another picture postcard. This one had a close up photo of the Lincoln Memorial and the message said:

> *Thinking about your fun in the sun!*
>
> *Hope you haven't forgotten to use enough suntan lotion. Those rays can be quite strong at this time of the year, opportunity only knocks once. Love and Hugs,*
> *The old man*

Under the postage stamp he wrote: Do) *kažu da stric*

*****

Translation of the second response postcard Mark received from his Dad:

> *Thinking about your, (I hope you know what you are doing) fun in the sun! (sounds like you are playing with fire – don't get burned.)*

Hope you haven't forgotten to use enough sun-tan lotion (Be prepared to take every precaution). Those rays can be quite strong at this time of the year (Be prepared to be as thorough as you can,) opportunity only knocks once, (it might not be pos-sible for us to have a follow up meeting for a while). Love and Hugs (Whatever it is – I'll be there for you,) The old man

Under the postage stamp he wrote: Do) *kažu da stric* (Ser-bian: until the bastards say uncle)

*****

That Saturday afternoon Mark went to the old art house/ movie theater to see "Abbot and Costello meet Franken-stein". He purchased a large popcorn and drink combi-nation and took a seat in the third row. When he walked into the dark theater there were eight other movie goers in various locations: A young couple making out in the last row on the right; a man and three young children in the center of the theater; and an old couple along the aisle in the center.

About halfway through the film a tall, slender man walked into the theater and sat down beside Mark.

"Hi Sparky", the man said, in a low voice as he reached into Mark's popcorn container and took out a handful of popped kernels.

"Hi Dad," Mark said, with a broad smile.

As in the old days, they sat through the second showing and the third. There were only two young college students working the lobby, the concession stand, the projection booth and covering cleaning duties for the theater itself as well as the rest of the building and parking lot. Neither seemed to be very interested in Mark or any of the other movie goers in or out of the building that day.

Slowly, methodically, Mark brought his father up to date. He knew that his father would not interrupt him while he told his story and from past experience he understood he would be expected to be concise but complete in the details that mattered.

When Mark said all he had to say they sat still, both staring straight ahead at the screen, for what Mark thought was an eternity. Finally his father took the drink from Mark's hands and after a long sip said, "Tell me more about the blue van. Start with the license plates."

"Maryland plates, mud covered most of the license plates but Max did make out the first two letters and the last numeral. The first two letters are 'O' and 'O', and the number at the end of the plate is 1. We have had plenty of time to look closer since it has been camping out on our street but still can't get close enough to clean off the mud so that we could see the full plate number."

"And what did he see inside the van?"

"Max only got a quick look inside while they were holding him but he said he could see a group of video screens fastened to the inside wall facing the door."

"Could he make out what was being broadcast on any of the screens?"

"I didn't ask and he didn't say."

"Was it color or black and white?"

"I don't know. Does it matter?"

"Everything matters!" his father barked. "Did the lead guy have earphones on or near him?"

"I didn't ask, Max didn't say."

"Was the motor running while the door or doors were open?"

"I don't know."

"Were there any signs that they had been camped out in the van for any length of time? Empty food or beverage containers; coffee cups; cigarette butts in or around the van?"

"I don't know."

By now Mark felt and clearly sounded rejected. His father turned to look at him, "There's an awful lot you don't know and yet you have let yourself get involved with who knows what! Did you consider that this might just be some college prank?"

"Now look Dad, someone definitely bugged the house; there is a shiny blue van watching our comings and goings; Max's room *was* trashed, as well as Sam's store – does any of that strike you as a sign of a 'frat boy' lark?"

"Don't get ruffled son, you just need to be certain of a lot more than you seem to know or have shared with me before you pick a fight with anyone – that's all."

"Now Dad, none of us *picked* this fight. Someone or ones entered our house and that was the start of the fight. Are you suggesting that we enticed them in some way?" Mark asked indignantly.

"Look, something either Max did or didn't do sparked a flash reaction. You don't know, or if you do, haven't told me what it is or even might be! You don't know, or if you do, haven't told me who these adversaries are or even might be. How can you possibly plan to fight much less expect to win before you know the 'who, what, where, when, or why' of it?"

Mark handed his father a computer disk. "Here's a copy of the diary pages. On these pages there are references to all kinds of big shots – Governors, Vice President's, even a former President. You have to assume some stuff but it does seem clear that whoever is involved tried awfully hard to cover it all up."

"You have any reliable confirmation of the involvement by the names that are mentioned in there?"

"Max is working on that now. What is certain is that a blue van has been parked on our street almost nonstop since the first break in."

His father interrupted, "I know, I have been watching your block since the first postcard."

"Really?" Mark said.

"Really!" His father said.

"And what have you learned about the 'blue van'?" Mark asked, sarcastically.

"It's registered to a lobby group on 'K' Street."

"How do you know that?"

His father smiled, "You don't want to know!"

"What else do you know, Dad?"

"These people are drowning in money. They have at least nineteen separate Swiss numbered bank accounts, maybe more; there are forty-two listed partners but only one has signing power or easy access to their funds; that same person is also named as a member of a total of 409 boards of directors. That is 409 of the current 'Fortune 500' companies. They regularly contribute massive sums to both parties, and seem to have direct ties to numerous Senators, Congressmen, Governors, Mayors all the way down to local School Board people all over the country. These guys are connected."

"Holy shit, what have we gotten into?"

"A lot more than just 'agency paper pushers' Mark, this could be worse than anything I ever had to deal with."

"So what do you think we should do?"

"How soon before Max can confirm that the diary is for real," his father asked.

"He has been really secretive about where he is and how he is doing but I am hoping that he'll be back soon."

His father thought a bit, then said, "Max is in New York; he has been spending a lot of time with a retired teacher in an old age home in Brooklyn."

Mark gave out a gasp, "How do you know this? And if you know this how can we be sure that no one else knows this?" His whisper was getting louder. "The blue van guys could be following him right now."

"Calm down and lower your voice," his father demanded. "No one else has been following him, at least not yet. Your blue van guys don't even know he is out of town yet."

"How can you be so sure?"

"He isn't being followed right now, of that I am convinced."

"How can you be so sure?" Mark's voice was rising again.

"Hey, calm down! I am confident that they are not following him right now." He then put his hand on Mark's arm and added, "He is only being followed by people loyal to me, okay? Just let's leave it at that."

"Dad, I know I am over my head here, but I need to know how you can be so sure!"

His father sat quietly staring at the screen.

"Come on Dad, tell me. I need to know."

"Hey, the less you know about some things, the better – for you and for your friends."

"But Dad...."

"Okay, I have been tracking the transmissions from the blue van. It really wasn't very hard to do. These guys act like they're invulnerable, they are connected... they are powerful... that makes them arrogant... but the arrogance has also made them sloppy. I was able to attach a black box under their bumper and I have been plugged in to every signal that has entered and left that vehicle for days now. They think it is strange that they haven't seen Max come or go in a while but they seem to be satisfied that he is cramming for his finals and is still in the house."

"So what made you aware that Max was on the move?"

His father smiled, "Because I know Max and I also know Ferde. Ferde would never have told you guys to go to hell. That isn't Ferde. And Max wouldn't sit still once he knew what was in the 'Becky papers'. He must have known how damaging all of this could be in the wrong hands. That is Max."

"Are you bugging the house too?"

His father laughed, "No, I'm not bugging your house. Your blue van guys are and I am just tapping into their transmissions."

A weak smile began forming on Mark's face. "How long do you think we have before the blue van guys figure it out?" Mark asked.

"They're arrogant but they're not ignorant, Mark. Max will need to show his face soon."

Chapter 18
Wednesday, November 12, 1997,
(the old courthouse)
Washington, D.C. – 6:10 A.M

Gloria waited for Max and Mark to get to the old court-house then led them down to the basement level. She opened the woman's bathroom door and in a loud whisper called out, "Anyone here?" She waited a few minutes then walked inside, carefully looked under each of the stalls, then waived Mark and Max in.

She felt along the wall by a series of sinks and pushed up on the edge of the last sink until it slowly began to rise revealing a small opening in the wall. She pulled out a flashlight and pointed it towards the opening and said, "Here it is, follow me."

The opening exposed a rickety wooden staircase leading down into a dirt lined passage. Two huge rats scurried along the path in front of them. "Hey, I didn't promise you a rose garden," she whispered as Max gasped. At the foot of the stairs she pulled down on a heavy rope and the bathroom sink lowered, blocking the opening from view.

Gloria seemed to know her way around the winding corridors and about twenty minutes later they were in front of a pile of loose bricks. Gloria motioned to the two young men to help move the bricks to a space against the wall. Before long all of the bricks were completely moved forming a ledge wide enough to support a person. She climbed on top of the ledge and reaching up pushing in a section high upon the wall. As she did an opening appeared about 10 feet to their right exposing a rusty steel door. Gloria moved her hands along the top of the door and lifted off a key. She inserted it into a lock in the center of the door and it popped open. She waved them past her into a cold and dark space leading to a tight passageway. Gently pushing them inside, she closed the door behind her.

They came to a wider walkway that led into a small room. Gloria gently guided the two men into the room, closed the door behind her and as they each brushed themselves off she flashed her light along the floor in front of them and led the way another few yards. Reaching above her she found a heavy chain and gently pulled on it. Instantly they were all bathed in bright lights.

"Make yourselves at home guys," Gloria said with a broad smile. "And welcome to the old homestead." Max and Mark looked around at a gleaming array of metal tables.

"Holy crap," Mark yelled. "Where are we?"

"Not so loud, we are in my father's embalming room," she whispered. "You wanted safe and secluded. Here is extremely safe and very secluded," Gloria continued in a loud whisper. "To the best of my knowledge, none of the visitors to this room have ever breathed a word about it." She laughed.

Max asked, "You grew up here?"

"Well not in the embalming room!"

"It would explain a lot about you," Max said.

Max moved slowly around the well lit room. "It is every bit as scary in person as I might have imagined it to be," he finally said.

"Okay, okay, a lot of dead people have been pushed and probed on these stainless steel tables, but I can guarantee that dead or alive there is no safer place for us now than here."

Mark shuddered, "Let's just concentrate on staying alive."

"Why is it so cold in here?" Max asked.

"Let's just say that 'warm and toasty' and dead bodies don't always make for a pleasant combination," Gloria whispered, "and don't talk so loud. The room is very well insulated but my Mom and Dad's bedroom is right above us and we don't need them coming down and finding us here." She pointed to a door halfway across the room, "Go through that door, it's a small storage room, you'll find a light switch inside to the right of the entryway. I'll just close up here."

Max walked forward, hesitantly, reaching around for the light switch. The new space was much warmer and less intimidating than the larger room they had just left. Gloria quickly joined them and pointed to a group of folding chairs in a far corner. "No one uses this room anymore. We will be okay here for as long as we want, sorry though, no tea and cookies."

Max asked, "What if your Dad comes down here?"

"He'll make us wish we were being embalmed," Gloria said, "starting with me."

"Seriously, Gloria," Max said. "What if he finds us here?"

"Not likely. He has been semi-retired for a few years but even when he had an active business, Sunday morning was a 'work-free time'. But if he or anyone else in the house were to come down and find us here I would just tell them we are working on a school project."

"Working on a school project so early on a Sunday morning?"

"How about we worry about it if and when it happens,

meanwhile we are safe and very secluded. Now, let's talk about what we need to do next." Gloria moved towards a small work table. "Grab a folded chair and sit," she said.

Mark asked, "Are there any dead bodies here?"

"Do you see any dead bodies here, Mr. Brave Heart?"

"Come on guys," Max said, "let's just concentrate on our live problems."

Over the better part of the next hour they each took turns bringing the others up to date on their individual findings. Mark went last, telling them what his father had learned, then he asked Max if he had any idea how this was likely to play out.

Max was quiet for a while and then said, "I think we need to give these bullies a taste of their own medicine."

"Meaning?" Gloria asked.

"Meaning", Max said, almost playfully, "we do more than just react to what *they* are doing; we make them react to what *we* do."

"Are you out of your mind?" Gloria asked.

"Think it through, they are not going to stop until they squash us," Max said. "We have been a seemingly clueless and predictable target. They see us as a few dumb college kids. Let's make them question how dumb or clueless we really are and how *un*predictable we *could* be."

"And we do that, *how*? Gloria asked.

"We *begin* to do that by turning the tables on them, by using the sharpest tools in our arsenal." Max said.

"What am I missing here, what tools? She persisted.

"We hit them with surprise and Mark's Dad!" Max said.

"We surprise them?" Mark asked.

"Are you listening to yourself?" Gloria asked.

"Yes I am listening to myself and I have listened to each of you and given this a great deal of thought. We have been allowing them to set the agenda. Let's give them something of our making to spend their time and attention on. At the very least it will buy us some more time and more time plus surprise can improve our chances for longer term survival. At the very least we need to slow them down if not stop them in their tracks – we may even be able to turn the tables on them." Max said. "Sure as hell beats cowering in the corner and waiting for them to finish us off."

"Yes, it would be better but I don't see how we can do that." Gloria said.

"We move them off of us and onto something else." Max persisted.

"How you expect to accomplish this?" Gloria asked.

"We begin by exposing who and what they know and stripping them of their seemingly endless bankroll."

"And how do you plan to do that?" Mark asked.

"You just told us that your Dad unearthed a bunch of Swiss accounts. Do you think he could get us account numbers and passwords?"

Mark thought for a while and then said, "I suppose he could, how would that help us?"

"For starters, we could try to move their money around; maybe just hide it long enough to make them begin to see their own vulnerability. You think they would spend very much time harassing us if they thought that their bankroll had just evaporated... add to that, what if we told them that we were responsible?"

"Wouldn't that make them even angrier at us?" Gloria asked.

"Sure – but it isn't likely they would do anything about it at least until they got their money back."

"What about their powerful friends?"

"We could take a page out of their book and make them disappear." Max said.

Mark stood up quickly, almost turning the chair over as he got up, "Hey, I don't want to play any part in a murder."

"Don't be ridiculous, all we have to do is put a spotlight on the relationship these high and mighty friends have with the likes of the blue van guys. I think that if we are able to do that, and I admit it is a big *if*, I think that these friends of theirs would scurry away like a bunch of roaches when the light is turned on."

Max sat up straight, took a deep breath and said, "Here's what we need to do..."

Chapter 19
Thursday, 15, September, 1775,
Benedict Arnold's March to Quebec – 9:47 P.M

At 19 and just 3 years out of the College of New Jersey, theology student Aaron Burr volunteered to join Benedict Arnold and a group of "nationalists" planning to advance just beyond the Canadian border to locate and return the body of General Montgomery who had been killed in action.

Colonel Benedict Arnold organized more than eleven hundred soldiers of the Continental Army at Fort Western in Maine where they began their march north to Quebec. It was a long and hard journey. They had to battle the weather, and unfriendly terrain, fatigue, disease and exhaustion. By the time they reached Quebec, deaths and desertions shrunk the force to about 600 hungry and tired men. One of the survivors was Aaron Burr, idealistic, seemingly fearless, quickly making a reputation for himself as a firebrand.

By the following year he had progressed to General George Washington's personal staff. Unfortunately for Aaron Burr, General Washington developed an almost instant dislike for the eager recruit. Among his fellow officers, Washington referred to Burr as an agitator, a rabble-rouser, someone not necessarily to be trusted. Within weeks, Burr was transferred out of the camp.

By the time Burr shifted into his new assignment in Orange County, New York, word about the systematic killings of British soldiers by a band of colonists calling themselves OOTAP had spread throughout the colonies. It seemed like everyone was talking about the *latest carving* – vicious stabbing - along the Boston Docks. Even though British patrols were doubled in many Boston neighborhoods and tripled along the docks, there seemed to be no way to stop or even slow down the successful attacks on British fighting men. Every day one or more mutilated body would be found, each stripped to the waist with the words, 'WE WILL LIVE FREE - OOTAP', carved onto their upper torsos.

Aaron Burr eagerly took part in the debate but never shared what he knew about Megan Melsh, her Uncle, or the rest of the murderous doings hatched in the TAP ROOM at Melsh's Tavern. He and many of his fellow recruits hoped that by repeating and even embellishing on the spreading folklore it would help mobilize more colonists in a way that Washington's forces hadn't yet been able to. He also daydreamed about personally contributing to the murders and overall demoralization of the British troops anywhere within the colonies.

It seemed to make perfect sense, as long as the British couldn't feel individually safe they wouldn't be able to effectively rule over the colonists. However, instead, it only made the British hungry for more colonists' blood.

Frustrated because they were unable to isolate and capture the actual killers, independent bands of British soldiers began burning entire neighborhoods to the ground in hopes of turning the colonists against OOTAP and everything it stood for. By early 1776, neither side felt safe from the growing number of hit and run attacks.

No history books ever documented the OOTAP murders or the other acts of civil disobedience by those who called themselves the organization of true American patriots with their battle cry, "WE WILL LIVE FREE". However, for those living in fear of both OOTAP and the British it became clearer each day that war between the colonies and their British ruler was inevitable. Given the history of the British fighting forces, no one believed that the colonists could or would come out on top in the end. This *reality* only increased the numbers now loyal to the British king.

Burr unofficially formed his own group of troublemakers. They never personally took part in the violence themselves but instead they were able to effectively instigate local unrest and generally encouraged and even financed others to commit cruel and brutal acts against anyone and anything British. Predictably, even just "thinking" favorably about anything British was enough to result in violence against a person, their businesses, even their homes and immediate family members. Burr concentrated on spreading doubt and fear. He funded the printing of pamphlets and paid to have them distributed throughout the colonies.

There were three strong themes running throughout Burr's pamphlets:

> *The OOTAP founders were "patriots of the highest order"...*

> *"OOTAP was bravely fighting to protect innocent families and neighbors from an invading army"...*

> *"The British soldiers as well as British sympathizers were merely serving the interests of a despotic King and his insatiable and unholy appetite"...*

> and the warning, *"those who did not support OOTAP were just not serving the best interests of what is right and just and saintly... and so would be dealt with even more harshly".*

Each pamphlet had column headings in dark bold type that were designed to further enrage and infuriate the public. *"Support OOTAP or perish under the tyrannical rule of a distant King"*, *"The redcoats deserve everything OOTAP has in store for them"*, gradually escalating up to *"Death to the British"*, the almost comical taunt, *"Have you killed a redcoat today?"* and *"The only good redcoat is a dead redcoat"*. The one comment most often repeated but never credited to Burr, even though he wrote it, was, *"Send a clearer message to the King by carving it onto the backs of a dead British cadaver."*

Somehow Burr was never personally tied to his many activities in support of the movement even though the first thing he did after leaving the army was to use his growing influence to help build OOTAP into an effective secret society. OOTAP, under Burr's influence, eventually became an active force within most every major aspect of life within the new nation. Aaron Burr might not have personally killed a single British soldier during these early confrontations but for those few people "in the know", his prodding and financial support from the sidelines turned the movement from an unruly band of hooligans into an international political and financial force whose equal had never been seen before and might never be equaled in the future.

Even though he loudly denounced anyone who might even be *thinking* favorably towards anything British, it did not seem to affect his own choice for a wife. In 1782, he married Theodosia Prevost, born and raised in Albany, New York. She was the widow of a British officer.

Theodosia enthusiastically supported his behind the scenes activities on behalf of the growing secret society. She also played a key role by concentrating on the wives of leading bankers and industry tycoons. She founded the *persuasive wives club* and used it to help build a power base that proved to be invaluable to Burr and OOTAP and even contributed towards making him the junior Senator from New York in 1791.

The Burrs made a strong and effective team. Theodosia picked up useful gossip from the ladies, while Aaron used it effectively against the power brokers to get what he wanted. And what he wanted was to get OOTAP sympathizers into Board Rooms of leading businesses, financial and religious institutions, the influential press and finally into virtually every level of Government. Before long they could place or squash any story and make or break any person. They did it all in the name of patriotism but in reality, once the power was in their hands they used it to gain favors and influence for themselves and when power was not enough to get what they wanted, they used fear to open each influential door.

By late 1805, when 30 year old Illia Sharpell was tapped to take over the movement his mother had founded shortly before he was born, it bore little resemblance to its initial *charter*. Although less than a handful of people even knew there was actually a structured organization it was able to influence or control virtually every major aspect of the life and spirit in the young nation. OOTAP sub-councils now existed in almost every town and local settlement. They all answered to a national board and the national board ran it all with an iron fist. A growing number of 'elected' officials served at the pleasure of their local OOTAP council. The national OOTAP board made the key decisions and insured that to one degree or another, nothing happened without clearly benefiting itself and occasionally one or more OOTAP council and its key decision makers, individually or collectively.

Illia believed he shared his mother's dream for a free America. But the more he personally got involved in the day to day dealings of the Council the more he questioned the extremism and outright greed of those in control. Council leaders were beginning to believe that as his influence grew it could threaten the Council and expose them to the outside world. At first it was hoped that he could be convinced to accept their vision. When it became clear that he could or would not, the council met and decided that Illia Sharpell had to be silenced.

It was actually his mother, Megan Sharpell, who cast the

deciding vote to issue a death decree upon her only living son. Although Illia was the baby literally born out of the movement, he would not be permitted to bring it down. And so, late in the evening on the 9th of January in 1806 two men whose sole responsibility had been to protect and serve him methodically beat and murdered him during his evening walk along the banks of the Potomac River. They emptied his pockets to make it look like a robbery and threw his lifeless body into the river.

When asked by another council member how she could possibly have taken part in such a decision Megan stared straight ahead and said, "Illia was a nice boy – his father would have been very pleased with how he turned out. But, we need a man to lead us forward. Unfortunately, Illia was not to be that man."

Chapter 20
Friday, 24, January, 1806, 'Buck Spring',
near Warrenton, North Carolina – 4:18 P.M.

Soon after Jefferson left the new Capital City to return to Monticello, Nathaniel Macon, the sitting Speaker of the House, made plans to return to his family home, "Buck Spring" in Warrenton, North Carolina.

Nathaniel Macon, like Aaron Burr, had attended the College of New Jersey and like Burr, the Speaker was an enthusiastic supporter of OOTAP even though he publicly spoke out against it. He convinced others to join and contribute huge sums of money and held back legislation which might have curtailed OOTAP'S activities or threaten either local or national Council leaders.

As soon as they knew he was back in Buck Spring OOTAP's regional Council leaders and a steady stream of their lieutenants *dropped by*. They sought and received Macon's promise of full support to do whatever was necessary to keep the Illia Sharpell *incident* from becoming a larger story than it already was. The words may have been different but the message was the same - "This is to be treated like a simple robbery, no more, no less. The investigation must be short and sweet and above all else, tightly controlled. In a few days or a couple of weeks at the most, the public's attention will be on to something else; doesn't matter what, as long as it is *not* on this." The Speaker was told, in so many words, to support their single clear message so as to get past this minor *distraction*. "This will all just blow away."

With each visitor, Macon's comfort level dwindled but he did his best to hide his fears.

"I understand what must be done," Macon responded to each of his visitors. "I fully understand." But he didn't understand and every instinct told him that this particular murder was very different from any that had come before. He was far too politically savvy not to understand what others could not or would not acknowledge. This matter can not go away soon and even if the all-powerful Council could in some way reduce the aftershocks, there would almost certainly be some collateral damage.

He also knew that if OOTAP fell so would he. However, he also knew that they had more and better options to cushion their possible loses than he did. He had a front row seat to the angry reactions from President Jefferson and his attorney general. No, no, no; this would not simply blow away. The Speaker had little doubt that if it was the last thing he would do, Thomas Jefferson would see to it that someone or some *ones* would be made to pay for this crime. He could not get the look of genuine anguish he had seen on Jefferson's face out of his mind. The Speaker couldn't remember ever seeing this President in as agitated a state as during their long meeting twelve days earlier.

"Where is Jefferson on this?" Each of his visitors wanted to know.

The Speaker's response was short and soberly delivered. "He is not at all happy." Over and over again, each visitor reminded him, "If *your* president's *unhappiness* results in trouble for us it will create even more trouble for you."

*****

Seven and a half hours later...

Almost at the same moment Jefferson and Breckinridge were struggling with their options, Macon was meeting with his inner circle to determine what best to do. He met with the four men he trusted above all others around his kitchen table, late on the first night of his return home from the Capital City.

With him now was Wharton Glover, a close friend and confidant for more than 25 years. Glover owned a group of Taverns along the Macon trail and benefited largely from his close relationship with the current Speaker of the House. They were soon joined by John Macon, the Speaker's brother and almost as soon as his brother sat down a knock on the door brought brothers Joseph and Benjamin Hawkins, childhood school mates and personal friends of both Nathaniel and John Macon for much of the previous 50 years.

The Speaker welcomed each of the four men with the same message, "It is not in any of our interests for a word about this meeting to leave this room."

Benjamin Hawkins laughed mockingly. "And who would be the most likely to spread such a rumor?"

"You know what I mean," the Speaker growled.

"Cut it out you two!" Joseph Hawkins yelled, "We have no time for petty squabbling. The last thing any of us need now is for us to waste valuable energy and the little time we may still have attacking each other."

"It was unnecessary and senseless and will bring us all down. This time, they went too far." Macon growled. "Look," the Speaker then whispered, "I watched Jefferson the day he first learned about this pointless crime and I can tell you that he is as close to ringing all of our necks as he may ever come."

Benjamin Hawkins waived his hands, "And you want us to do *what*?"

"Do nothing," cut in Joseph Hawkins. "Damn it, I want you

two to do nothing! If either of you can look beyond your own noses for just one second you'll see that the minute we hint at even the slightest criticism the Council will do to us what they did to Megan's boy. Is that what you want?"

Glover pounded both fists on the table, "Now, now, ain't none of us neither that stupid nor that brave."

They all looked to the Speaker for a response, but none came. Finally, his brother broke the uncomfortable silence. Gently placing a hand on top of his brother's arm he said, "Nate, just tell us what you want us to do – or better yet – what you *don't* want us to do?"

Nathaniel Macon had been the center of attention and in charge for as long as any of the men at his table could remember. As one of the most powerful politicians in the country he rarely was questioned, by anyone. Most of the people with whom he came in contact during any given day feared him and did exactly what he told them to do - without the hint of a question. But here in his own home, surrounded by the riches he had accumulated and the few men in his life whose opinions he knew he could trust, his every instinct said that he could now lose it all – especially his precious power. Like all elected officials, he swore an allegiance to the Constitution upon taking office but he also knew that he served at the pleasure of the OOTAP Council and could benefit from that power only as long as the OOTAP Council would permit.

He began to speak slowly and without emotion, seeming to choose each word carefully, "This thing will not go away easily. This time, the council has made it very difficult... no, make that impossible for any thinking man to look away."

"But murder ain't new for them, Nathaniel," Glover interrupted.

"No, it isn't," the Speaker said, "but to expect that no one outside of the Councils would continue to ask questions until some degree of justice was done is simply foolish. To drop that body on the President's doorstep, so to speak, and to remind the rest of us that we could be next, all of that is new and challenges us to do what we should have done years ago. Secrecy was always the council's strongest weapon. But fear of the threat of what they could do was even more powerful."

"So now they'll have to step into the sunlight for a week or two," Glover interrupted. "It won't amount to a hill of beans, I assure you. The sheep will quickly move on to a tastier pasture before you know it."

"Listen to me," the Speaker shouted, "Jefferson and Breckinridge are meeting this very moment at Monticello and I can assure you they will do something. I am telling each of you, when all of the dust finally settles we need to be on the right side of this."

Glover waived his hand, "The Council is better insulated from harm than the President himself, and maybe it's the President who should think twice before he challenges them."

Macon stood up and began to pace, "I know that each of us have prospered beyond our wildest imaginations because of our ties to the Council. Over the years we made our choices and looked away. But this is different, very, very different. We just can't look away anymore."

Benjamin Hawkins stood and walked over to Speaker Macon. "You must think long and hard before you do anything, old friend. No one knows better than you how much pain they can extract. You don't want them to ever question your loyalty. Not one teeny tiny itty bitty bit. If they can kill Megan's son they are not likely to stop at anything in order to hold on to their power and fortunes. Just remember: the

Council never forgives and they *never* forget."

Each was quiet for a while and then Glover spoke, "I have followed you along this path with my eyes wide open, Nathaniel, but I can't promise that I would join you in a suicide mission if you even hint about taking sides against the Council. Not one of those people could or likely would accept such an act of mutiny without making certain we were crushed."

Joseph Hawkins quickly chimed in, "And they would not stop with us – we would be putting every member of our families at risk. You know what they are capable of and even the thought makes me shudder."

"What makes you think they don't already know how we feel about this?" the Speaker's brother asked.

The Speaker slowly sat down, folded his arms in front of him, and stared up at the ceiling. Each of the men sat for a long time without saying another word.

Squatting down, in the garden, just outside of the open kitchen window was Wharton Glover's son-in-law. He made a few notations in a small note book, carefully placed the book into his jacket pocket, then slowly stood up and walked towards a bank of trees where he had tied his horse earlier that morning.

*****

At 4:17 A.M. on Saturday, January 25th, Nathaniel Macon awoke in a deep sweat. He reached for his glasses, feeling along the small table by his bed. "Where are those darn things?" he mumbled. He stared straight ahead, rubbing his eyes. He thought he noticed something moving in the far corner of his room.

Since the Illia affair began he was never without a dueling

pistol within easy reach. During the day it was strapped to his ankle. When he slept, it was usually tucked under his pillow. He slowly reached for it. He was almost consumed by fear as he realized that the gun was not there. He slid his hand from side to side under and around the pillow but it was gone. His panic grew when he heard a voice coming from the shadows.

"Is this what you're looking for, Mr. Speaker?" It was a man's voice, but he couldn't seem to put a face to it.

"Who is there?" he screamed.

"I'm just a very disappointed constituent, Nate."

"Who are you and what are you doing in my bedchamber?"

"I told you who I am – I am a very disappointed and I have to say, disenchanted and unsatisfied constituent."

Fear was a new emotion for the Speaker. He had enjoyed knowing that he could be responsible for creating fear and even terror in others, but since Illia's body washed up along the Potomac River he understood that terror might well be his new constant companion. His hands were shaking, and a cold and clammy sweat was covering his entire body.

Slowly, the man at the other end of the small room walked towards the bed and sat along the edge. He calmly handed Macon his eye glasses. He then removed the bullets from the Speaker's gun, dropped the bullets into his coat pocket, opened the small drawer of the night stand on the side of the bed and dropped the gun into the drawer, closing it quickly. Macon was visibly shaking now as he recognized the chief enforcer for the national Council. He wanted to say something but the only sounds he could make were barely audible sighs. Then with much effort he asked, "Are you going to kill me?"

His visitor gently placed his hands over Macon's mouth. "If we wanted you to be dead, Nate, it would have already happened. No, at least for the time being, we do not want you to be dead." Then with a hearty laugh he added, "Well, not within the traditional definition of dead, at least not yet. But politically, I'd say you are now deader than a doornail. As you know, we were considering you for the vice presidency and maybe even the presidency in not too many years. However, without a single doubt, that is never going to happen now.

"No Nate, you will not be dying tonight, certainly not from unnatural causes. But beginning tomorrow, when you return to the Capital City – and you *will* be returning to the Capital City tomorrow - you will be our handmaiden, even more so than before. We will tell you when to wake and when to sleep and what to say and when to say it. Deviate from any of that by even a syllable and you and everyone you hold dear – including the memory of your dearly departed wife – will disappear. Eventually, no record of your ever having existed will be found in any book or article or whisssssper." He emphasized the word whisper as he stared into the Speaker's eyes.

With his hand still covering the Speaker's mouth, the visitor moved his face closer to Macon's. "By a simple nod, I want you to let me know that you *do* understand me, Nate."

Nathaniel Macon, with tears running down his face and urine beginning to fill his bed, repeatedly nodded his head up and down.

He was still nodding his head as his visitor removed his hand from Macon's trembling mouth, stood up and left the room.

*****

The following morning, Macon went to visit his wife's grave as he did each and every day when he was in residence at Buck Spring.

He shuddered at the site before him. Both of the plots, the one for his wife, now dead for almost 16 years and the adjoining one for their son, had been ripped up, the headstones destroyed. Centered on each grave were the remnants of what had been a giant burning cross.

*****

Wharton Glover lived above one of his roadhouses. He lived modestly but had one major extravagance, a collection of privately commissioned "boudoir" drawings and paintings by French artist Jean-Honoré Fragonard.

A mysterious fire began just after 3:00 A.M. on January 25th, 1806. Glover's roadhouse and everything within it burned to the ground. Neighbors came across a pile of broken frames and damaged canvases that were believed to be part – if not all of his famous oil painting collection. The piled high remnants seemed to be carefully placed inside a pig pen just south of the main house.

Although his body was never found, it was assumed that Wharton Glover died in the fire that morning.

Later the same day, separate fires destroyed three more road houses which had been owned by Glover. A total of 47 people, most of whom Glover never personally knew but whose only mistake seemed to be that they were in the wrong place at the wrong time, died in that series of fires.

The remaining estate of Wharton Glover was confiscated as a result of a series of legal judgments which surfaced over the next few months.

Just a few days shy of seven months later, on August 22,

1806, Jean-Honoré Fragonard died of mysterious circumstances in Paris, France. Even though he received commissions to paint for luminaries of the time such as Louis XV's mistress, Madame du Barry and played an essential role in the founding of what later became the world famous Louvre, references to him as a major painter of his times virtually disappeared from all texts until more than 50 years later.

*****

John Macon regularly spent his Sunday mornings attending early church services. Not a particularly religious man during most of his life, he did believe that there was a God and as he grew older hoped this God would be understanding of his many and varied lapses of honesty.

He had become known as his brother's enforcer and played upon that reputation to build a small fortune from real estate holdings throughout the state for himself and his children.

At 7:15 A.M., Sunday morning, January 26th, 1806, he was sitting in his usual pew, third row from the back. Three young men, each dressed in priest's garments, entered the church. As each entered, he knelt down, made the sweeping sign of the cross and, lowered his head in prayer. Gradually, raised his head, once again made the sign of the cross, stood and took a seat. One sat behind John Macon as the other two moved to sit on each side of him. Several minutes later the 'priest' behind Macon carefully looked around the sparsely filled church and quickly wrapped a thick wire around Macon's neck, crossing his hands as he pulled it tightly into a noose. The other two 'priests' held onto Macon's arms until all life left his body. Minutes later, each stood, made the sign of the cross, and backed out of the church.

Although the various OOTAP councils controlled and manipulated most aspects of power and commerce in the America of the early 1800's, one small but specific group within the population was recognized to be off limits to OOTAP and its high central Council, it was the Quakers.

In 1806, by way of their settlements in Western Ohio, a small group of North Carolina Quakers settled an area along the Whitewater River. The Hawkins brothers had previously established a working relationship with two Quakers who were among these first settlers - John Smith and Jeremiah Cox.

As soon as Benjamin Hawkins learned about the brutal deaths of John Macon and Wharton Glover he began working on a plan to move his family and his brother and his brother's immediate family to Europe. The two brothers quickly gathered what few belongings they could and with their wives and children in tow filled three carriages and raced towards the new Whitewater River Quaker settlement. Stopping only when they had to rest the horses, the Hawkins brothers and their charges safely reached John Smith's log cabin just before midnight, on Saturday, February 1st.

Towards the end of the year, Joseph and Benjamin Hawkins decided that it was now safe to leave the Quaker compound and move the group to New York so that they could arrange passage to Europe for the final leg of their escape.

Another slim area that was free of OOTAP's influence and control was the New York City Watch, established to keep the peace in 1802 under the supervision of High Constable Jacob Hays. By 1806, Hays was in his fourth year in charge and was a rarity for his time – an honest and conscientious civil servant. He developed many of the earliest criminal detection methods and brought numerous criminals to justice. In the eyes of this detective, the law was not for sale or for rent and no one was above the law, including the rich and powerful.

The Hawkins brothers first met Hays during one of the early battles of the war for Independence. They developed a high level of mutual respect and at least once each year met either in upper New York State or in the hills of North Carolina to fish and hunt.

Just before Thanksgiving, 1806, Benjamin Hawkins got word to Hays asking for his assistance. He sent a confidential message saying that a criminal gang in North Carolina was threatening their lives and said they were planning to travel to Europe in order to keep their families safe. Hays agreed to help them if they could make their way to New York, and so, during the early morning of December 21, 1806, the caravan of three coaches arrived at the service entrance of St. Peter's Church, the only parish at that time that existed in New York for practicing Catholics.

One of Constable Hays's most trusted Lieutenants chose Christian Luswanger, a new law enforcement recruit, to keep watch over and protect the Hawkins' families until they could board their ship to Europe. Luswanger regularly brought food and supplies into the church basement and worked as the brother's agent to negotiate final travel arrangements with a Spanish ship's captain.

Try as they might, OOTAP could not find a single clue to lead them to these two men or their immediate families. A series of accidents occurred involving some of their friends, distant relatives, and neighbors, but still, no leads to the brothers' whereabouts. All of that changed two days before Christmas, 1806 when a member of St. Peter's church in New York City reported to his local Council that he thought he saw Benjamin Hawkins's wife during mass early one morning.

Built in 1785, the church had been the object of anti-Catholic feelings among predominately Protestant New Yorkers. On Christmas evening, 1806, as parishioners began entering the building for midnight mass, a group of young toughs circled the church with signs and chants against Christians in general and this specific church in particular.

Mayor DeWitt Clinton called out the Watchmen to keep the two sides apart and return order to the neighborhood. Instead of order, a riot broke out. By the time the dust settled every member of the two Hawkins families were dead along with their sole defender – Christian Luswanger. Luswanger had been stabbed to death, making him the first New York City policeman to be murdered in the line of duty.

The Mayor, son of a former New York State Governor, (both of whom owed their political fortunes to OOTAP), offered a reward for any information leading to the arrest and conviction of the person or persons responsible for Luswanger's death. Ten of the rioters were arrested but no one was ever charged with the crime and it was never officially solved.

*****

It was now less than a year since the five men met around the Speaker's small kitchen table. Four of the five men along with most anyone close to them, were now dead. The point would be driven home; OOTAP and their ruling council did not forgive... and it would not forget.

It would be almost two hundred more years before a serious challenge would be posed against the secret society.

*****

The speaker survived for another 31 years, but in every other way he died that predawn morning of January 25th.

Chapter 21
Saturday, 25, January, 1806,
Monticello, – 11:59 P.M.

When he first decided to return to Monticello, the President was not certain how long he would be away from the Capital City. What he did know was that he wanted to be alone with his thoughts. He knew he could close out anyone in his immediate circle merely by decreeing it, but he couldn't close out Sally Hemming.

He neither arranged for her to stay in Washington nor gave orders for her to accompany him back to Monticello. This made it easier for her to request a riding horse several days after he departed and to take off for Monticello on her own. Something was happening; she did not know what, but she did know that whatever it was she could bring comfort to Jefferson if she were by his side.

Sally Hemming reached Monticello just before midnight.

She went looking for him as soon as she arrived. She found him sitting in front of the fire in his study. Horace was in his usual place, seated inside the room by the door. She looked at Horace and nodded. Horace gave her a friendly smile and a brief nod.

She moved closer to Jefferson and whispered, "You can talk to me. You said it always helps you to talk to me. Whatever is happening should not change the fact that you CAN... TALK... TO *ME*."

She stared at Horace and whispered into Jefferson's ear, "Please send Horace out of the room for a little while. I want to comfort you..."

"I did not come here for comfort; I came here in hopes that

this friendlier place could help me think through some concerns of state." Jefferson said.

"Then at least send him away long enough for me to talk with you. I can't speak freely with him here." Horace looked at her sadly but did not move from his seat.

Jefferson said, softly, "I do not wish to involve you in the matters I came here to resolve. Horace's presence here is needed. It would be wrong to chase him away at such a time."

"Are Horace's feelings now more important to you than mine?" She asked.

He gave her a stern look, she had now gone too far and she knew it.

Leaning closer she said, "You are the one who taught me that all man's problems have solutions."

He reached out for her hand and held it tightly. "Oh, I have solutions, several in fact. But one is more odious than the next. What I have here is a problem without any tolerable solution. It is like the condemned man on the gallows. There are ways he might die *other than* at the end of a rope. There is always a possibility that he could fall from the scaffolding as they walk him up to the top of the gallows or the rope could break, the fall would kill him; or his heart could give out, or lightning could strike. But dead is dead, no matter the circumstances. Like condemned man, I do have some alternate outcomes but each one is more deadly than the other."

"Now, now," she said, as she gently touched his face with her hand. "No man will ever bring you to a hangman's gallows."

He looked into her eyes and leaned forward to kiss the top

of her head. "The time might now be here for me to be my own hangman."

She started to speak but he gently touched her lips with his finger. "When all is said and done, each of us must accept the final responsibility for being our own judge, jury and even chief executioner."

"And that time has come for you?" She asked.

He looked deeply into her eyes, and after a long silence whispered, "Yes, dear Sarah, that time has now come for me."

She shuttered as if a chill had just filled the room, then smiled, "I like that you speak my given name."

She settled down at his feet and rested her head in his lap. They sat quietly staring into the fireplace. Somehow, without a word of advice or council, she had helped him come to a conclusion. He now knew exactly what he would have to do and how best to do it. While still staring into the fire he spoke to Harold in a clear and firm voice, "Have the carriage prepared, we will begin our return to the President's house, now."

"Now, in the middle of the night?" Sally asked.

"Now", he repeated, "Yes, now."

"I only stopped once to rest my horse." She said, meekly. "He will need to be fed and allowed to rest." She said. "Will I be returning with you in your carriage?"

He shook his head from side to side, "No, I do not want you in Washington until I work through the problem that brought me here."

She knew better than to question him further, especially with Horace in the room.

"I have already waited too long." He said, then motioning to Horace he added, "No more delays, we will leave as soon as the horses are in place. Send word ahead, I want the Speaker and that horrid Philthrow and Aaron Burr to be sitting on my doorstep when I arrive. Ask the Attorney General to join me for the return trip."

Chapter 22
Monday, December 1, 1997,
Washington, D.C. – 5:32 A.M

Max rose early enough to turn off his alarm, shower and dress and entered the kitchen of the townhouse with 10 minutes to spare. Mark's father, had already been there for several hours and sat quietly in a corner of the room. He was holding an electronic call box in his lap and wearing an oversized pair of headphones.

A pot of coffee was noisily percolating by the time Max entered the kitchen.

Mark's dad motioned for Max to come closer to him. He suggested Max go out of his way to tease and belittle the blue van group during each and every time they now communicate with them – but especially today and tomorrow. "Make it personal." He stressed, "Don't pull any punches. You need to make them angry – when angry, people do dumb things. Talk down to them, treat them like stupid children. Be spiteful, mean, as unpleasant as you possibly can be. Be sarcastic. Mock them every chance you get. They will expect you to fear them. In fact, they are counting on that. Make them believe that you think they are not worthy adversaries. *It will work.*"

Gloria and Mark entered the room within minutes of each other. Max whispered what Will James had just told him and both nodded silently to Max and the older man. By 6:00 A.M. they were ready to begin.

Max poured himself a cup of coffee, took a long sip, and then began speaking directly into one of the listening devices they found in the kitchen light fixture. "I would like to call this special meeting together; it is 6:00 A.M., according to the clock on the wall. My name is Max Barnes; I am sitting in the kitchen of my rented townhouse with a group of good friends. It is my understanding that listening in from a blue van parked indiscreetly up an adjoining street are the loyal stooges of an organization known to a precious few as OOTAP. If I am any judge of character – and you fools are definitely characters - you are now looking at each other wondering how I know who you are and even that you are there at all. I am not certain if the overweight tub of lard - that top banana of your bunch – is physically in the blue van at this early hour," Max looked over towards Mark's father who was holding up a clipboard with the words: THEY ARE CALLING HIM NOW, written in big block letters. Will James pointed towards his earpiece and made the hand sign for being on the phone.

Max continued speaking, "No, of course he wouldn't be up and around at this early hour. That is probably why his gofers in the blue van are now calling him."

*****

The two men in the van sat staring at each other shaking their heads. The lead person was holding on to the car phone. After a few rings he heard, "Who the hell is this calling me at 6:00 A.M.?"

"It's Myron, P.H."

"Well this better be damned important, Myron."

"I am here at the college kid's stake out…"

"I know where you are Myron, I put you there. What I don't know is why you woke me up at this ungodly hour!"

"Something has gone terribly wrong here, P.H."

"Now Myron, what can possibly go wrong? You are watching a group of dumb ass college kids. All you have to do is watch the front door and report back as to who came and who went..."

The driver of the van broke him off in mid sentence. "We are also monitoring the bug we installed in their kitchen and they seem to know we are here."

"What are you talking about?"

"Here is the playback of what we heard just a few minutes ago..." The man in the van pressed the replay button on a Wilcox reel to reel recorder and fed the audio into the phone line.

P.H. screamed into the phone, "I'll be right over, do not leave your location!"

Back in the townhouse, Will quickly scribbled a message on the clip board and held it up for Max to see: "Their leader is on his way in. His name is P.H."

Max read the sign and mockingly said, "Wow, P.H. is on his way! I bet you guys in the blue van will now have some 'splainin to do!"

Less than half an hour later there was a knock on the van door; they looked through the peep hole and quickly opened the door to let the heavy man in. "I don't know how you could possibly have screwed this up, but you clearly have. Quick, give me a headset."

Will James held up another sign: P.H. has arrived.

Mark broke the silence, "Well, well, well, the big man has arrived – good morning P.H."

One of the men in the van quickly jumped out side of the van and took a quick look around. He returned to the van and whispered in the fat man's ear, "Aint no one around P.H."

In the van, the three men looked at each other and shook their heads in amazement.

Mark spoke again, "Let's cut to the chase, P.H. You are no longer a mystery man. Yes, a group of 'dumb ass college kids' are about to 'out' you and your band of criminals.

But, before you moan and groan about that let me share even worse news. Yes, it can get worse; in fact, it already has. 43 of your numbered Swiss bank accounts have been drained dry. Well, not totally dry, we did leave the equivalent of one U.S. dollar in each of the accounts, so I guess I can't say that you are now penniless – you have at least a hundred U.S. pennies still in each account. But, don't take my word for it. Pull up your balances on that fancy computer of yours."

Max held up both hands and Mark and Gloria gave him a long distance high 5."

In the van, the heavyset man slumped in his seat in front of his computer screen as he moved from one account to the next only to see the same result on each of the balance sheets.

Mark's father held up another note that informed the rest of the group that he now had 7 additional account numbers and as he put the note down he quickly drained those accounts of all but one U.S. dollar each.

Max waited until Mark's father nodded towards him and then continued speaking, "OOPS", he yelled, "I guess we initially missed seven of your Swiss accounts. Well, they are also down to $1.00, U.S., now."

In the van, P.H. retyped the seven account numbers that just showed eight and nine figure balances only to find each one now down to a single U.S. dollar.

"O.K., now that I *really* have your attention, and before you do something stupid like rushing the house and trying to kill us all let me remind you that if you try to take any or all of us out and succeed then you will never see your money again. I am not saying you will ever see your money again even if you do not kill all of us; you might and then again you might not. But of course, you would give up any chance of a positive ending if you try to harm the only ones who know where it is. Let me give you a few minutes for that to sink in. When you are ready to learn more just hit your horn three times."

Mark's father sent a thumbs up signal then scribbled a quick note on the pad and showed it to Max. It said, "You are doing great —keep it up."

Soon three short horn blasts broke the early morning silence.

Max nodded to him and began speaking again, "Okay, now listen very carefully. I will only say this one time. Sometime tomorrow we will give you meeting instructions for your P.H. to follow. I will speak into your listening device and then we will remove and destroy the listening device – along with the other 13 scattered throughout the house. You will be told where to go and when to be there. Any deviation from our instructions and you can kiss your money goodbye. If between now and then any harm comes to any of the inhabitants of this house or your other favorite haunt – the Nodal bookstore - then you can kiss your money goodbye. We want P.H. to return to his New Jersey home tonight, so he is ready for our instructions in the morning. We expect P.H. and only P.H. to follow those instructions – to the letter. If you send anyone else then you can kiss your money goodbye. If you send any additional members of your band of bad old boys with P.H. then you can kiss your money goodbye. Do anything further to annoy us and, let's say it together, that's right, YOU... CAN...

KISS... YOUR... MONEY... GOODBYE! Now, if you understand and accept these orders honk your horn three times."

Almost as soon as Max stopped talking three short horn blasts could be heard.

Max smiled and then said, "Good, very good. We will see you tomorrow, now, DON'T have a nice day!"

The three friends stood and hugged each other. Then, one by one, each walked over to Will James and shook his hand.

Chapter 23
Monday, December 1, 1997,
Washington, D.C. – 7:10 A.M

Max, Gloria, Mark and Will James were still in the kitchen when they heard a sharp knock on the front door. No longer concerned about the blue van group Mark opened the door. Standing with his head down and arms at his side was the heavy set man from the blue van.

Mark started to close the door as the man quickly spoke up, "I wouldn't do that if I were you. You can clearly see that I am all alone here. I only want to speak to you guys – that's all, no funny business, hear me out and then I'll leave as peacefully as I came."

"Just a minute," Mark said, "wait here – and no funny business, understand?"

"Don't worry", the man said, meekly. "I am not looking for trouble. I seem to already have more than enough. Thank you very much."

"Wait here!" Max said as calmly as he could. Mark quickly closed the door and rushed into the kitchen. "He's here," Mark said in a loud whisper.

"Who's here?" Max asked.

"It's one of the guys from the van. I think '*the*' guy himself."

Mark's father quickly stood. "This makes no sense," he said.

"He claims that he only wants to talk," Mark quickly said.

"Yeah, and a hangman only wants to measure the condemned man for a new neck tie as he slips the noose around the condemned man's neck," Will James whispered. "You don't want him in here, not while we are all together."

"What do you suggest?" Max asked.

James quickly gathered all of the notes from the table and stuffed them into a paper bag as he whispered to Max, "Go talk to him outside, stay firm but allow him to play out his hand. This is definitely not what I expected, and frankly, I expected plenty of twists and turns from this group. Don't forget; treat him like he is beneath you. Get him angry and you win. Remember, you have taken his money away from him and other than power; money is the most important thing in his arsenal. You did it without their having a clue that you would or even could do such a thing. Use that to your advantage."

Max walked to the door, looked back at the others and smiled weakly, "Here goes nothing!" He took a series of deep breaths and then opened the door just wide enough to step outside, quickly closing it behind him.

The man spoke first, "So... you gonna let me in?"

"Now, now", Max responded, "you were told very clearly to wait until tomorrow for further instructions. Are you really foolish enough to push the envelope like this?"

The man looked directly at Max. "Look kid, you got us by the short hairs. I don't know how you were able to clean us out but it looks like you did."

"Just for the record," Max said, "we didn't clean you out. There is still the equivalent of one United States dollar in each of those accounts. We *could* have cleaned you out and didn't. We still can and will if you foolishly try to pull anything like this again. Now move along, we'll give you further directions tomorrow. Do you understand?"

"Yeah, yeah, but I just told you I don't want any trouble," the man said. "All I want to do is talk."

"So talk," Max said.

"Let's be more civilized than that , not here, not out in the open like this," the man protested.

"It would really be a change of style for you guys to do anything 'out in the open' wouldn't it?" Max said in a mocking voice.

"Hey kid," the man said, poking his finger in Max's chest. "Don't overplay your cards. I came here in good faith to try to work something out. You want peace, I can give you peace. You want war, I can give you war."

The two glared at each other for what seemed to Max to be an eternity. Max looked up the street and saw the blue van begin to move closer.

"Just let me come in," the heavy set man said, finally breaking the silence.

"Forget it! Now, I strongly suggest you turn around and wait for your further instructions. We already showed you we can access your funds, do you want us to show you how easily we can 'out' some of those elected officials and community *leaders* you have had at your beck and call? How long do you think they will stand beside you if they can no longer hide in the shadows?"

"I said that I don't want trouble," the man yelled, then held both hands up, in a mock sign of surrender. "Just give me 15 minutes."

"We have nothing to talk about today. Tomorrow is another day. Have your blue van parked in its regular space, down the street. I want you to be in your New Jersey home, connected to the sound system in the van. I will give you further instructions sometime between 5:00 A.M. and 10:00 A.M. tomorrow. Not one minute before and not one minute after. Now get off my porch."

"You and your buddies are completely over your heads," P.H. yelled. "I tried to give you a chance here. You're playing with fire, kid, and if you aren't careful you *will* get burned. Bigger... better... more powerful people than you have tried to stop us and each and every one of them ultimately dropped to their knees and begged for mercy before we crushed them into the ground. DO YOU REALLY THINK YOU CAN DO WHAT NO ONE ELSE HAS EVER BEEN ABLE TO DO?"

"Tomorrow you will hear our demands. Now get off my porch!" Max said, then turned and went inside.

The man stood in front of the closed door and yelled, "Think about it! Just think about the chance you have just walked away from! You may have won this round, you stupid little shit, but you WILL NOT WIN THIS WAR! I promise you that!" He turned to walk away, then stopped, looked back at the front door and added, "Don't overplay your hand, kid. The very last thing you should want is *me* for an enemy."

The blue van was now along the curb in front of the town house. The man opened the side door and clumsily jumped inside and slammed the door shut as the van quickly pulled away. By the time the man clicked his seat belt the van was making a sharp turn at the corner of the street. The driver yelled back, "How did it go, P. H.?"

"Shut up and drive," the fat man yelled. "Just shut up and drive."

Max leaned against the closed door for a long while before returning to the kitchen. He was shaking uncontrollably now. As he entered the kitchen he found himself all alone. There was a small note on the table that read, "Get high in the dull place in 4.5."

Max crumpled the note and slumped down in one of the chairs. "What now?" he asked out loud, "What now?"

Chapter 24
Monday, December 1, 1997,
Washington, D.C. – 11:32 A.M

Other than the two young men working the various stations within the building and three people sitting in the front row either absorbed by an old World War One movie or just deep in their own thoughts, the downstairs portion of the theater was empty. Max slowly walked towards a flight of steps and up to the balcony. He spotted Mark and Gloria and sat down next to them. Almost as soon as he was seated he could see Will James edging his way towards them from the back of the balcony.

Gloria whispered, "Hi stranger, new in town."

Max turned towards James, "I don't want to sound overly dramatic, but I looked in that man's eyes and I believed I was looking at evil itself."

James smiled, patting Max on his shoulder, "From what I could hear you did fine. You never lost your head as he did. But then again, he has a lot more to lose than you do."

"I have my life to lose."

James smiled, then whispered, "I will do everything possible to make certain that does not happen. Now listen, they're bad all right but not invincible. We are about to bring them down and the good part is that they now know it and can't seem to understand either how we got the edge over them or what to do about it."

"Why do you think he just walked up to our door and asked to talk with us directly?" Max asked.

Although Max was directing his question at Mark's dad,

Gloria quickly answered, "What better way to measure up an opponent than to stand right beside them?"

"Good girl," James said. "The only time you and he were eye to eye was when they cornered you in the park. That time they had you by surprise, you were alone and they assumed vulnerable. Just the way they like it. You have since shown yourself to be an unpredictable opponent. This time he was hoping to find out how he underestimated the situation and to see if he could make the most of a situation that was spiraling out of his control. With these guys it is all about control."

"I tried to stay firm but my insides were running for cover," Max said.

"Well I think you have handled the situation as bravely as you could. I think all three of you have squarely faced perhaps the most powerful force around and proved yourselves to be worthy adversaries," James said, with a broad smile, "to one degree or another some very brave and smart individuals had tried to put them in a hole like this before and did so with zero success."

"We didn't do it, *you* did it," Max said.

"Hey, I may have been the mechanic, but you guys drove the car, and you did it without the safety of cover. That takes a lot of spunk, and they have been crushing spunk for more than 220 years. They aren't down or out but they have been shaken and they are not likely to make any moves against you at least until they get their money back. They *must* get it back but even more importantly, they need to find out how you drained their accounts in order to protect against it ever happening again. We bought ourselves some time."

"So what's the plan now?" Gloria asked.

"I didn't get anything from the listening device after they drove away. Either they found it or he was so wound up that he just wanted it to be quiet so that he could think. Whatever it was, tomorrow we need to deliver the landing punch. Let me do a little more probing. I will leave here first. Wait about half an hour and then the rest of you leave separately. Let's plan to get together again later today, say 7 or 8 o'clock tonight. I suggest the ice cream parlor. An ice cream parlor in the dead of winter isn't likely to have many people around in December and so it will be easier for me to determine if they are lurking around," James said, "any questions?"

Max was the first to speak, "I just don't understand, how you moved that much money without leaving a trail?"

Mark's dad laughed, "If the money doesn't leave the bank then there is no trail."

"I am now even more confused. They all but acknowledged that their money was there one day and gone the next, so if it didn't leave the bank, where is it?" Max asked.

"Can you answer his question, Mark?" his dad asked.

Mark smiled, "Let me try to answer your question. When I was a kid my father played a game with me that he called, *where's the leaf?*"

"Is that supposed to clear everything up?" Max said clearly irritated.

Ignoring Max's comment Mark continued, "The first time we played the game, he told me it was to teach me to think out of the box. He asked me to imagine that he had just handed me an envelope filled with dried leaves and said that he would give me $20 if I could name a place where I could hide these leaves without his being able to find them. My answers were all met with the same response from

him, 'I can still see them!' Ultimately, I gave up. He asked
me to think about it the rest of the day and if I could come
up with the truly best and safest hiding place he promised
to give me the money after lunch the next day. That damn
riddle kept me up most of the night. The next day, after
breakfast he asked me if I had a better answer and I listed a series of places I had thought about during the night.
With each one he laughed and said, 'I can still see them!'
Finally, he said, 'Come for a ride'. Maybe if I take you to
the park you'll relax enough to think of the right answer?
We drove to the park and walked among the trees. At one
point he bent down and picked up a fist full of leaves and
said, 'what if you hide your leaves here, among these – I
might not be able to pick them out and so they would be
hidden from me, right?' Then I finally understood; if you
want to hide anything, place it with more of the same; if
you want to hide a leaf bring it to a forest; so if you want to
hide money..."

Gloria and Max finished the sentence, speaking in unison,
"Hide it among a lot of other money!"

"Exactly," Mark's dad said, "and that is what I did. There
were many accounts with gigantic sums already in those
banks. It is unlikely that the holders of those accounts
check their balances minute to minute or if they do there
is even less chance that they would quickly withdraw the
new funds and run away with them. I moved money into
some of these large accounts within the same branch. If
someone checked their account they certainly wouldn't
complain if their balance somehow expanded over the
night; nor would they complain if it disappeared the next
day – after all, with active accounts and huge balances
there are fluctuations up and down all of the time. Also,
when the bank begins to double check *their* holdings they
will be hard pressed to notice how the blue van accounts
lost anything because the bank's total deposits would com-

pletely match the previous day's total, to the penny. It's a bowl of jelly beans that is a mirror image of the previous day's bowl of jelly beans. They have no pressing reason to question how many are blue today that were green yesterday. All that matters is that the net amount of jelly beans are present and accounted for. The first thing the bank will want to confirm is that no assets left its vaults. Eventually they will go account by account but by that time we will have broken the tyrants in two. Remember, all of this is either going to blow up in our faces or their faces as early as tomorrow."

Gloria asked, "Will we ever give the money back to them?"

"Give it back to whom?" James asked.

"To the blue van guys?" she asked.

"In a pig's eye," he laughed. "That bunch is lucky I left them with a dollar in each of their accounts."

"Why did you leave a dollar in each of the accounts?" She asked.

"Because zero balances in otherwise active accounts would have set off a stream of red flags and automatically would have triggered a thorough bank audit."

"So you do not plan to return the money to them?" Gloria persisted.

"I told you, 'in a pig's eye'."

"If not to them, then who will wind up with it?"

"How about the people they actually took it from, starting from the family assets they robbed from those who wouldn't play ball with them or tried to expose them; or the hungry and homeless that their greed created by killing jobs and destroying businesses? There are towns in this country that have dangerously rotted bridges and all sorts of other neglected infrastructure because they were drained dry of assets by these evil bastards. I can think of many places for that money and not one of those places would be back into *their* Swiss accounts."

They all sat quietly, thinking about the power they now had. James got up and slowly walked towards the stairway and out of the theater.

"What a cool dad," Gloria said.

"Thanks," Mark said, "and I'm his spitting image."

Gloria smiled, "In your dreams!"

Chapter 25
Monday, December 1, 1997,
Washington, D.C. – 4:19 P.M

Over the years, O.O.T.A.P. had become a 'family business', handed down from generation to generation. Its strength came from the iron-fisted control it had over the lives of so many other inhabitants on the planet. They regularly crossed borders, moved from one language to another, taking what they wanted, when they wanted, from anyone, anywhere. Since the early 1970's O.O.T.A.P., or the 'Touring Company' as it now preferred to be known, was run by Phineas Illia Harper, or "P.H.". He was a direct descendent of Megan Scheit, nine generations removed and without question the most malicious and wicked of all his predecessors. .

Although O.O.T.A.P. had substantial control over a number of foreign banking entities since the 1920's, it wasn't until P.H. took over the day-to-day operations of the Touring Company that their foreign interests far outweighed those within the borders of the United States. He used his political, business and banking connections to open the doors to China. First by bringing a former United States Vice President and Presidential candidate into the highest ranks of one of the world's largest beverage corporations and then, years later, making certain that the very same former Vice President would be elected president, so that he could spark a series of mutual trade agreements between the U.S. and China.

The beverage company opened a series of bottling plants on Mainland China, then other seemingly innocent and on the surface, unconnected agreements followed. Before long, China was in the modern world with both feet - or to be more accurate, China became the newest and most fertile branch of the OOTAP confederation' of councils.

*****

P.H. sat alone in his modest home along the New Jersey shore. Try as he might, he just couldn't understand how so much went so wrong, so quickly. How those little shits did what kings, princes and even popes could not do, he thought, as he sat staring out of his living room window.

For the eighth time today he dialed up each of his numbered Swiss accounts only to see $1.00 in the balance column. "One dollar!" he yelled at the top of his lungs, "One dollar!"

His call to Henry Bourgess, bank president at the Swiss bank Wagelon and Company did not go well at all. "I'll ruin you, Henry," he screamed into the phone. "You will *not* tell me that there is nothing you can do. One day you are holding billions of my dollars in your 'so called safest bank in the world' and the next day I am wiped out! You WILL NOT tell me that this can happen without your full knowledge! DO YOU UNDERSTAND ME?"

Knowing full well that this American could easily do whatever he threatened, Bourgess tried to calm his caller down. "I swear on my mother's eyes that I know nothing about this, P.H., nothing! But I assure you that I will get to the bottom of this."

"I don't want your assurances, Henry, I want my money back and I want it back now! I want it back this minute! I do not care what you have to do or who it will come from. I JUST WANT MY MONEY BACK, IN MY ACCOUNT, NOW! Do you clearly understand me?"

"I do, but..."

"Don't 'but me' Henry. I will expect your call in one hour

– or less - and the only message I expect to hear from you in one hour – or less – is that the money is back in my account and whatever had happened will not... cannot... ever happen again!" P.H. slammed the phone down with all of his might.

*****

Henry Bourgess sat on the edge of his bed, still holding the telephone receiver, almost as if in a trance. His wife propped herself up on her elbow and asked, "Henry, what's the matter, dear?"

"It is not good, Hilda, not at all good."

He slowly stood up and walked into the bathroom. Turning both faucets on full, he buried his head in the basin. As he toweled his head dry he said to no one in particular, "Poppa was right, 'If you lay down with dogs, you wake up with fleas'."

*****

Bourgess reached for his robe and went into his study. He sat at his desk and reached for the phone several times, each time lifting the receiver and then gently putting it back in its cradle.

He looked at the clock; it had been 27 minutes since the call came in from the American. He opened the right top drawer of his antique desk, the very same desk that held the bank's first deposits when it opened for business in 1741. He removed a small metal box from the drawer and placed it in front of him. He slowly dialed the opening combination and lifted the cover. Inside were a few documents, a thick stack of crisp new American hundred dollar bills, several old military medals, a photo of his wife and a small antique revolver.

It was now 52 minutes since the call from the American.

He picked up the gun with his right hand, tightly held his wife's picture in his left hand, put the end of the barrel into his mouth, gave out a howl and pulled the trigger.

The end of the barrel shook between his teeth, chipping two teeth, but to his surprise, nothing else happened. He pulled the trigger again, and again, nothing happened. In a fit of despair he threw the gun against the wall.

His wife rushed to the door, "Henry, are you all right?" she screamed.

The phone rang, startling them both; on the fourth ring he slowly lifted the receiver. The voice was calm and steady, "Time's up, Henry, where's my money?"

Chapter 26
Tuesday, December 2, 1997,
Washington, D.C. – 8:52 A.M

Gloria was the last to enter the kitchen. She pulled out a chair and sat opposite Mark and Max who had already been in place for the better part of an hour. They stared at the clock on the wall without speaking a word.

Just before 9:00 A.M. they each held hands. Gloria smiled reassuringly at Max. Mark nodded his head.

"Good morning, sunshines," Max said into the listening device they had removed from behind the stove, "rise and shine – today is the first day towards the end of your lives."

"The next song is going out to my new best friends in a blue van," Max said mockingly. Then, to the tune of "Knock Three Times", Tony Orlando's 1970's hit song,

> *"Honk three times... if you want to see your moneeee*
> *Look at the bal-ance,*
> > *if you want to feel poorrrrrr,*
> > > *everybody...*
> > > > *honk three times...'*

Then silence.

"What's the matter?" Max yelled into the listening device, you have never heard the delightful tune *by Illia Sharpell and the true Patriots."*

Within a few seconds they could hear three separate blasts from a nearby car horn.

"Splendid," Max said. "Now we are cooking with gas. Okay, here are the rules and the penalties, first the penalties. As promised yesterday, I will say this just one time – you are to follow all rules to the absolute letter. If you are foolish enough to refuse to comply, then you will lose all chance of ever retrieving a penny of your ill-gotten gains. If you are still listening and understand the potential horror you all face, honk three times."

They heard three short bursts from a car horn.

Max closed his eyes tightly and continued speaking, "Okay, let's begin. I know that the fat man is not here in Washington with you; he is in New Jersey at his pleasant little cottage beside the ocean. I assume he is listening in on this conversation. If I am correct on both counts you are to honk your horn two times. I'll wait."

There were two blasts of the horn.

"These instructions are for you, *Mr. P. H.* - here we go. In exactly 5 minutes you are to put your wide body into your silver Lexus sedan. Bring your cell phone and wear a white shirt, if you can find a white shirt that fits. Drive the SUV out in front of your home. You are to drive it yourself. Open all doors and the trunk and stand inside the trunk and move around the trunk to show those of us who have you under surveillance that you will be driving alone in the car. There must not be anyone else with you in the Lexus. Do you understand so far? If so please honk the horn two times."

There were two horn blasts.

"You are to drive north on Route 9; stop at the *Jersey Freeze* ice cream shop in Freehold, New Jersey, park your unlocked car at the rear of the building. Get out of the car and go around to the front entrance, order a large vanilla soft serve cone, have them dip the cone in chocolate and add whipped cream and two cherries. Return to the car. Hold the cone up above your head so that those of us having you under surveillance know that you are keeping to the letter and spirit of these instructions. Then place the cone under the driver's side wiper blade. Get into the car and wait until 11:45 to give the one holding you under surveillance a chance to call in your position. At exactly 11:45, without removing the cone from the windshield, you are to drive to the Woodbridge Shopping Center Mall, park near the Sear's Department Store, leave your cell phone on the driver's seat and walk into the men's clothing department where you will receive your next instructions. You will be observed every minute from the time you leave your home until you arrive at the Woodbridge Shopping Center Mall. We have timed the drive and if you leave now you should arrive at the Jersey Freeze close to 11:30 A.M. If you are more than ten minutes late all bets are off. Remember, we will definitely know if you are not alone in the SUV or if you speak to anyone else on your cell phone or at the Jersey Freeze. Follow these instructions to the letter and you will receive your final instructions while you are in the Sear's men's department. Make the slightest move that is not in keeping with these instructions and your money will be gone forever."

There was a brief silence.

"Now, two short honks of the horn followed by a longer honk, wait to the count of ten and then honk two more times if you understand the instructions and again three times if they are clear to you as well as to 'fatty'."

Within a few seconds they heard the first series of sounds that had been demanded. Less than a minute later they heard the remaining sounds.

"Very good, now, for you in the blue van, you are to drive away and if we see you or any of your cronies within a mile of this house ever again you will be very sorry indeed. One last item on the agenda, I want you all to listen very carefully to this." Mark stood up and placed the listening device in the microwave oven, set it for 10 seconds, closed the door and hit the start button. Soon sparks flew and smoke came rushing out from the appliance. "That will refocus their beady little eyes and keep their floppy ears ringing for a while," Will James laughed.

Chapter 27
Tuesday, December 2, 1997,
Freehold, New Jersey – 11:27 A.M

P.H. arrived at the Jersey Freeze in Freehold, New Jersey just before 11:30 A.M. He parked in the rear of the building, as per the instructions, got out of the car and sneaking a look around the parking lot; he walked towards the front entrance. Even though the day was overcast and he couldn't imagine anyone else in an ice cream store in the middle of winter, there was a line of people in front of him. Mostly young mothers with young children trying to make the most important decision of their young lives – what flavor ice cream will they have today?

"Can I taste the strawberry mocha delight?" one asked.

"Why don't you make the fruity tooty double chocolate cheese cake low fat yogurt anymore?" one of the adults asked from the back of the line.

Then there were the endless questions about today's special toppings and after all of that came the need to choose between a paper cup or a plain cone or a chocolate-dipped waffle cone. He felt as if his head was about to explode. Finally, when he thought he couldn't stand one more minute of this he pushed to the front of the line and bellowed at the top of his lungs, "I don't have all day here, let me show you all how this should be done!"

He reached through the service window and grabbed the young attendant by his lapels. With less than an inch between their faces he said, "Large vanilla cone, dipped in chocolate, with whipped cream and two cherries, NOW."

When P.H. returned to the car, he waved the cone above his head then placed it under the windshield, as per the instructions, and got into his car.

A few minutes later Will James lifted his head from the back seat and said, "Hi, Chubby."

P.H. jumped; looking back he started to reach into the glove compartment.

"You're not looking for this, are you?" James said, pointing the gun at the back of P.H.'s head. "See what happens when you leave your car unlocked?"

"What do you want from me?" P.H. growled.

"Gee, I don't think you have anything left of any value for me to want."

"I could have my guys squash you all like the loser bugs you are." The fat man squealed.

"Let me see," James said, rubbing his chin with one hand as he pushed the gun into the back of P.H.'s head. "If you asked Manny, your number one goon, he could certainly hurt me and would rush to do it, but at this very moment he is hiding in the Sear's menswear department in the Woodbridge Mall. Then there is Sid and Mike. No, they can't rush to your side because you told them to crouch behind some cars in the Woodbridge Shopping Center parking lot. So who does that leave? Oh, my, the rest are still in Washington where you left them." James gave out a hearty laugh, "Sorry Phineas, you're out of muscle for the moment. I'm afraid it is just you and me right now. Oh, yes, and your little glove compartment friend here. Now, give me the ignition key and get out of the car."

"If it is all the same to you I prefer to be called P.H."

"No problem, Phineas", James said, mockingly, "I just think Phineas has a more melodious sound to it."

James got out of the car and shoved P.H. towards a small car several spaces away from the Lexus. Motioning towards the driver's side James whispered, "Get into the driver's seat."

James watched P.H. try to squeeze his girth into the much smaller front seat, then barked, "Bring the seat closer to the steering wheel."

"It's as close as it can go," he complained, "if I push it in any further I won't be able to breathe."

"Breathing isn't all it's cracked up to be, Big Guy", James laughed, "just do it!"

Holding the gun at his side James quickly settled into the rear passenger seat, then handed the key to P.H. and said, "You drive, I'll direct. Now, turn the engine on and begin to drive, that way, out of the lot."

When they got to the edge of the parking lot James told him to turn left. "But the Woodbridge Shopping Center is to the right," P.H. grumbled.

"So it is, sooooooo it is." James said, poking the gun into the fat man's neck, "But we are going left. Is that O.K. with you, Phineas?"

"I asked you *not* to call me that. I told you that I prefer P.H."

"So you did, sooooo you did." James was intentionally trying to keep the big man on edge. "Tell you what, Phineas, just in case you haven't picked up on it as yet, I don't give two hoots or a holler what you prefer. Now, turn left and await further instructions. Kapeesh?"

*****

P.H. was told to drive into an almost deserted bowling alley parking lot further south on Route 9. They came to a stop in an area slightly shaded by a small clump of trees. "Give me the key," James demanded. After placing the key in his pocket, James moved out of the rear seat, walked around the car and got into the front passenger seat.

"Now give me your recording device," James said.

"What recording device?" P.H. asked.

"The one you told Manny to put fresh batteries into at 7:09 this morning."

"I don't know what you're talking about," P.H. insisted.

James reached into P.H.'s breast pocket and pulled out a mini cassette player, and said, "I was talking about this, Phineas."

"Here's the deal Phineas, you are over and done with. You and the band of *bothers* you have led off the cliff are over and done with; and most of all, O.O.T.A.P., or whatever you call yourself these days, is over and done with. Your money is gone and you still have your life," James said.

"You can't be serious, YOU'RE threatening me? Do you have any idea how far up my connections go?"

"Phineas, Phineas, Phineas," James said mockingly.

"P.H.!"

"Phineas, Phineas, Phineas," James continued. "How long do you think those really important sheep are going to hang around with you if it looks like you're going down?"

"Just tell me what you want, specifically." P.H. said.

"First I want you to lay off those college kids."

"That's all you want?" P.H. said dismissively."

"No, it is not all I want. In fact, I am just beginning. Next I want you to close up your hate machine and walk away."

"And if I refuse?" P.H. smiled.

Matching his smile with an even wider grin, James said, "I guess you need a little more convincing. Good, I will have so much fun with the rest of your holdings."

"That will *never* happen."

"Phineas, it has already happened. I think you just need another sample of what we are able to do."

P.H. began to laugh heartily. "Fool me once, shame on you. Fool me twice, shame on me. You were lucky, you caught me off guard, and I'll give you that. But, let me put it this way, if you can get the better of me again I'll eat your hat."

"And you will close down and walk away?"

"*If* you are able to get the better of me again and live to tell the tale, yes, I will close it down. But you aren't better than me so that is never going to happen."

"It's a deal!" James said. "Now if you will just get out of the car I will be on my way."

"You're leaving me here, stranded?"

"Phineas, don't take me for a complete fool. You can just use the cell phone you have hidden in your right sock to call one of your peeps to come pick you up."

P.H. glared at him, "I will make you pay for this. If you had half a brain you would know that."

"I'll tell you what, if this time tomorrow I am the only problem you have on your mind I will call you, tell you where I am and beg you to come take me out of my misery," James said.

"Now that's a deal!" P.H. roared.

"Meanwhile leave the kids alone," James said.

"You have no idea what you have started." P.H. yelled.

"Correction," James said, defiantly, "Phineas, it was *you* who started this. Now, *we* will finish it."

"If I were you I would be very careful from here on out," P.H. said with venom in every word. "I would be very, very careful. For you this may be some lark or, at best, a 'Don Quixote' moment in an otherwise empty and meaningless life, but for the loyal Americans I represent, you are little more than a distraction, a bug in the headlights. If you walk away now I promise to make your punishment quick. However, if you insist..."

James grabbed P.H. by the lapels and brought him closer, then said, "You are a disease, and this bug in the headlights intends to bring you down along with all of the so-called patriots who hang on your every word either because you own them or scared them shitless along the years. You are no more or less than a street bully. Your days are coming to an end. Up to this minute all we have deprived you of is 'money'; you still think you have an army of protectors. By this time tomorrow they too will be gone. Deprived of both money and influence and the 'power' both made possible, maybe then you will begin to feel the terror you and your kind have spread over others for so many years."

James put his hand up to his ear, "Do you hear that? That sound is history finally locking you in your place and throwing the key away. Enjoy the last few moments, while they last. By this time tomorrow it will be crystal clear to even you that you are through and there is absolutely nothing you will be able to do about it."

"I don't know what you and your young friends are smoking but if you think you can bring us down I suggest to you that it is time to sober up," P.H. said as he struggled out of the front seat. "For your information, we own or control almost two thirds of the 'Fortune 500' Boards of Directors – lock, stock and barrel! Most layers of government – from local district men to the White House. Did you hear what I said you ignoramus, the White House! We own 30% of the U.S. Congress, almost 20% of the U.S. Senate. Hey, we even control a third of the Supreme Court! You and your group of boy scouts gonna fight that?"

"I don't believe you!" James taunted.

"Remember that 'phone in my sock' you empty headed twit? I have the private cell number for every one of those I have just referred to. Yes, including the President of the United States!"

"Yeah, sure!" James smirked.

"We are your army and your navy – are you not aware of the 'privatization of the military Mr. Shithead?" P.H. yelled. "It started with the jobs nobody wanted to do – peeling potatoes, scrubbing toilets, slowly, slowly up to road building and finally killer patrols and protecting visiting dignitaries. You and your diaper patrol gonna reverse all of THAT?"

P.H. was on a roll now. "Who do you think clothes and feeds your military? We do! It started from a foot in the door to owning the door and everything behind it in just a few generations. You think you can bring all of that down in a day, or in a week or in a hundred years?"

James reached into his pants pocket, grabbed a fist full of small change and threw it out the window towards P.H.. "Here, use my money to buy yourself a newspaper tomorrow – I promise you will not be bored."

P.H. laughed, "You think one of *our* papers will pick up your story? Maybe you expect one of *our* TV or radio stations to spread your lies. It will never happen! We are in control here. We have been dummying down the population for years. We own the minds and carcasses of the 'great unwashed'. YOU DON'T HAVE A CHANCE."

James moved into the driver's seat and drove off.

"Words," P.H. yelled after the car, "empty words and empty threats." With great difficulty P.H. reached down to retrieve the small cell phone he had hidden that morning in his sock.

*****

James drove about a block and then pulled over. He looked at the cassette recording device he had taken from P.H. He hit the rewind button, then the play button. "Thanks P.H.," he said to himself. "No one would ever have taken us seriously without this."

He started the engine and as he made a wide turn at the corner he felt something hit against his foot. Looking down he noticed a small silvery object. He pulled along the side of the road, turned off the motor and got out of the car. He reached down to pick up an object on the floor. It was a small cell phone, realizing that it must be P.H.'s cell phone and probably fell out of his sock either when he struggled to get into or out of the car, James retrieve the contact list. "Wow, thank you again, P.H. This looks like an 'A list' if I ever saw one. We really didn't need this but it will definitely speed up the process. Let's see how long this herd of sheep will stick with their fat little shepherd."

He began to laugh so hard that tears were streaming down his cheeks. "It is going to be a very long walk back Chubby", he yelled out of the window, "very long indeed!"

Chapter 28

"He who permits himself to tell a lie once, finds it much easier to do it a second and third time, till at length it becomes habitual; he tells lies without attending to it, and truths without the world believing him. This falsehood of tongue leads to that of the heart, and in time depraves all its good dispositions."
−Written by Thomas Jefferson in a letter to
Peter Carr, his nephew, 19 August, 1785

Wednesday, 29, January, 1806,
Washington City, District of Columbia − 4:17 P.M

The carriage ride took longer than usual. As a result, Jefferson and Breckinridge did not return to Washington until late in the day, Wednesday, the 29th of January. Each was tired, hungry and concerned about all they had to do as soon as they reached the White House. There had been bitter words expressed during the trip. It was not unusual for the two men to disagree − but it was rare for them to be disagreeable with each other.

It was true that O.O.T.A.P. had prospered during their watch but it was also true that it had not been permitted to grow as much as with the previous administration. During this carriage ride the two men argued about the options facing them now − Breckinridge believed that O.O.T.A.P. could and would take Jefferson down with them; Jefferson believed he had to rid the earth of Philthrow, once and for all, even if it cost him an honorable place in history.

As soon as Jefferson's carriage came to a stop in front of the President's mansion Jefferson was informed that Aaron Burr, Jefferson's first Vice President and Burr's long time aid, James Philthrow were waiting in the President's public reception area. He was also informed that the Speaker of the House was on his way and was expected shortly.

Before leaving the carriage Jefferson told John Breckinridge, "I would like you to meet with the two scoundrels first. I am counting on you to put the fear of the all mighty into their hearts and minds?"

Breckinridge grimaced, "Tom, do you really think anyone can accomplish such a lofty goal? These thugs fear no man - I am sorry to say – not the President of these United States much less an old country lawyer like me."

"Lofty or not, today must be the day we either end their domination or we must begin to personally accept the consequences for the damage they have and will continue to inflict on the population."

"And if they laugh in our faces?" Breckinridge asked.

Jefferson leaned back into the carriage and put his hand on Breckinridge's arm, "All tyranny needs in order to gain a foothold is for people of good conscience to ... remain silent." Jefferson thought for a moment, and then added, "If being the president does not give me the power to end this thing of theirs today then what good is being the president? I might as well go back to Monticello and tend to my gardens."

"Look, Tom," Breckinridge said, "there may have been a time when you or any of a hundred men could have put a stop to this bunch. We knew it and yet did nothing. Partly because they were no direct threat to us and partly because we believed that they were doing what needed to be done to our mutual enemies." Breckinridge thought for a moment, and then added, "Let me put it in even simpler terms – we had rodents in our midst and with our eyes wide open we agreed to allow an elephant to roam around freely to rid us of the mice. Now the mice are gone but we are faced with elephants that refuse to leave. The power now lies with them and they are NOT about to either share or relinquish that power, not for me and not for you. I don't know what you hope to accomplish here today but if it is to get them – even some of them – to voluntarily stop their evil work then you are about to learn that it just cannot be done. We have passed the point of no return. So, what do you plan to do next?"

"I can no longer stand by - no, make that, I WILL NO LONGER STAND BY – and allow there to be one set of laws for them and another set of laws for the rest of us," Jefferson said.

"So I ask you again," Breckinridge demanded. "What are you planning to do?"

They sat staring at each other for a while before the footman tenderly knocked on the carriage door and said, "We have arrived, Mr. President."

Jefferson was halfway out of the carriage when he stopped and turned to reenter the carriage, closing the door behind him. Then in slowly delivered, measured speech he said, "I am prepared to exterminate Philthrow."

"Just like that?" Breckinridge challenged.

"Just like that!" Jefferson repeated. "They had the gall to murder young Illia and leave him floating within sight of my home, where my children and their children could cast their eyes on his bloated body. And you seem to be able to write it off as little more than the cost of doing business. Well I am not. And I expect more from my Attorney General!"

"And I expect more reality from my president!"

They glared at each other and then Jefferson turned and exited the carriage. "I will be in my study for a short while. Prepare them for a reckoning," Jefferson yelled over his shoulder.

Breckenridge went directly to the public reception area. Without formally greeting the two men he motioned them to join him by the window. "You must know," Breckenridge began, "that the president cannot allow the recent incident to go unpunished."

"So the President is now the Safety Director for the Capital?" Burr mocked. "I hear that it was just a robbery gone badly. Does he know something that the rest of us do not?"

Philthrow moved between the two men and said, "*We* will resolve this matter. The robber or robbers who did this will be found, will face justice and will pay the ultimate price for this deed."

Breckinridge put his hand up, "Stop it! Don't take us all for fools, we are not fools. You have gone too far this time. He cannot ignore what has happened, and we all know this president well enough to accept that he will not walk away from this. You have gone too far!"

"Is he prepared to acknowledge his long standing relationship with the Council?" Philthrow asked, stressing the words 'long standing'.

"If you are asking if he intends to assume responsibility for letting your criminal gang have free range for all of this time," Breckinridge said, "I believe he is."

"If we 'go down' so will he," Burr said.

"He understands all of that and I believe that he has made his peace with it," Breckinridge said.

Burr looked at Philthrow, and then said, "He cannot expect us to just accept for ourselves whatever he is willing to accept for himself. The Council has too much invested to give it all up. He is misjudging the resolve and reach of the Council, a very big mistake."

Breckinridge raised his voice, "Don't threaten him or me!"

"Do not look upon this as an idle threat, Mr. Attorney General. It is a fact and if he is foolish enough to test us, he will lose. He will lose badly."

Just then Horace entered the room. He informed them that the Speaker had arrived and that the president requested them all to join him in the sanctuary.

*****

By the time Breckinridge, Burr and Philthrow reached the sanctuary the Speaker was walking up the hall towards them. Horace took his usual place by the door. Jefferson was slumped in an easy chair beside one of the fireplaces.

Staring into the fire, Jefferson was the first to speak and as he did, he emphasized each word. "You know, 'Little Burr', that 'Council' of yours may have a mountain of hidden funds and several armies of influential co-conspirators, but none of that is going to help them or you – this time."

"Now, Tom—" Burr began, only to be interrupted by Jefferson.

"Don't you call me Tom, you immoral and corrupt thug."

"And how do you wish me to address you?" Burr asked.

"Don't address me at all!" Jefferson screamed, now glaring directly at Burr.

"Come on, Tom... er...a...Mr. President," Burr continued. "It is just a robbery gone badly. It is unfortunate; it is a terrible turn of events, but what is to be gained by destroying so many careers? Not the least of which will be yours."

"You think my career is or could be a prime consideration for me at this time? Are you so foolish to believe that anyone in their right minds will believe this 'robbery' scenario of yours? I might expect such drivel from the snake standing by your side here today," Jefferson said, pointing at Philthrow. "What he lacks in integrity he more than makes up for in greed and dishonesty. I gave you credit for more than that. This hogwash you are spouting is beneath even you. Let me say it clearly; you will not get away with this. Do you hear me?"

Philthrow walked forward. "Let's understand each other, Mr. President. You may not trust me; you may not like me; but to try and fight the Council – especially over something like this – is pure folly. It is madness and completely unnecessary."

"We confide in our strength, without boasting of it; we respect that of others, without fearing it," Jefferson said.

"Oh, Mr. President, we can take care of this and given your strong feelings about it, I assure you that we *will* do so promptly. It isn't as if you were unaware of our methods." Philthrow said.

Jefferson stood up and walked towards Philthrow. "You are addressing the President of these United States, you slimy bastard. That still carries some weight around here."

"And you are creating deep concerns in the minds of those governing the Council, Mr. President, and they too carry considerable weight around here – and beyond." Philthrow said, then with added emphasis, "You know, Mr. President, we patriots deserve your support every bit as much as Illia Sharpell does, if not more."

"Patriotism is not a short frenzied burst of emotion, but the long and steady dedication of a lifetime," Jefferson said, "this Council of yours is not patriotic; it is nothing less than a criminal force, a band of thieves and greedy rebels. Everything you stand for is dishonest and self serving."

"You didn't seem to feel that way when we were more effective than your General Washington at breaking the will of the Redcoats," Burr said.

Jefferson returned to his chair beside the roaring fireplace; once again staring into the flames he waived the visitors out of the room in obvious disgust.

*****

PART TWO

Chapter 29
Wednesday, December 3, 1997,
Washington, D.C. 8:20 A.M.

"I see it but I still do not believe it!" Max yelled. He was looking at the front page of that morning's Washington Post. The front page consisted of a single banner headline:

EXTRA!
EXTRA!
EXTRA!

CORRUPTION INC.
U.S. INFLUENCE PEDDLING RING
EXPOSED!

*****

UNITED STATES
JUSTICE DEPARTMENT
EXPECTS INDICTMENTS SOON AGAINST
19 CURRENT U.S. SENATORS! 132 CURRENT
U.S. CONGRESSMEN! 3 SITTING SUPREME
COURT JUSTICES! 312 of the 'FORTUNE 500'
BOARD CHAIRS!

Almost the entire edition was devoted to what the editorial page described as the story of the century! Specific Swiss bank account numbers were referenced; there were details that suggested influence was bought and paid for to insure the passing of specific pieces of legislation. Articles connected groups of powerful men to a secret American based, international crime organization.

Scattered around the kitchen of the townhouse were copies of that morning's *USA Today, The New York Times, The Chicago Tribune, The Los Angeles Times and The Wall Street Journal*. Each had similar banner headlines and follow up stories.

"All of these papers agreed to run the story without worrying about their own involvement?" Gloria asked James.

James smiled, "Not exactly. You know most nationally distributed papers now use satellites to get newspaper content to their printing presses. I merely intercepted and replaced the stories they were planning with our own story."

"So won't they just print a retraction in their very next edition?"

"They could, but that is very unlikely to happen."

"How can you be so certain?" Gloria asked.

James smiled broadly, "First of all because at least one of them, if not most of them, will probably win a Pulitzer for the breaking coverage. It is also unlikely because the rush is already on between some of the best lawyers in the country and officials of the justice department to negotiate the best possible terms for their high profile clients. The lawyers fully understand – although their clients are just beginning to get the message – the first to confess and turn state's evidence has the best chance to avoid lengthy prison sentences. One thing I do know is that by end of day today members of the House, Senate, and the Supreme Court will almost certainly be announcing their early retirement, and even a willingness to be witnesses for the prosecution when the cases come to trial. And numerous cases will almost certainly be going to trial."

"Of course that is likely but how can you possibly be so confident that it is going to happen this quickly? These people have so much power and such high and mighty contacts... I wouldn't question that it will happen in a few months or even a few weeks, but today?" Gloria said.

James smiled and whispered in her ear, "It is simply human nature – the bigger they are the quicker they run for cover."

"Come on Dad, Gloria is asking a really good question." Mark said.

"Okay", James said, "Your Mr. P.H. was kind enough to leave me his cell phone. It had the direct numbers for many of the public persons on his payroll. I called as many as I could last night and 14 members of the House, 3 Senators and a Supreme Court Justice agreed to resign today if I did not mention their names in the first round of stories. They also promised to testify for the government when this all goes to court."

"I think it is safe to say that the 'Touring Company's' days are over," Max yelled at the top of his lungs.

*****

In his New Jersey shore home P.H., surrounded by many of the same newspapers was being inundated by calls from the press as well as some of the public figures blaming him for letting it all get out of control. He finally ripped the phone out of the wall and drove to his nephew's home.

*****

Over the next three days follow up stories connected a series of foreign leaders and banking institutions to the schemes. By the weekend, another 47 members of the House, 4 Senators and 2 more Supreme Court Justices announced their early retirement.

When authorities came for P.H. early the next day, his home was boarded up and he was nowhere to be found.

Chapter 30
Monday, December 7, 1997,
Brooklyn New York, 3:15 P.M.

Max picked up Mrs. Abondola early in the morning and together they drove around the old neighborhood. By 3:15 they were in front of P.S. 16, in the Williamsburg section of Brooklyn. They were watching children play in the fenced in schoolyard while sharing a cheese danish from Flaum's Appetizers on the corner.

"So what do we do now?" Mrs. Abondola asked. "No more dragons to slay. Are we ever going to be able to do ordinary things again?"

Max laughed, "How we gonna keep them down on the farm after they see Pareee?"

"Seriously, though, what's next for you?"

"Some of the answer depends on how we handle Mr. Jefferson's part in this story."

"Yes", she said with a sigh, "I guess it was only a matter of time before we had to face that question up front and personal. I will follow your lead, Max, what is your suggestion?"

"Let me see," Max said sarcastically. "If we tell all that we know about his involvement we would almost certainly be prime candidates for a Pulitzer – maybe even share the cover of Time Magazine, the couch on the Tonight Show and speaking fees in the tens of thousands of dollars. Or, we could say nothing and stay poor and unknown. How will we ever be able to decide?"

They both laughed.

"I'm an old lady, Max, my needs are being met and frankly the thought of instant fame scares me."

Max put his hand on hers, "Me too!"

"But is shoving such an important story under the rug really an option?" She asked.

He thought for a while. "Remember what you said when I first told you about this mess? You told me that you supported true and honest reporting. If what we uncovered could help future generations gain a new insight into the actions of a leader, then we owe it to history to report it."

"I also told you that if that person is no longer around and so, can't defend him or herself, then history should only be corrected if the new information is truly relevant and not just idle gossip," she added.

"Well, doesn't this pass all of those tests?" He asked.

"I just wish we had more than these diary pages to back it all up with." she said.

"We need to decide," he said, "I will agree to whatever you recommend."

"That's a lot of responsibility for an old lady." She said.

"What do you think Jefferson would do?" He said.

"Judging by how completely he hid his participation in the entire affair I think he would cover this up as well. But that shouldn't be the measure. We need to be true to our own standards for what is right or wrong." She said.

They sat quietly for a long time, still watching the children in the play yard. Finally it was Max who broke the silence. "I would like to think that history might best be served by not tarnishing his reputation."

"Can you live with yourself if that is the decision? I am not certain that I could," she said softly.

"I have given this a lot of thought. I suggest that we reach out for a respected Jeffersonian historian; tell him or her what we have; present all of our support documentation; let him or her punch whatever holes in it that he or she can; let that historian advise us if it passes the 'need to know' test."

"I like that approach," she said.

"And let them pick up the Pulitzer." He said.

"I like that even more," she added.

Max gave his old teacher a hug and kissed her on her cheek.

Chapter 31
Saturday, December 8, 1997,
Washington, D.C., 11:25 A.M.

"If I live to be a hundred I will never understand you young people," Sam Nobal said.

"First you kill yourself to find some little previously undiscovered morsel about Thomas Jefferson. Then you find, not a morsel, but a seven course meal and what do you do? You hand it over to some fancy shmancy historian. Can you explain the sense of that to me?"

Max laughed. "It was just the right thing to do, Sam."

"That's no explanation, Mr. College Boy." Sam argued.

"It's the best I can come up with on such short notice."

"So what is the plan now?"

"Like so many others in my position today, I have a, how would you say, 'fancy shmancy' diploma and no job prospects."

"I don't think there are that many in your position, Max." Sam said. "You could write your own ticket if you would only get in front of the Jefferson story."

"It just wouldn't be right, Sam."

"Well, from where I am standing it is just dumb to walk away from what is technically, legally, fairly and in any other way you choose to define it, legitimately yours. Hey, you could have been killed by these shysters."

"Maybe so," Max sighed.

"Are you planning to stay in the area?"

"I would like to, and if I can get a job in town I would stay for a while."

"You could work here. I would even consider sharing part of the business with you." Sam said.

"50/50 partner?" Max asked.

"50/50, 99/1, it is all relative. Or another way to look at is the more percentage to you the more of my debt becomes your responsibility." Sam laughed. "With you here we would attract more young people; I'm not what you would call a young person magnet, you know?"

"I've noticed," Max said, looking around at the few customers in the store.

"We could change the name of the store to Nobal and Barnes. How would you like that?"

"Or we could change it to Barnes and Nobal", Max said.

"Barnes and Nobal", Sam repeated, "it does have a nice ring to it. Now, where have I heard that before?"

"I would guess you may have seen the giant signs for the big mall store on the other side of town?" Max said.

They both laughed.

Chapter 32
Late summer, 1998,
somewhere in Djibouti, North East Africa

In the mid to late 1970's, just after he took control of the operation, P.H. invested heavily in Djibouti, first by almost single handedly financing the rebels, helping them get their independence from France; then propping up the country's first President, Hassan Gouled Aptidon. Hassan quickly installed an authoritarian one-party government dominated by his own Issa community and privately swore his allegiance to O.O.T.A.P., in general, P.H., in particular. Repeatedly thanking P.H. for his guidance and support.

P.H. never really believed he would need a safe haven from the U.S., but he did want a quiet place in which to 'get lost' whenever the need arose. Djibouti seemed to fill the bill. Although the United States maintains diplomatic relations with the small country it did not and still does not have an extradition treaty with them.

In 1978 under a series of untraceable identities he scattered more than twenty-five million dollars in gold bars in various safety deposit boxes around the country. 'Mad Money' at the time – survival funds now. He was pleased to see that these assets had escaped the college kids' claws. When he ran away from his New Jersey shore home he left almost everything except a pouch of uncut diamonds, about four hundred and forty-four million dollars worth; six hundred thousand dollars in 9.50 silver, two thousand American $100 dollar bills and a hand written note guaranteeing his personal safety signed by the Secretary General of the United Nations. Fortunately, he did not need to use the letter and so he had every reason to believe that his current location was known only to himself.

P.H., or Patrick Hernaldo, the name on his expensive new credentials, had gotten into a comfortable routine since arriving on this off the beaten track speck on the East Coast of Africa. Each day, just before dawn, he woke to watch the sun rise and then enjoyed a small breakfast of fresh fruit and berries followed by a long, leisurely swim. An hour or so nap almost every day in the mid-afternoon; a strict two hour regimen at the hotel gym; followed by three or four hours working on his new hobby, building boats in bottles; then a light dinner and off to bed, usually by 8:00 P.M.

He had dropped almost 50 pounds since leaving the U.S. and felt twenty years younger.

It took him a while to get used to doing things for himself but even that felt good now. Occasionally, while walking along the coastline he would try to think of ways to get even with the "little shits" who brought him and his empire down. But he was almost ready to accept his current status.

Almost.

PART THREE

Chapter 33
Sunday, December 24, 2006, Christmas Eve, Washington, D.C.

Phillip Haskins began most mornings gazing into his floor to ceiling mirror. He liked what he saw. His own mother would not have recognized him now, but it wasn't his mother he was trying to evade, it was the United States Federal Bureau of Investigation.

The plastic surgeon did an amazing job. It was a shame that he had to be killed as soon as the operation was declared a success. No loose ends, which was the only way to insure his safety. He planned it well. No detail too small. This time no one would get him. No one!

The hardest part at the beginning was the strenuous exercise regimen. However, today with a body that would make anyone half his age jealous and more energy than he could ever remember having was far tastier than the dozens of Krispy Kreme doughnuts he had consumed almost every day in his former life. He also enjoyed the way heads turned his way when he walked into the gym or lounged on a beach.

P.H. had finally returned to Washington, D.C. with a new face... new name... an entirely new identity... 6 pack abs and a clear purpose... to get back what those "little shits" took from him. They must pay for taking what was rightfully his, was the one and only thought consuming his every waking moment. They must be made to pay for every day – no, every single second - he was forced to live outside of the country he loved so much.

"I *will* live free once again!" He yelled into the mirror.

Chapter 34
Wednesday, December 27, 2006,
Washington, D.C.

The small bookstore had prospered under the partnership of Sam Nobal and Max Barnes. Other than a small salary for each, all profits were reinvested into making it a favorite stomping ground for young and old alike. Eventually they took over the stores on either side of the original location, broke down the connecting walls and developed strong video and music sections as well as a small café.

From time to time Federal agents came by to ask if anyone from O.O.T.A.P. had surfaced but after P.H. went underground the rest of the organization seemed to have dried up.

In late 2003 Sam had a heart attack; although not fatal it did bring his work schedule to a halt. He now only came in when he was bored and even those visits were short and rare.

Max believed he had lucked out when he hired Jeffrey Gendreau, a disabled veteran, who recently moved into the area from Martha's Vineyard, Massachusetts. He didn't seem comfortable talking about his war experiences or how someone could exist on a minimum wage salary and still afford to have lived in a part of the country that had earned a reputation as a retreat for presidents as well as the rich and famous.

What attracted Max the most was that Jeffrey seemed to know about most types of music and could describe and compare individual artists and groups even if their popularity was limited to a single record or album. He attended as many concerts and small club performances as time permitted; somehow had even gained access to various closed door rehearsals and recording sessions. Jeffrey knew his music and almost single handedly built a music department for Max that quickly became a major source of very profitable income.

*****

Now that he was safely back in Washington and looked nothing like his old self, P.H. regularly visited Sam and Max's store. He made huge purchases from the music department and occasionally bought a book or just sat at one of the small café tables, usually nursing a Turkish coffee. It made Jeffrey nervous, but he knew better than to complain. He knew all too well how easily his uncle could lose his temper.

Jeffrey was the only living person who knew that P.H. and Patrick Hernaldo and Phillip Haskins were one and the same person – his Uncle Phineas. He was also the only one who knew about the plastic surgery. In fact, it was Jeffrey who actually arranged for the plastic surgeon to be killed – just as soon as his uncle's bandages were removed. Jeffrey's Uncle Phineas told him what to do and when to do it. Jeffrey always did what his Uncle Phineas told him to do – most people did.

Chapter 35
About seventy years earlier...
Wednesday, September 9, 1936,
Swan Lake, New York 8:20 A.M.

Esther Miller Harper's soon-to-be birth was the talk of the neighborhood. There was no doubt that it would be welcomed with open and caring arms, plenty of love and outward signs of affection. Ellinor and Benjamin Harper, the parents to be, couldn't wait to share the blessed news with their friends and neighbors. The Harpers were long time residents of the small upstate New York community; they were regular churchgoers, rarely missed a Sunday service... these were good American *simple folks*. Benjamin grew up in the modest one level home at the end of a cul-de-sac, which had been built by his great, great grandfather, on his mother's side.

They owned and operated a small general store in town – also started many years before by Benjamin's great, great grandfather. There were no other such stores for many miles around. Over the years there had been talk about large national retailers coming to the area but each time the permits proved to be hard to get, building regulations seemed to change each time the advance people met with local inspectors, and opposition from the general public was fierce and seemingly organized. What was super unusual was that in spite of their *monopoly*, the Harper's retail prices for just about anything the store had to offer were at least half the going rate.

What no one outside of their tightly knit family ever knew was that the clothes closet in the smallest of the four bedrooms had a wooden staircase which led down to a four level living and working space from where the past few generations operated an international federation of power brokers and money launderers – the modern day version of O.O.T.A.P. - the *real* source of the family's income,

The new bundle of joy would be born into a simple church going family with a personal net wealth somewhere north of one hundred and three point six billion dollars – and growing.

No one imagined that this birth was the result of some master plan. At 44, Ellinor, thought her child-bearing days were long gone. If it was a surprise to Ellinor and her friends and neighbors we can only imagine how staggering it was for Benjamin, Ellinor's husband of almost 31 years. When he first learned that he would soon be a father again it was just weeks away from his own 80th birthday.

Medically, the pregnancy was not going well. Ellinor's doctors expressed their concerns. This was quickly turning into an unmanageable medical problem for the barely functional back-country hospital and well beyond the knowledge or experience of any one on its small staff. Ellinor was told to stay in bed for the remainder of the pregnancy.

"We need to buy more time," her doctor told her. "Every day the fetus remains in your body it gets stronger. Today, this baby is too small and too weak to survive on the outside."

Benjamin contacted his son's friend from the Phillips Academy Andover, Benjamin Spock. He told Spock that he was having nightmares about leaving his wife in the hands of the backwards medicine men in charge. "I think we waited too long, Ben. I should have moved her to Manhattan weeks ago. Now that she's further along I think the trip would make matters worse – if that is even possible. Help me to make the best decision for Ellinor, please."

"Of course I will and I will stay involved as long as I can be helpful," Spock assured the father of his old friend. "I've delivered enough full term pregnancies and preemies to know that a 44 year old mother-to-be increases the number and degree of risks many times over. What we need is a medical 'vunderkind', one who regularly sees many such difficult births." The phone went silent for a while and then Spock spoke again. "I may know just the guy. Let me call him and see if he can break away."

"Just let him know, clear as a bell." Benjamin pleaded, "I can and I will pay him anything he asks if he will help us, *anything.*"

Less than an hour later Spock called back; "Great news. I just connected with the best guy for this; I filled him in and he is willing to catch the next plane to the states."

"He is taking a plane to the states; where is he coming from?" the nervous father to be asked.

"He is coming from The Hôpital des Enfants Malades de Paris."

"Why do we need to go all the way to France? Aren't there any doctors here, in this country to help my Ellinor?"

"Now listen to me, as much as I would love to be patriotic and claim that we in America have the best and the brightest in modern medicine, the unfortunate fact is that we are actually quite backwards, especially when it comes to preparing for potentially difficult deliveries or any childbirth involving mothers in their thirties and forties. This doctor I am recommending is the one for your Ellinor, of that I am convinced. The Hôpital des Enfants Malades de Paris was the first pediatric hospital in the Western world and it has consistently been heads above those that followed. They wrote the book and the sequel and no one else is even close. They have also led the way in attracting and developing the best doctors in this field. If Ellinor were my wife, my choice – my one and only choice - would be Jacques Pilron, their new guiding light. He is one of the best diagnosticians I know and thoroughly dedicated to upgrading the practice of medicine. He studied under René-Théophile-Hyacinthe Laennec, for God's sake – the guy who invented the stethoscope. You don't know how lucky we are that he is willing to take the next plane out. In addition to his tremendous work load within this outstanding teaching hospital he still finds time to go into the poorest neighborhoods in Paris to provide quality care for many destitute women and children. In my opinion, and you *did* ask for my opinion, you need a miracle man right now. There really is no one better."

"Okay, okay!" Benjamin yelled into the phone. "Give me his contact information and I'll arrange for a plane to pick him up and rush him here."

"Stop organizing for one bloody moment. Go hold your wife's hand and tell her help is on its way. I will make the necessary arrangements."

"Money is no object, Ben."

"Has it ever been any other way with you?"

*****

Spock called Dr. Pilron back and told him a private plane would be provided to rush him and his team to the patient's side.

"Just one thing more, Jacques," Spock added. "Ben Harper is rich and powerful and *always* gets what he wants. He can be very generous, especially when it comes to his family's needs, but he can also be overpowering at times."

"With all due respect, Dr. Spock, I will *not* be there to hold Monsieur Harper's hand. I will be there for the comfort and medical needs of the femme enceinte, how they say, mother-to-be and if we can perform a miracle here

- her baby. Monsieur Harper will be a far distant third consideration."

*****

They flew through the night landed on the small landing strip O.O.T.A.P. used to ferry money and drugs into and out of the country. As soon as the plane landed a series of waiting station wagons sped them and their luggage directly to the small hospital.

Chapter 36
Saturday, September 12, 1936,
Swan Lake, New York 3:14 A.M.

Dr. Pilron wasted no time. As soon as he and his team arrived they examined Ellinor and began evaluating the status of the yet to be born baby. Benjamin was asked to leave his wife's room and told to wait outside. He paced back and forth until the guard at the door finally suggested he sit in order to allow them to focus on keeping the area free of unwanted stragglers.

The team quickly took over an entire floor of the small building and set up a special emergency care unit within the hospital's little used operating theater. Benjamin hired 6 guards from the Pinkerton National Detective Agency to stand guard around the clock and insure that the visiting medical team had anything and everything they requested – regardless of the cost and specifically without consideration to the needs of the rest of the hospital.

What seemed like an eternity passed until Pilron left Ellinor's room and walked towards Benjamin, motioning for him to remain seated. They shook hands rather formally and Dr. Pilron moved a chair closer to the nervous husband and sat down. "Monsieur Harper, my concern is your wife. 44 is not the ideal age for a pregnancy even under ideal circumstances, and as you already know, these are not ideal circumstances. However, even that is *not* my major concern. Her overall medical condition is my prime concern. She is too weak and her body may not be able to withstand the rigors of a birth – especially a troubled birth as I am certain this will be. I am also concerned about a premature delivery so early in the process. As best we can calculate, your baby is just at 30 weeks and if it is delivered now it will be incapable of sustaining life on its own." He stared at Benjamin, waiting for a reaction and not sure if his words truly connected.

Benjamin sat up straight, stared into the young doctor's eyes and said, "This is not her first birth, doctor. She is tough and in excellent health. Just do your job."

"I beg your pardon?"

"You heard me; you're supposed to be the best at what you do. So go and do it. You barely just arrived and already you sound like you are giving up."

Pilron sat back in his chair, a broad smile began to form. "Monsieur Harper, do you have any idea how dangerous this matter is? This is not *just another pregnancy*. First of all, a baby taken anything near 30 weeks will certainly face respiratory stress. The lungs are not yet fully developed. It would also be vulnerable to infection. And if that isn't enough, even if the baby can survive childbirth it will still need assistance as soon as it leaves the womb to gain weight and strength and maintain its body temperature. Weight gain is concentrated in the last weeks in utero so this early in the process it is still extremely underweight. To make matters worse yet, infants this age can be sluggish feeders, capable of taking only very small amounts at a feeding and using a lot of their energy to do so."

Doctor Pilron stopped to gauge how much Benjamin was absorbing, and then continued. "Put simply, *both* the fetus and the mother-to-be could die."

Benjamin held up his hand as though to stop Pilron, but the young doctor persisted, "We are looking at a very high risk of morbidity and mortality here and that is just to make it through the trauma of the birth process. My team and I have helped many women in similar situations and so we are a little more confident that we can save your wife but the baby is an entirely different matter and not just during the delivery. Even *if* we successfully deliver your baby it will face major obstacles to enjoying a full and healthy life. The relatively few prematurely delivered babies that survive childbirth have had to endure considerable health problems as they age. Almost certainly, some milestones in the first 2 years will be delayed. And even if it can make it to adulthood, there will be other medical hardships to face for the entire span of its life. Unfortunately, the odds are *not* with us."

"Stop it!" Benjamin demanded. "Enough," he yelled. "You are scaring the shit out of me. Can you not put forward *any* hope?"

"I am still sitting here, Monsieur Harper, am I not? As long as I and my associates are here, there *is* hope."

"Is there nothing positive to share with me other than *your presence here*?" Benjamin demanded.

"What I have just shared with you *is* my optimistic view." Dr. Pilron said.

"So what are we to do?

"Our challenge is to buy time. Every day spent in utero will make a big difference to this baby's ability to survive, every day it remains in your wife's womb will help. Yes, there are ways to delay the birth, but at some point – and I do not believe we have yet reached that point – it will be out of our control. When the baby is ready we will just have to respond as best we can." Almost as an afterthought, he added, "To make matters even worse, from what I can see, the people and equipment in this hospital will not increase our pool of options."

"So where should we go?" Benjamin pleaded, "Name it – anywhere in the world."

"Monsieur Harper, as bad as it is here, moving your wife at this time only reduces the slim chance we have for any level of success."

Benjamin put his hands up and said, "So you have bad news and worse news. What I need is *good news!*"

"No, Monsieur Harper, what you need is the truth."

Harper moved closer to the doctor and in a hoarse whisper said, "Let me be perfectly clear with you, dear doctor. I do not want there to be any misunderstandings, not now, not ever. I brought you here to save my wife *and* my baby's life. Ben Spock, whom I know and respect, says that you might be my best chance to do that. I will settle for nothing less. I don't care what else might be happening in your life at this moment and I certainly do not care what it costs. You have my full support as long as you fight for their lives as though your life depends upon it – because it does, and just in case you doubt that or do not already know who I am, I can assure you that I am a *very powerful man.*"

Pilron sat back, stared intently into this old man's face, and said, "Monsieur Harper, I came here, voluntarily, with possibly the best available team of medical professionals in existence today for the kind of medical need your wife faces. On any given day, I and every man and woman in this medical team deal with more high risk pregnancies, from fertilization to birth, than most of your American hospitals do, or, possibly even collectively, among all other hospitals in the world. That is an easy fact to check. Perhaps you should have checked it before you asked us to come."

He stood slowly, stared angrily down at Benjamin, and then leaned down with his face inches from Benjamin. "Monsieur Harper, I can leave or stay but whatever I do, will be *my* decision. Permit *me* to be perfectly clear with *you*, because I also do not want there to be any misunderstandings either, not now, not ever, I DO NOT DO THREATS VERY WELL!"

"Goddamn it, stop calling me Monsieur Harper."

"I am being respectful, sir. How would you prefer to be addressed?"

"Call me Benjamin."

"As you wish, *Benjamin*."

"All I want is the best for my wife," Benjamin said almost apologetically.

Doctor Pilron placed one hand on Benjamin's shoulder and began speaking in soft, measured tones, "I came here knowing full well how difficult this would be. I came anyway because Ben Spock, who is a hero of mine, asked me to come and told me that he believes that I can make a difference here. I will not leave until I have exhausted every possibility. But, I owe it to you and your wife to be honest, perhaps brutally honest. Modern medicine in this specialty is still developing.

"I am a man of means and influence Doctor..."

Doctor Pilron raised his hand to stop Benjamin in mid sentence. "Did Ben Spock not tell you anything about me?"

Benjamin looked confused, "I don't have to know anything besides your ability to save my wife and baby – past successes give me hope but they are no substitution for your ultimately being successful here and now – and once again I want you to know that the fee is meaningless to me, all I want is my wife and baby to live to tell the tale."

Pilron sat down again next to Harper. "A countryman of mine, Alexandre Lion, invented what he called an incubator system to care for premature infants. It is not really a new concept, there have been similar inventions over time, but this one seems to be better than earlier attempts. I cannot understand why hospitals have not yet fully embraced its use. It was presented in this country at the Trans-Mississippi Exposition in 1898 in Omaha, Nebraska. That was almost 40 years ago but as of this moment it is still considered experimental, unproven in a formal scientific way."

"I don't understand, what is an 'incubator'?"

"An incubator is like an artificial womb to assist premature babies – it can mean the difference between surviving and *not* surviving."

"And you think this machine can help my wife?"

"Not your wife, the help it gives is entirely for the new born baby. If your baby insists upon leaving the safety and nurturing surroundings of your wife's womb earlier than 37 weeks gestation, the Lion incubator may be just what we need to help what would be a dangerously premature baby to survive on the outside."

"How does it work? Benjamin asked.

"It works on the principle of ..."

"No" Benjamin interrupted, shaking his head from side to side; "I don't have to know how it works. Just tell me how we can get one here."

"The whole concept is still considered to be experimental. There aren't that many working units in the entire world. We have two such units in my hospital back home but they were specifically built to be operated on our electricity delivery system which is not at all like yours. Converting it to meet your system would just take too long and there is no guarantee that it could work effectively after the conversion. I will send out a series of telegrams to try to locate one. Negotiating the use of one could take weeks if not longer."

"Let me send out the telegrams," Benjamin broke in.

Pilron put his hand to his mouth to hide the amusement on his face, "Benjamin, I promise you that those few who must receive such a telegram will respond far quicker to one signed by me than one from an anonymous person – rich and powerful as you may be – from the very little town of Swan Lake, somewhere in Upper New York State of the still quite backwards and I would add, insensitive United States."

"Doctor Pilron," Benjamin shrugged and said, "Then just find us one and leave the rest to me."

Chapter 37
Sunday, September 13, 1936,
Swan Lake, New York 6:11 A.M.

Dr. Pilron alerted Benjamin that he located a Lion incubator which was currently in a teaching hospital in Seattle. "Unfortunately the hospital administrator refuses to make it available so I am still pushing all other possible leads."

Benjamin asked, "This machine in Seattle, will it meet your needs?"

"From what I was able to learn it has been in use on an experimental basis for several months and is performing well."

"How long will it take you and your staff to set it up once it is here?"

"It won't be here, Benjamin. I told you, they refused to release it. But I will continue—"

Benjamin broke in, "Dr. Pilron, I promise you, as God made little green apples, it *will* be here!"

Benjamin asked a series of follow up questions as to the exact location of the machine and who and what would be needed to properly crate the machine and send it on its way.

Dr. Pilron scratched his head as he watched the octogenarian push past the orderlies and their cart. "Sacré bleu," Pilron said to himself. "Save me from these self-possessed American barbarians. When will they learn that blank checks and brute force are not the answer to everything in life?"

*****

Tuesday, September 15, 1936,
Swan Lake, New York 2:27 A.M.

"Doctor Pilron, wake up." Nurse Siemon gently tapped his arm.

"What time is it? Ah, what *day* is it?" The sleep-deprived doctor slowly raised himself on his elbow and stared into the young woman's eyes.

"Doctor Pilron, it just arrived, the incubator from Seattle, it is here and the delivery men want to know where to set it up."

"The Seattle Incubator?" Pilron asked in amazement.

"Yes, yes, yes!" She said.

"Don't be ridiculous," he said, incredulously as he turned over to get back to sleep.

"It is here, Doctor. Come see for yourself."

*****

Later that morning Dr. Pilron was meeting with his team when he heard Benjamin in the outer corridor. He quickly rose and rushed into the corridor towards Benjamin. "How in God's name did you do it?"

Benjamin gave out a hearty laugh, "Let's make a little pact between us – just you and me. I promise not to doubt you anymore, and you will have to promise not to doubt me anymore. I told you I was a man of influence."

The two men hugged. "Now we have a chance?" Benjamin asked as tears began to run down his cheek.

"It is still an uphill struggle." The doctor said softly, "But at least *now* we have a fighting chance."

Chapter 38
Thursday, October 29, 1936,
Swan Lake, New York 1:14 A.M.

Benjamin was in his usual nighttime place, in the reclining rocker next to his wife's bed when he awoke to see a flurry of activity in the room.

The lights were on and Pilron was barking orders to his staff.

Rubbing his eyes Benjamin pulled Nurse Siemon aside. "What is happening?" He asked.

She gently eased him back into the recliner and said, "Monsieur Harper, for better or worse, the time has come. Your little baby is yearning to breathe free."

"What can I do to help?"

She smiled an all-knowing smile and suggested, "Perhaps a prayer for all of us, Monsieur Harper."

*****

Thursday, October 29, 1936,
Swan Lake, New York 5:17 A.M.

Pilron slowly walked towards Benjamin. When he was within inches of the old man he flashed a broad smile and reached out to shake Benjamin's hand.

"Just tell me how my wife and baby are." The old man pleaded.

"Your wife is a trouper, Benjamin. She is doing better than I could have hoped for."

"And the baby how is the baby?" Benjamin asked, haltingly.

"You have a little girl; every bit as much a fighter as her mother. It was touch and go. Not once but several times. However, as of this moment, both mother and child are doing okay."

"Just okay?" Benjamin whispered.

"Benjamin, Benjamin, Benjamin." The doctor teased, "Okay is already a blessing."

"When can I see them?" Benjamin asked.

"Wait a while. They have each been through hell and back. Allow them each to rest right now, perhaps in a few hours they will be ready for company."

Benjamin gave the drained doctor a bear hug. "I can never thank you enough."

"We are not yet out of the woods, Benjamin. Let's not provoke the fates by celebrating too quickly. Right now, I just want a large glass of wine and a soft bed, and maybe not in that order."

*****

Ellinor was able to go home just shy of three weeks later. Esther Miller Harper remained in the hospital for 97 days longer, as did Pilron and most of his team.

The day after the baby was safely reunited with her mother and the rest of the Harper family Benjamin handed the doctor a signed check. The amount was left blank.

Doctor Pilron looked at the check, smiled and handed the check back to Benjamin with a pat on the back. "My fee will require a series of checks like this one."

Benjamin offered the check back to the doctor and said, "I assure you, no matter what number you write on this check, it will clear any bank in the world."

The doctor thought for a moment and then said, "My fee, Benjamin, is your commitment to help bring this facility of yours into the modern times."

Before they returned to France the doctor and his executive team worked closely with the original hospital staff in an effort to improve the future quality of medical care for the community. Several established doctors from leading medical facilities in Boston, New York, and Chicago were hired and relocated to the small community, along with their families, all at Benjamin's expense. Modern equipment was ordered and installed, also at Benjamin's expense, and a fund was created to insure further improvements for many years to come.

Several weeks after he returned to France, Doctor Pilron received a hand written note from Benjamin along with the very same signed blank check that had been initially offered to him by Benjamin. The note said:

> *"I appreciate your willingness to leave without suitable payment – but you and your team worked hard and deserve to be properly compensated. Such payments are the very least to be expected and I always pay my debts.*
>
> *Please fill in any number you wish and cash the check. No matter what number or amount of zeroes after that number, I will never be able to fully repay you for the blessing you delivered."*

Less than a week later, Benjamin received the check, ripped in half along with a bottle of Champagne and a hand written note:

> *"It should please you to know that a number of the procedures my team developed in your hospital while caring for your lovely daughter will now help many others in the days and months*

to come. That is the best payment of all.

Consider your debt to be fully paid."

The note was signed, *'from one headstrong human being to another!'*

Gradually, very gradually, the baby grew. The proud new parents and Esther's 4 year old brother, Phineas, known to all as "P.H.", showered the new arrival with love and attention. Although P.H. had never been very close with his other siblings, he simply adored Esther.

Chapter 39
Saturday, October 1, 1949,
Swan Lake, New York

Raised as a Protestant, shortly before her 13th birthday, Esther announced that she wanted to convert to Judaism. Partly because her parents believed that it was just a passing fancy but mostly because it was what Esther wanted; she was promised the full support of her non denominational parents and atheist older brother, P.H.

They learned later that her interest in the new religion began when she met Norman Palp, a member of the Hasidic community in nearby Liberty, New York. They were initially brought together by a shared commitment to animal rights issues. Activism in this common cause led to a rich and mutually supportive friendship and finally turned to love.

*****

Three years later, 16 year old Esther and 17 year old Norman came to Benjamin announcing their desire to get married.

Benjamin, 96 years old at the time, and his 60 year old wife went to 19 year old P.H. and asked him to talk his baby sister out of it. "She'll listen to you," they begged. "Dearest Phineas, please, she is only 16."

"And you were only 13 when you married Dad," he reminded his mother. "And that marriage didn't go so bad did it?"

"She is so young, Phineas. Please, talk to her. Make the Jew go away. You could do it. At least make them agree for her to finish school first."

Before Phineas could bring it up with Esther, she reached out to him for his support in convincing their parents to allow her and Norman to marry. "They'll listen to you, P.H. Please help us. He is a good and caring man and I love him so much," Esther pleaded.

Unable to deny his baby sister any request, Phineas visited his parents later the same day. "She says she loves him," he told them. "How can we stand in their way?"

"She is only a child herself," his mother cried.

"And how will they support themselves?" His father asked.

"I'll make certain they never starve, Pop."

"And what if he treats her badly?"

Phineas put his arms gently around his father and whispered in his ear, "He'll *never* treat her badly, Pop. I guarantee that."

"How can you be so certain, my son?"

Phineas flashed a wide grin. "Pop, rest assured, he will *never* treat her badly. I'll bet his life on it."

*****

Phineas set the young couple up on a small farm in the Catskill Mountains. They raised chickens and a few cows and several small crops. They lived modestly, producing enough to feed themselves with a bit more left over to barter for what else they might need. There was also enough land to provide safe housing for lost and abused animals that were fortunate enough to cross paths with the caring couple.

Although Esther's health continued to be a concern, she and her husband thrived on the farm. From time to time, Phineas would visit, and with each visit he could see that their love for each other was real and without limits.

*****

Tuesday, May 24, 1960,
Catskill Mountains, Upstate New York

When his sister called to say that she and Norman were expecting a baby, Phineas was overjoyed. Soon, a healthy son was born to the happy couple. Richard Benjamin Palp named for Norman's uncle and Esther's father.

Esther and Norman wanted a large family but that was not to be. "After Richie was born, her doctor warned them that given her health situation, she might not survive another pregnancy.

"Well, she decided, if I can't make more babies of my own then we should help raise other people's babies."

Soon the local churches and human service agencies knew where to send habitual runaways and children considered 'unadoptable' because of age or physical or emotional problems. Each one was welcomed into the Palp home with unconditional love and understanding.

By the time Richie was 10, he had 14 *brothers* and *sisters* living on the small farm with him, his parents, and the many stray animals. Some of the children were older, some were younger; any problems in their past was theirs to keep to themselves or share as they chose; all that mattered was that while in *this* house, as part of *this* family, love would be given unconditionally; they would only have to account for what they did here and now.

Esther and Norman organized a Co-Op with 9 other neighboring farms. Every summer the farmers would combine many of their common duties so that each family could take a full week to travel or visit relatives while the rest of the Co-Op members filled in during their absence. The Palps had a huge motor home, courtesy of Phineas.

They usually spent their 'free week' camping in Upstate New York. On one such trip Norman suffered a massive heart attack while driving in a powerful rainstorm towards their campsite. Norman and Esther along with 4 of the children died instantly as a result of the crash; 2 other children died of their injuries over the next few days. Phineas found homes for the remaining children and arranged for Richie to come live with him. That was the beginning of a permanent bond between Richie and his Uncle Phineas.

At first Phineas shielded Richie from the family business. But in time, Richie was brought in and under his uncle's tutelage showed real talent for it.

Chapter 40
Thirty seven years later...
Wednesday, December 3, 1997,
Toms River, New Jersey – 11:52 P.M.

Several hours before he planned to slip out of the country to escape to Djibouti, Phineas met with Richie.

"We have to assume that those little shits somehow picked off all of the numbered accounts. It is too much of a risk to even try to get into any one of them now. They will be in the New Jersey house within hours – if they aren't already there. Fortunately, I kept several safe houses in and around Washington, D.C. and the small apartment in Martha's Vineyard. The ones in Washington may be compromised but I feel confident that Martha's Vineyard is still safe. I packed a *travel bag* which can keep me for a while."

"A travel bag?" Richie asked.

P.H. laughed, realizing that it might be his last laugh for who knows how long, he quickly added, "Yes, a travel bag; I emptied my safe in New Jersey of some precious metals – pure gold and silver coins, some cash, and a dozen or so video taped conversations which will make it harder for some really influential worms to pretend not to know me. These are likely to avoid the current witch hunt and they may be in a position to help us somewhere down the road."

P.H. gave Richie a hug then looked deeply into his eyes and said, "You haven't asked me about an exit plan for you, how come?"

"Frankly, I haven't given that much thought." Richie answered, innocently.

"Well, fortunately for you, I have." P.H. put his hands on

Richie's shoulders, "I set aside a few dozen - plus or minus - small bags of uncut diamonds – all clean and untraceable gems. You can find them inside the spare tire of the 1955 Chevy along with several hundred thousand dollars in U.S. currency. No one would ever look for any of that in a beat up old car. The car is garaged at the Mobil station we were using as a drop off place in Toms River. It has clean registration under the name Jeffrey Gendreau. In the glove compartment is a set of credentials, including a clean driver's license and passport, each in the Gendreau name with your picture. These credentials should pass the tightest scrutiny. The keys to the car and the Martha's Vineyard apartment are in a metal box under the rear passenger's side bumper. Drive it away tonight. I have also arranged for a set of your dental records and fingerprints to be stored in a Toms River police department employee file under the name Jeffrey Genreau. As long as you publicly distance yourself from me and all of this you will be safe."

"How will we keep in touch?" Richie asked.

"We won't. The less you know about where I am the safer it will be for you."

"Is there no one left to fight for you?" Richie asked.

"Too risky to count on anyone now", P.H. said, "not that I ever really trusted any of the others on our payroll - not the armed squad... not the legal eagles, definitely not the politicians or business big wigs – the *so called* partners - I never trusted anyone but you."

"So this is the end of the road?"

"Maybe for a while, but not forever; we'll be back, bigger and stronger." P.H. added.

"How can you be so certain?" Richie asked.

"If you know anything about human nature you know that everyone has a price. For some it is just a few bucks... or some favors... find the *price* and the rest is just a matter of negotiation." P.H. said. "We couldn't have lasted as long as we have if greed and weak leaders and a population of sheep did not exist. Oh, we will be back all right, just a matter of time. This is only a temporary glitch, Richie. Maybe we are down but we are far from out and when I return – and I will return - we will get even."

They hugged; tears streamed down Richie's cheeks. This was the very first time in his entire life that he would be on his own. The thought scared him.

*****

Richie Pulp ceased to exist as the shredded remnants of his old driver's license and various documents were sprinkled with gasoline and set afire. As the ashes were released into the Atlantic Ocean Jeffrey Genreau was born. He spent the rest of the day cleaning out his small furnished apartment of anything that might be incriminating. Other than some small mementoes – which easily fit into an average sized shoe box – there were only a few changes of clothing which he tossed into a Goodwill bin on his way out of town.

He had a taxi drop him off about a half a mile from the Chevy. After the taxi drove off he walked the ten blocks or so to the Mobil Station, and then began his drive to Martha's Vineyard, Massachusetts.

He slept in the car for a few days waiting to see if there would be any activity around the Martha's Vineyard apartment. Finally, convinced that he was reasonably safe, he went into the building and entered the apartment. He tossed his coat onto the couch and plopped into bed. He slept through the rest of the day and into the night.

At four in the morning he woke up in a deep sweat. Reality was setting in and he was suddenly famished. He went into the kitchen and found a can of Campbell's Chicken Noodle Soup and a can opener. He poured the contents of the can, plus a can of water, into a small saucepan, heated it up and hungrily consumed every bit. Still hungry, he opened a can of tuna fish and a large can of Libby's Fruit Salad and ate impatiently out of the open cans.

He stepped outside onto the screened patio and stared out into the darkness. *It is all over* – he thought to himself, *it lasted for more than two hundred years, through numerous wars and depressions, good times and bad times. Unfortunately it didn't make it past our watch... the shame of it all.*

*****

Jeffrey locked himself in the apartment for the better part of the next six years. He only left the apartment for food and an occasional walk along the water's edge; most of the time he sat in front of a blazing fireplace and watched television.

By fall of the sixth year P.H. sent him a secret message directing him to work his way into the book store so that he can be positioned for whatever they may come up with.

By Christmas, 2003, Jeffrey packed up and left the solitude of the apartment for the *war zone*. He began the long drive to Washington, D.C.

Chapter 41
Four years later...
Sunday, January 7, 2007,
Washington, D.C., 2:15 P.M.

Jeffrey and P.H. were having a late lunch in the Happy Harvest Café, their usual Sunday morning haunt. Each seemed absorbed in a different section of the New York Times when P.H. gently folded his section of the paper and broke the silence.

"I have been thinking about how best to proceed and I have the beginnings of a plan."

Jeffrey looked up at his uncle; he slowly removed his reading glasses and tucked them into his pocket as he said, "Ready to share with the rest of the class?"

"Yes," P.H. said as he stood and placed two twenty dollar bills on the table. "Let's get some fresh air."

They crossed the busy street and entered a small park, soon surrounded by a thick wall of tall trees. "You've been there long enough to earn their trust. You have also had a chance to get to know them, really know them. What would you say was most important to the ringleader?" That was how P.H. referred to Max Barnes. He had a pet name for each of the members of the group that collectively ended his life of power – or the 'treacherously disloyal rats' – his other name for those who brought his organization to a screeching halt and forced him into early retirement – of sorts.

Jeffrey thought for a while and then said, "His squeaky clean reputation, his belief that he is on the right side of the argument – every damn time. He sees himself as the one who could have really gotten rich if he brought down Thomas Jefferson but chose instead to disassociate himself from any possible personal gain or fame."

"Exactly!" P.H. said quickly. "His holier than thou maybe even saintly and squeaky clean moral reputation. We need to drag him through the grime and the mud just like he and his group of rats did to me and our family's life work."

They continued walking for some time before Jeffrey asked, "How do you plan to do this, Uncle Phineas?"

"I fully intend to do it with much pleasure, Jeffrey, with very, very much pleasure."

Chapter 42
Monday, January 8, 2007,
Washington, D.C., 3:18 A.M.

Jeffrey tossed and turned most of the night. He kept waking up; deeply disturbed, agitated, going from chills to heavy sweating and then back again to chills. This was not like him, not like him at all. He knew that the day would come for payback. It was only a matter of time. "Revenge is essential," he could still hear Phineas raging on and on. "It is our right, no, make that our responsibility, to get back at this group of treasonous rats. And when we are done with them they must be made to howl in pain like the wretched beasts they are."

Jeffrey got out of bed and began pacing. It is only right for us to get our pound of flesh, he thought. "P.H. was made to give up so much; would have been forced to give up even more; might even have been thrown into jail; for what, for caring so much about his country?" He was talking out loud now. He went into the kitchen and filled a large glass with cold water. As he began lifting the glass it slipped out of his hands and fell to the ground; surrounded now by broken glass and a small pool of water he put his hands to his face and began to sob. "Get a hold of yourself," he heard himself saying. "This is the right thing to do. I must maintain the honor of the family and take vengeance for all of the evil that was done to us."

Usually he enjoyed plotting with his uncle, the more ghastly the details the better. After all that had been plotted against Phineas it was only right for them to want to get back at the disgusting group of rats. He went back to bed and tried to sleep but each time the only image he could see as he closed his eyes was his mother's face. "She wouldn't have been pleased," he thought. She never knew everything her family did but knew enough to consider it to be wrong, terribly wrong. No, she wouldn't have been one bit pleased.

Jeffrey finally fell asleep just minutes before his alarm went off. When it went off he grabbed the small windup clock and threw it against the wall, then pulled the covers over his face and went back to sleep.

He woke again at about 11:30 and slowly got out of bed. He paced for a bit then called in sick and returned to bed. He stayed in bed most of the day. "What am I going to do?" he kept asking himself. "What am I going to do?"

Chapter 43
Wednesday, January 24, 2007,
Ashland, Virginia, 7:30 A.M.

The morning news/traffic/talk shows all opened that day with the same lead. "Regina Blankly, 27 year old night admitting clerk at Greater Laurel Beltsville Hospital, 5 feet 7 ½ inches tall, about 120 pounds, shoulder length blond hair, green eyes; last seen a week ago leaving her apartment on 8th Street in Laurel, Maryland. She has 'Type 1' diabetes and may or may not have her medicine with her. She was last seen wearing white pants, a light green raincoat and green canvas shoes. Police have no reason at this time to suspect foul play but at her family's request have set up a special hot line for any information about her whereabouts."

*****

Her 6-year-old bronze Chevy was found three days later near the Laurel Centre Mall saturated with blood.

Her head was found in the woods at the end of Larchdale Road by a jogger almost a month later. Positive identification was made with the help of dental records.

*****

Friday, March 9, 2007,
Washington, D.C., 11:10 A.M.

Phillip Dorn, a Prince George's County Homicide investigator accompanied Sgt. William Trall and Det. Steve Mordinelli, both from D.C. Homicide, into the busy bookstore. Quickly flashing his badge, Trall asked to see Max Barnes.

A few minutes later Max came to the front of the store and introduced himself.

"Hi, I'm Max, how can I help you?" he asked.

"We are here as part of an investigation of the Regina Blankly murder."

"I have been reading about it, such a horrible, horrible story."

"Yes," Detective Mordinelli said dryly, "a horrible story." He turned to his fellow detectives and rolled his eyes. "We have some questions for you. Would you mind coming to the station with us?"

"Can't we speak here? I don't know how I can be helpful."

"When was the last time you saw Ms Blankly?" Mordinelli asked.

Seeming to be surprised by the question Max said, "I don't think I ever saw her."

"You don't think you ever saw her? Don't you know if you ever saw her?"

"I guess she could have come here to shop or browse but to my knowledge we never met."

"That seems strange, Mr. Barnes."

"Strange or not, it is the truth."

"Mr. Barnes, there were three framed photographs of you in her apartment." Pointing to the monogram on his sleeve, "There were two dress shirts hanging in her closet with the same monogram as the one you are wearing to-day. Are you saying that you did not have a relationship with Ms Blankly?"

Max held on to the counter to steady himself. "Yes, that is exactly what I am saying. How can anything of mine be in her apartment?"

"That is what we would like to know."

People were beginning to stare.

"We also found an American Express charge receipt from the day before she was declared missing. Seems she purchased three books and a CD from this very store," Mordinelli said.

"So she shopped here, a lot of people shop here. I don't necessarily know each of those who do," Max said defensively.

Trall smiled, "Do they all use *your* American Express card to pay for their purchases, Mr. Barnes, because, in this instance, Ms Blankly paid for her purchase with *your* American Express card."

Phillip Dorn spoke for the first time, "It might be best to take this conversation to a more private location. Let's just go to the station house. I am sure you will be able to clear this entire situation up rather quickly and then you can return to your store."

Jeffrey was watching from the other side of the store. He glanced over to his uncle who looked like he was just browsing along the wall of books with little or no interest in the drama taking place in the front of the store.

Max, visibly shaken, finally nodded his head and said, "Just let me get my coat."

*****

Matters quickly went from bad to worse. With a warrant in hand the D.C. police searched Max's apartment; they found a toothbrush with the dead woman's DNA along with articles of her clothing in his room and various other articles with her fingerprints throughout the apartment.

One last piece of evidence seemed to seal his fate. It was a handwritten note found in one of the books by his bed, threatening to leave him if he didn't stop dealing drugs to children, signed, *'With a love that wants so deeply to forgive, if not forget. Love, Regina'*.

Chapter 44
Monday, April 14, 2008,
District Court of Maryland,
Greenbelt, MD, 1:18 P.M.

With Max insisting that he did not know Regina Blankly and, as the District Attorney phrased it, "a mountain of physical evidence showing that he knew her quite well indeed," the trial moved along quickly.

"A woman was *decapitated*—in a peaceful, middle-class Washington, D.C./Baltimore suburb," he reminded the jury during his plea that moved back and forth between heated and emotional to passionate and touching. "Regina Blankly could have been your daughter," he said pointing to one juror; "or yours," pointing to another. "She was more than just a face on a missing person's flyer, she was someone's sister, friend, neighbor, and coworker, and by all accounts, she was a kind and gentle young woman who will surely be missed. You heard one coworker remember her as being caring and considerate as well as funny and good natured."

The D.A. told his wife that morning, "Today's closing statement is my ticket to the governor's mansion." He looked around the court, put his notes in his breast pocket and in a slightly trembling voice said, "Regina Blankly held a number of jobs, working as a clerical typist in a dentist office prior to becoming a night admitting clerk in the busy emergency room at Greater Laurel Beltsville Hospital—a job that she rightly considered much more than simply filling out insurance forms. Colleagues recalled that she never failed to console families of the sick and injured, bringing them coffee and allowing them the chance to talk about their anxiety and grief. You heard the testimony from a staff doctor who noted the countless cases of gratuitous and senseless violence that the emergency room saw on any given night shift; and that Regina Blankly was always caring and concerned for all the people she met... never cynical, even when patients or their families seemed undeserving of her patience and thoughtfulness. The people of Maryland can accept nothing less than the death penalty for the wild animal responsible for this evil and fiendish crime."

He started to walk towards his seat, paused, and then walked back to face the jury. "Regina Blankly is no longer able to speak for herself. That ability was taken from her. It is now your chance to speak for her. Tell that evil man," he said in a low, trembling voice, pointing towards Max, "tell that evil man, that what he did was wrong and that he must be kept from civilized people so that he can never commit such a dastardly crime again; never, never, never again."

The DA demanded and Max's jury of his peers agreed, Max Barnes must die as soon and agonizingly as the law permits.

*****

Max was ultimately sent to death row at the North Branch Correctional Institution, Cumberland, Maryland. Built and opened in 2003 as one of the most technologically advanced maximum security prisons in the world, it housed the most serious offenders within the State of Maryland.

His cell was slightly larger than 60 square feet, constructed of cast concrete so that there were no seams in which to hide contraband. The cell doors were made of ballistic-resistant glass to allow easy observation and boost officer safety.

Life in prison was especially hard for Max. Although most of the prison population claimed innocence, he knew he was innocent.

Shortly after being brought to prison he was transferred to death row.

*****

**Wednesday, March 18, 2009,
North Branch Correctional Institution,
Cumberland, Maryland, 11:10 A.M.**

Will and Mark James followed the case but neither of them came to Max's defense. The combination of Max's denials against the overwhelming evidence presented by the State's attorneys and the gruesome nature of the crime itself made it impossible for them or anyone else to come to any other conclusion except that their former friend was guilty as charged.

It was the persistence of Gloria Salizar, now Gloria Steadman, who pushed Will and Mark James to "at least consider" that in all of the interactions they had with Max, at times during the most difficult of circumstances, he never, even for a split second, demonstrated a level of evil that would have been essential for committing such a crime.

"This just isn't Max," she kept insisting. "And you, of all people, who knew him decades before I ever met him, should know that he could never have done such a thing."

"Look," Will said, "any of us is capable of doing terrible things, given the right circumstances. Hey, her toothbrush was in his apartment. How in God's name can he claim he never met her?"

Finally, reluctantly, they agreed to go with her to the prison and speak to Max.

Their first site of the prison was while driving along Route 220. Mark broke the uncomfortable silence that had existed for most of the ride from D.C., "This looks like Alcatraz on steroids."

*****

They were led into a small area with a thick glass partition separating them from the prisoner. Max was already seated on the other side of the glass. They could see heavy chains linking his hands to his sides. It had been some time since they had seen him and both men were surprised by how old and dazed he appeared to be.

The guard reminded them that their conversation would not be confidential. There would be two guards on his side of the glass and one guard on the visitor's side of the glass; both sides of the conversation would be recorded and could be used by the state in any future appeals actions. Each was asked to sign a document acknowledging what they had just been told.

Finally, they faced Max. "How are you holding up?" Gloria asked haltingly.

"I'm getting through it the best I can," Max quickly responded.

Will moved closer to the thick glass between them and Max. He was clearly moved by the current sight of this once vibrant young man. What sat before them now was a frail man with a slight tick in his right eye. Max's hair was cut short allowing them to see a deep scar running along the right side of his scalp.

"I don't want to beat around the bush, Max," Will said. "I have known you since you and Mark were in grade school. I don't want to believe that you did this thing, but Jesus Christ, they seem to have you dead to rights."

Max smiled and responded almost mockingly, "Of all

people, I thought you would be the first to recognize that things aren't always as they seem."

"So fill in the gaps for me - for us. We are here because Gloria shamed us into it but of course we want to help if we can. Gloria has never believed that you did this thing, never, not for a moment. Neither Mark nor I *want* to believe otherwise, but it does look cut and dry."

Max started to raise his hand then quickly turned to one of the guards on his side of the glass and asked for permission. Both guards nodded their approval. Max slowly raised his hand, "I swear to you on everything I hold dear, I never met that woman; I did not kill that woman; she was *never* in my home or my life. I cannot explain how her things got into my apartment or my things got into hers. That is the truth and I will take that truth with me to my grave. I cannot explain any of this. And, yes, if I were you I probably would also doubt my story. BUT - I - DID - NOT - KNOW – HER! AND THAT IS THE TRUTH, I SWEAR TO YOU."

Will took a deep breath. "We are only permitted 15 minutes and then they will be chasing us out. But Gloria has gotten herself assigned by the court as an aid to your new appeals lawyer and so she will be able to return as often and for as long as you both would like."

Max began to cry, "Thank you for believing in me Gloria, thank you, thank you, thank you."

"Hey, don't go all soft on me. The last thing you need now is false hope. I can't promise anything but a flood of legal filings. I am here with the 'deadly duo'," she said glaring at the two men by her side, "because I am hoping they will be able to shed new light on some of this. There must be something here that I keep missing. If anyone can jiggle the puzzle pieces to make more sense out of them you know that these guys can. I will do whatever I can, let's just hope it is enough."

"Or in time," Max interrupted.

"Oh, don't worry about the time," Gloria shouted. "These appeals can take decades. We have plenty of time and I don't plan to waste a minute of it."

They said their goodbyes and watched while Max was led out of sight. Finally, they were instructed to stand and walk out, in a single line.

Nothing was said until they were back in the car and Gloria asked, "What do you think?"

Mark answered first. "He looks thirty years older. Everyone knows that he could have avoided the death penalty if he had just accepted responsibility and apologized in open court. They never put him at the scene of the murder or offered witnesses that ever saw them together. They never even found the rest of the victim's body. He sealed his fate by sticking to his claim that he never knew her."

"So, doesn't that tell you something?" Gloria asked.

"All it says is that he missed a chance to avoid all of this," Will broke in.

"Please," Gloria yelled, "would *you* have taken responsibility for something you did not do? I think he stuck to his story because it was the truth and the truth was all he had."

"Maybe so, maybe so, Will said.

*****

They had agreed to stay overnight in the area and checked into the Holiday Inn on George Street in Downtown Cumberland, about a ten minute drive from the prison. The check in clerk gave each of them a sign in card and said, "We don't get many tourists, are you visiting someone at the prison?"

"What do we look like?" Gloria responded.

"To be honest, you each look like you could use a good hug and a hot meal," the clerk, a middle aged woman with a thick Russian accent, said.

"Is the hotel restaurant the place for either or both?" Gloria asked.

"It's a nice place to eat but I think you would do better right now if you went to the Queen City Creamery. It is family owned and run and has been for many years... in addition, they make the best ice cream in Cumberland."

"How far away is it? We've been on the road much of the day and a long drive is not what any of us really want right now," Will broke in.

"You can leave your car right where it is then," the clerk said, laughing, "Lean in that direction. It's right across the parking lot – just a few yards from the hotels side entrance."

Mark and Will shared one room and Gloria rented a connecting room. They were all tired and hungry and agreed to quickly drop their bags off into their respective rooms, freshen up a bit, which for Gloria meant calling home, and then they agreed to head out to get something to eat.

While they were waiting in the lobby for Gloria, Mark turned to his father. "I have been wondering," he said, "that the entire case against Max is just too clean."

"What do you mean, *too clean*?" Will responded.

"There are no questionable or fuzzy edges." The so-called

facts all seem to be cleanly cut and perfectly placed. I just don't think that life is ever that neat."

Will thought about what his son was saying. "Be more specific."

"It would be a no brainer *if there was* a relationship, for Max to just acknowledge that he knew her; that alone would not necessarily label him as her killer, a good suspect sure, but not automatically her killer. So his stuff winds up in her place so that he can be found and charged; her stuff is strategically found in his place so that a relationship can be confirmed. It's just too clean."

"I guess I have been thinking along the same lines," Will replied. "Max's insistence that he did not know her is probably the weakest position he could have taken. That is of course unless it is true. Max really never talked about her to you?" Will asked.

Mark thought for a while then said, "Never, I certainly would have remembered. I think I know everyone Max knows but the first time I heard her name was during the lead up to his trial. Of course it is possible that Max knew someone that I did not know; we do live separate lives but I keep coming back to questioning why he would keep her a secret."

He paused for a moment then continued, "She would have wanted to talk about it to her friends or co-workers or family members. That would be more likely than keeping it a secret relationship. They were each single adults, gainfully employed, active, why keep their relationship a big dark secret? The D.A. must have looked for people to confirm their connection. Given Max's insistence that he never knew her, all they had to do was put one or two friends or co-workers on the stand that said she had spoken of her new boyfriend, Max; or she was going to some event with her new boyfriend, Max; or she was having a *problem* with her new boyfriend, Max."

Will broke in, "O.K., so let's play with that for a while; let's assume that he never knew her and she never knew him. Then we would have to conclude that her things were *placed* in his apartment by someone or some ones unknown and his things were *placed* in her apartment by the very same person or persons. But if this is what happened then that someone unknown would have had to have free access to both apartments?"

"Since the District Attorney did not show that they had any common connections," Will answered, "It would have had to be a stranger to one or the other."

"So we should be looking for a stranger to one of them who was close to the other or a stranger to both him *and* her." Mark said.

Will smiled and punched Mark's arm, "Good, very good, and not only would it have had to be someone with the ability to access both apartments but also someone who was willing and able to decapitaste this woman in order to put Max on death row."

Just then Gloria walked into the lobby. "First we eat, and then we talk," she yelled.

Both men laughed.

Chapter 45
Wednesday, March 18, 2009,
Queen City Creamery,
Cumberland, Maryland, 4:22 P.M.

The Queen City Creamery was in a red brick building at the other end of the parking lot from the hotel. Walking into the building was like stepping back in time into a 1940's era soda fountain with its oak flooring, turn of the century style light globes, a soda bar and what looked like really comfortable booths. A woman with a wide grin was by the register. "Welcome home... hey, like I said to my first husband's horse, why the long face?"

"We're really not looking for a comedy club..." Will said.

"Okay, then", she quickly added, then just 'welcome home', is that acceptable?"

Will looked around and said, "We're really not looking for an amusement park, either."

Gloria broke in, "I'm sorry for old sour puss, but the truth is that we have had a very tough day, we're tired and hungry and not in very good moods."

"Sounds like my first husband," she grunted.

"How many husbands have you had?" Gloria asked.

The woman made a point of looking at her watch, "Just one, although the day is still young."

She pointed towards a back booth. "Sit there, the food is all freshly made; the desserts are like you wish your mother made." She handed them each a menu and with a warm smile added, "I'll make sure that the roller coaster does not run anywhere near your table."

*****

Will and Mark ordered soup and a sandwich and Gloria had a salad. After they finished their meals the waitress offered them each a mini-cone of custard, "It comes with your meal and it's really good."

"Thank you," Will said. "Maybe later, O.K.?"

"Of course," she said as she cleared the table.

Mark told Gloria what he and Will had talked about while they were waiting for her in the hotel lobby. "It would have had to be someone who could also access his American Express card. Remember the receipt they showed in court?" she asked.

"Who do you think could have dreamed up such a plot – much less pull it off so successfully without any of it sticking to him or her?" Gloria asked.

"The billion dollar question!" Mark said.

Will thought for a moment, then said, "Maybe not one billion – maybe 112 point 7 billion."

Gloria and Mark stared at Will, "You don't think the O.O.T.A.P. monsters are up and around again, do you?" Gloria asked.

"I wouldn't put it past them," Will said. "They have the motive; would have no problem committing another crime, even murder; and probably still have the means to pull it off."

"Oh my God!" Gloria said, slamming her hands down on to

the table. "What did we start?"

"We didn't start anything," Will corrected. "They started it all, remember?"

"We beat them once; think we can do it again?" She asked.

"Wait a minute," Will cautioned, "Thinking that they are the ones who did this and proving it are miles apart. We might have been able to get the better of them before because we caught them off guard. If they did this, and it is a major *if*, they have had a lot of time to plan and execute this plot and a lot of time to get away. So far it looks like whoever did this have been very smart and incredibly careful. It could have helped if we came to this explanation *before* Max was convicted but it is very different now. Especially since the man who actually put him on death row is now the governor of the State. He is the one who would have to agree to a stay of execution and I shouldn't have to remind you that he has a lot to lose if this thing is reversed."

"So Max is going to die because you waited too long to get involved?" She asked.

Will put his hand on her arm, "One step at a time; first let's see if there is any way to prove this theory of ours. We also would have to identify the key players. Then, and only then, can we hope to see what if anything we can do."

Chapter 46
Friday, March 20, 2009,
Washington, D.C., 2:13 P.M.

During the investigation and trial, and up until several weeks before the actual verdict and Max's conviction, Jeffrey was left in charge of the day-to-day operations of the store. With his uncle's help, the assets were channeled away from the business and finally the store was closed for good. A mysterious fire broke out the evening before a scheduled bankruptcy auction of the inventory and store furnishings.

*****

Neither Will nor Mark spoke very much during the long drive back to Washington. Although Max Barnes was in each of the men's thoughts, Mark was thinking about the early years of their friendship, consciously avoiding Max's current situation while Will was only thinking about Max's present state of affairs in an effort to think through what, if anything, he could do to make the best possible use of the remaining time before Max's almost unavoidable execution.

*****

Tuesday, March 31, 2009,
Washington, D.C., 7:13 A.M.

Will acquired a gavel to gavel transcript of the trial and asked a lawyer friend of his to go through each page to see if there was anything that might be used to justify a new hearing.

"It looks clean to me," his friend reported back. "He wasn't railroaded by the prosecutor nor poorly served by his legal team. If anything, his lawyer's seemed to be working feverishly in his defense and the prosecution appears to have gone out of their way to be fair but as long as Max held to his claim that he never met the victim; didn't know her; never even spoke to her in passing – that he could remember, his fate was sealed. They only had circumstantial evidence but it was evidence that pointed to the complete opposite of Max' story. In my opinion, I don't think that this or any other jury could have come to any other conclusion."

Meanwhile, Will accessed the case files in both Washington, D.C. and Prince George's county by hacking into their solved case records. He couldn't find a single incident that would point towards bad or lazy police work. The investigation was by the book, as best he could see. The investigators followed the clues and with each passing day it became clearer that Max was their guy.

Finally, having exhausted the obvious, he asked a forensic financial auditor he knew to go through the book store's bankruptcy filings. His friend first reported back that it seemed like the business just fell apart without Max. "Not all that unusual when a strong manager takes his or her eye off of the day to day operations and leaves it to a less experienced person for an extended period of time."

Two days later he called Will back. "I went through the financials again because the more I thought about it; the more it seemed to me that the collapse of the business looked too controlled to be natural."

"Hey," Will responded. "Can you restate that for me in a language I can understand?"

"There is a 'tempo' to a healthy business," his friend began, "It is not unusual for that tempo to change – sometimes for the better, sometimes for the worse – when a manager is replaced. Sales trends change as the new guy shifts the pieces, towards his or her specialty or comfort area."

Again, Will broke in, "You're not making it any clearer. Can't you dumb your message down a bit more so that I can understand what the hell you are talking about?"

"Okay, let me start again. This was a very successful book store with a quickly growing second tier of sales coming from the introduction of music and café departments when your friend was taken out of the picture. He was replaced by the person who actually built the music and café departments. You would have expected music and café to prosper the most from this particular management change. It would have been natural for the book sales to soften while the music and café sales grew, that was not the comfort zone of the new leader. BUT... THAT... DID... NOT... HAPPEN." He emphasized each word.

"Sales within the two departments didn't drop – but net revenue and particularly profits did drop. Gross margins for the music and café departments fell sharply. I kept asking myself how and why that would have happened. So I revisited the paperwork you got from their CPA, especially the weekly balance sheets. It turned out that the reason margins slipped was because all of a sudden markdowns in these two departments alone began to tank after your friend left the business. Digging a bit more I learned that *all* of the markdown monies were being given to a new customer they attracted after Max was removed from day to day operations. Digging even further, I learned that the new customer NEVER ACTUALLY PURCHASED A THING. There were no purchases to support the refunds."

"So margin dollars were being siphoned off; profits were being skimmed off of the top!" Will screamed into the phone.

"Exactly!" his friend responded. "Collapse of the business was inevitable; it was only a matter of time. And it looks like the shutdown was being timed to happen *before* your friend's trial concluded so that his almost certain conviction would cover up the failure of the business."

"After he was convicted of murder the last thing on his mind would have been to ask what happened to his business," Will said.

"Once again, EXACTLY CORRECT!"

Chapter 47
Thursday, April 2, 2009,
Queen City Creamery,
Cumberland, Maryland, 10:00 A.M.

Will was finishing his third cup of coffee when Gloria walked in. She walked quickly towards his table and gave him a big hug.

"No hello, no 'gee, you look great', no small talk," she pleaded. "Just tell me what you learned."

"Not yet," he responded, "first tell me what Max had to say about this Jeffrey guy."

"You're killing me," she yelled.

Jonathan put his finger to his lips, "Shhhhhhhhhh. We are not alone. Now, tell me what Max said about Jeffrey."

"O.K. seems Jeffrey had been a long distance fan of the store. He claimed that he always shopped there when he was in the area. Well some years back, Max got a bound business plan proposal from Jeffrey. He claimed to have just been discharged from the Army..."

"Jeffrey was never in the army, or the navy or the marines or any other branch of the United States Armed Forces. He interrupted.

"Well he certainly gave Max the impression that he was," Gloria began. "Anyway, each time he visited the store he complained that there wasn't anything but books available for sale. He said that it was time the store dragged itself into the new century and stocked some of the newer music, maybe even sold light snacks and drinks. So one day Max pulled him aside and challenged him to come up with a realistic plan to blend music and snacks into the existing footprint of the store. Within days, Jeffrey returned with drawings and even a financial breakdown of what it would cost to do and how quickly they could expect to see a return on their investment, this so impressed Max that he got a small bank loan and told Jeffrey to bring the plan to life and he would be allowed to actually run the new departments at a fixed salary plus percentage of the new revenue.

"The new departments did bring in new sales," Gloria continued, "and may even have helped build the overall store's profitability. When the shoe repair store next door closed down Max negotiated for the space and expanded his store into the newly emptied space, enlarging the music concept into a full department for Jeffrey to manage. A year or so later, Max bought out the rest of the lease from the deli next door, on the other side of his store. He threw down the connecting wall and turned it into a café, for Jeffrey to manage. With each move, the overall business grew. Jeffrey became a key player and when Max became a suspect in the murder it was only natural to turn to Jeffrey to take over the store until Max could return. Of course, Max never did return and the business died. Now, tell me what you found, pleeeeeese."

"I had a forensic accountant comb through the books of the business; seems that the *growth* of Jeffrey's two departments came from chunks of so-called sales through a string of untraceable cash transactions."

"What's the difference how sales are paid for, as long as they are paid for?" She asked.

"It only matters if the new sales aren't really sales at all but carefully orchestrated shams in order to make it look like the base was growing. Also, the store was built on giving credit to the students – it was Sam's way of doing business and Max just took the policy to its next logical stage by accepting credit cards. This influx of cash sales must have set off a red flag for Max. There were notations on the weekly balance sheets asking his accountant to look into it. However, when they opened the café shortly after introducing music to the product mix, and the café sales really did lend itself more to cash than credit, what initially raised questions just faded into a sea of improved bottom line results. 'If it ain't broke why fix it?' But according to my accountant friend, it really was 'broke'. Someone was juggling the numbers by adding monies to the till to make it look like the department was a huge success. When Max was taken to jail, the process was simply reversed and someone or some ones began skimming monies out of the business until it collapsed."

"So Jeffrey pushed it into bankruptcy?" She asked.

"He certainly helped it along that path," Will said.

Haltingly, she asked, "And Jeffrey is also responsible for the frame up."

"Not yet clear," Will answered. "That is a possibility but I cannot say for certain; at least not yet."

"So it has nothing to do with O.O.T.A.P. after all?"

"I don't know that, either. It would have taken a lot of money and someone a lot more financially savvy than Jeffrey seems to be to think this all up and drive it home. O.O.T.A.P. or no O.O.T.A.P., someone put a lot of thought and assets into these maneuvers."

"So," she asked, "what do we do now?"

"We dig into Jeffrey's past and see what comes up. I was hoping that Max had more about this guy than he has shared."

"Do you want me to go back and try again?"

"Yes, but make certain you don't give him false hope. After all, it is possible that this embezzlement plan that we have uncovered has nothing to do with the murder."

She thought for a while then said, "Some hope is better than no hope. Don't you agree?"

"Maybe so, maybe so."

Chapter 48
Saturday, April 4, 2009,
Washington, D.C., 4:10 P.M.

Will's effort to get more information on Jeffrey seemed to hit a wall at every turn. His first sweep unearthed absolutely nothing for the period before Jeffrey began working for Max and the trail stopped when the store and its inventory mysteriously burned down. Very curious, he thought.

Most of the store's personnel records were lost in the fire but Will was able to access an old personnel roster with social security numbers and emergency contact information for all staff members at the time. The social security number shown for Jeffrey turned out to be a bogus number. A little daylight shined through with the emergency information listed alongside Jeffrey's name, his uncle, Phillip Haskins was shown as the person to contact in an emergency. There was contact information that matched phone company records for an upscale townhouse in a northern suburb of D.C.

"No record of a driver's license or tax filings either before or after his time at the store. No credit card accounts - that I can find - and believe me, I looked," he told Mark and Gloria during a three way phone call later in the day.

"A real mystery man," Gloria said.

Mark broke in, "Do you have any photos of Jeffrey that we could use to look for him in or near the uncle's address?"

"Nope."

"There must be some way to pull him back from obscurity," Gloria said,

"Someone thoroughly scrubbed Jeffrey out of existence. If they missed a beat, I haven't found it. At least not yet," Will said.

Gloria agreed to go back to Max to ask if he could think of anything. Perhaps some comment Jeffrey might have made when they worked together; an interest in a hobby or event; something, anything that can lead them out of the blind ally in which they were currently stuck.

They agreed to talk again later that evening.

*****

Will drove to the address he had for the uncle. He circled the block and then parked a few streets away. He walked back to the address. It was a three story building with a door man. He glanced into the doorway as he passed by but did not stop. He continued down the street and walked into a small neighborhood bar on the corner.

He sat down on a stool towards the end of the bar. A stout man, about 50, walked over and placed a paper napkin in front of him. "What will it be?"

"What beer do you recommend?" Will asked.

"How about a nice micro brew with a bite to it, been selling a lot of it lately?

"Sure."

The bartender brought a tall glass of a dark brew and placed it on a coaster. He took a dish of nuts from behind the bar, placed it next to the glass and smiled. "You're new around here."

"Yes I am. I have been looking for an apartment. Know of anything on the market?"

The bartender laughed. "For someone to move into this area, someone else has to either die or lose an election."

"A lot of politicians live around here?"

"In this neighborhood you are either a politician or a lobbyist – which means you are a former politician or a lawyer – or a *wanna be* politician or a reporter," the bartender teased. "Which are you?"

"A reporter, of sorts."

"What is a reporter of sorts?"

Moving closer to the bartender, Will looked from side to side then said, "I do freelance work for a couple of the supermarket tabloids."

"We all do freelance work for supermarket tabloids," the bartender said. "That's how the doormen and delivery boys around here can afford to be doormen and delivery boys." They both laughed.

"What brings you here today?"

"Just checking out a possible lead."

"I thought I knew all the players in your field."

"I'm just in from L.A."

"Really", the bartender said.

"Really", Will said.

"Well, good luck." The bartender walked to the other end of the bar to greet a customer who just walked in.

Will put the glass to his lips and took a long swallow. He nursed the rest of the beer for the better part of an hour while watching the few customers through the huge wall mirror behind the bar. Finally, he got up, left a ten dollar bill on the counter and as he walked towards the door, said goodbye to the bartender.

"See ya in the funny papers." The bartender yelled after him.

So much for nothing, Will thought to himself.

The bartender watched Will walk across the street and thought he saw him slow down and stare into the three story building halfway up the block. He picked up a cell phone from under the bar and quickly dialed a number, pressed the phone to his ear and waited. He turned to face the back of the bar as he spoke softly into the phone. A few minutes later he closed the phone, put it back under the counter then took another look through the window towards the three story building. A few minutes later he returned to his customers.

Chapter 49
Saturday, April 4, 2009,
Washington, D.C., 11:25 P.M.

Gloria was the first to speak that evening during the phone conversation with Will and Mark.

"Max told me about an incident that happened when Jeffrey first started working at the store. Seems a policeman was harassing a homeless man in front of the store and Jeffrey went out to help the guy. Finally, Max went out to see what was going on and Jeffrey told him that he inherited his mother's soft spot for lost and forgotten souls, such as this homeless man. Max thought that was really nice and told him so. 'It has nothing to do with nice,' Max remembered Jeffrey overreacting to his innocent comment, 'but for the grace of God, that could have been me.' According to Max, Jeffrey pulled out his wallet, grabbed all of the bills inside and handed it to the homeless guy; really made an impression on Max."

"So we have a good hearted embezzler on our hands," Mark chimed in.

"Yea," Will said, "a kind of Robin Hood... gave what he stole from Max to the lost and forgotten souls. A bit of a mixed message, wouldn't you say?"

"It's all we have right now," Gloria said. "Can we use it to break through the brick wall we keep hitting our heads against?"

"Let me think about it," Will answered, "Let's all think about it. Every little bit helps."

*****

Their first real break came when Max told Gloria about a set of photos that were taken when they officially opened the café. "They are probably still in my computer," Max told her.

Accessing Max's computer, still in the Prince George's County Homicide evidence room, proved to be one more challenge for the trio. Gloria filed a formal request, claiming that she needed it to prepare for a stay of execution hearing in front of a federal judge. When Will thought the authorities were dragging their feet he threatened a petition campaign. Finally, seeing no possible harm, the chief of the department agreed to let no more than two members of Max's legal team have limited access. Mark and Gloria were led into a small room in the basement of the courthouse where they were told that they had 30 minutes – not a minute more.

It only took a few minutes for Mark to copy and send all of the contents of the hard drive to Will in a scrambled e-mail. They spent the rest of the time trying to look busy until the guard walked over and told them they had to close up and leave.

Chapter 50
Wednesday, April 22, 2009,
Washington, D.C., 5:11 A.M.

Will and Mark alternated with each other in 4 hour shifts within sight of the address they had for Jeffrey's uncle, armed with several thermos bottles of black coffee and a single head shot of Jeffrey taken during the café grand opening ceremony.

Shortly after 5:00 o'clock Mark sat up and dialed his father's cell phone. "I got him," he whispered into his phone.

"Great! Don't let him get out of your sight and definitely do not let him spot you. I'll be there as fast as I can."

Two men, one of whom clearly matched the photo of Jeffrey on Mark's sun visor slowly walked out of the front entrance and began jogging down the street. Mark got out of his car and followed several hundred yards behind.

Almost an hour later, as the men returned to the building, they waived at the doorman and he opened the door for them, Mark continued on towards his car. Will was already seated in the front passenger seat.

"That's him all right." Will said as Mark entered the car. "Can we assume that Jeffrey's uncle is the other guy?"

"I don't know. They seemed to be having a heated discussion during their jog. Whoever it is was by his side seemed to be in complete control of the conversation."

"What makes you say that?" Will said.

"Jeffrey seemed to be hanging on the other guy's every word." Mark said.

They sat staring at the building entrance.

"So, now what do we do?" Mark asked.

"I think we need to know if the other man is *the* uncle and if not, then who he is. After all, he may just be a guy letting Jeffrey crash for a while until he bounces back from the bankruptcy and resulting loss of steady income. You know, as Freud said, 'Sometimes a cigar is just a cigar'. If Jeffrey – alone or with help – actually did engineer a frame on Max and this other guy helped him to do it, uncle or no uncle, then we still have to find out why. And if Jeffrey, with or without anyone else's help did engineer a frame then we will have to get some proof before they disappear into the wind like old P.H. did. But proving any of that could take more time than Max has left." Will began reviewing a series of photos he had taken of the other man.

Thinking out loud, speaking to no one in particular, Will said, "I know I never saw this man before but he sure reminds me of someone I *have* seen before. This is really strange."

*****

Over the days that followed Will and Mark were able to map out a fairly regular routine. Each morning, rain or shine, the 'maybe uncle' and only occasionally, Jeffrey, walked and jogged for the better part of an hour, then returned to the building until the next morning. Each day's route never varied from the ones before. Will guessed that anything they might want or need was brought to them by one or more of the many delivery people who went in and out of the building during the day and night.

Although numerous people came and went to and from the other buildings on the block, there did not seem to be any other tenants or guests of tenants in the building Mark now referred to as, 'uncle's place'. The building's doormen changed shifts at 8:00 A.M., 4:00 P.M. and at midnight, on the dot, every day including weekends. Each one stood stiffly inside the entrance, more like trained guards than people whose primary function was limited to the opening and closing of doors and greeting of visitors.

There was a scrambler, probably on the roof of the building, which made it impossible to tap into any audio or video communications entering or leaving the building.

*****

Will kept thinking that something about the "maybe uncle" was familiar but he couldn't quite pin it down. It hung in the air until one hot day in late May; Mark bought two ice cream cones from a Mister Softie truck and gave one to Will. Will placed his cone on the dashboard in order to put his camera away. The cone fell over and smudged the windshield.

As he looked at the mess forming between the dashboard and the bottom of the windshield an image of the *Jersey Freeze* sign flashed into his mind. It was there for just a split second, little more than a blink. He quickly sat up, staring at the cone. Another single frame popped into his consciousness of Phineas Harper placing the cone under his windshield wiper. Will was breathing heavily now.

Mark stared at him and said, "Pop, are you alright?" Will said nothing for what seemed like an eternity and then began to pound on the steering wheel with both fists. He slapped his forehead with his right palm and began yelling, "That son of a bitch! That damn son of a bitch!"

"Hey," Mark yelled back. "Are you going crazy on me? It's only a little custard. We can clean it off easy. Here, I'll do it."

Will slammed his hand on top of his son's and held it in

place while grinning from ear to ear. "I think I just figured out who Jeffrey's uncle is," Will screamed, repeatedly banging his other hand on the steering wheel.

"Hey, you're making a scene here, calm down," Mark pleaded.

Will scooped up the remains of the cone and threw it out of the window. He started the car and pulled out of the parking space. "Damn him to hell, Jeffrey's jogging buddy is the one and only, Phineas Harper!"

"How can you be so sure?" Mark shouted to be heard over the traffic sounds.

"It's him all right. Phineas damn Harper. Evil has a new face but it is still him!" Will kept yelling as he headed towards the interstate highway. "That damn son of a bitch has been under our noses all of this time!"

Chapter 51
Wednesday, June 3, 2009,
Queen City Creamery,
Cumberland, Maryland, 9:27 A.M.

"Max confirms that the man you are following is Jeffrey. He remembers seeing the other man in the café from time to time but didn't think that the two knew each other away from the store. He wanted to know how you can be so certain that the other man is the O.O.T.A.P. guy we beat last time around. He didn't see any resemblance in the pictures I showed him, and frankly, neither do I," Gloria said.

"I can't explain how he converted himself from the mass of fat to this 'hard body specimen' with the posture of a Marine, but it is him all right; he may now be 70-75 pounds lighter and he may have a completely different face but that sneer, that evil mocking sneer is still there and there is also 'the walk'. I will never forget his distinctive self-satisfied, overconfident, walk; its smug and arrogant Phineas all right; the very same Phineas that we loathed before is back again and this time we need to make absolutely certain that he does not get away again."

"It would certainly answer how Max was framed in such a ghastly way. And yes," Gloria persisted, "I have definitely learned not to doubt you. But I have studied those pictures; Max has studied those pictures; there is absolutely no resemblance at all."

"With today's modern surgery techniques you can change facial features but the best surgeon cannot alter your DNA and we have independent confirmation that this person's DNA is a 100% match of the person we all knew as P.H."

"Please," she persisted, "tell me more."

"We have been following him on his morning jogs for a while now. He is a creature of habit. Very little change of any kind from day to day to day. Seems he has picked up an appreciation for Juicy Fruit gum. Every day we watched him put two fresh pieces in his mouth as soon as he hit the street each morning. He then crumbles the wrappers, stuffs them into his pocket – always the right pants pocket - and then the run begins. Each and every day, just before he starts his return, he spits the gum into the gutter and replaces it with two fresh pieces. Once again, the crumbled wrappers go into his right pants pocket, and off he goes.

On a few of these days we simply scooped up the chewed gum and had it analyzed. There is absolutely no doubt, our new 'fit as a Marine gum chewer' is the one and only fat blob we knew as P.H., no doubt, none, zilch, not a chance in a million, no, make that no chance in a billion, period, end of story."

"But that doesn't prove he was behind the murder and then arranged for it to be pinned on Max," Gloria responded.

"We will need real proof, Dad," Mark said, "and I can't see any way to get proof while he is living in that fortress of his."

"Even if we got proof," Gloria interrupted, "it would take a miracle to reverse Max's conviction."

Will sat quietly staring at the picture of Jeffrey's uncle. "Maybe not a miracle," Will said, a broad grin beginning to form, "maybe just a 'McSimmons'."

Chapter 52
Early summer, 1974,
Republican National Committee Headquarters, Washington, D.C.

In the summer of 1974, Theo McSimmons was the national chairman of the Republican Party. Trip Morganstein, a well-placed lobbyist, known around "K" Street as the president's favorite fundraiser with the full support and backing of the local O.O.T.A.P. organization, went to McSimmons demanding that he use a list, Morganstein would provide, as his primary source for picking state republican financial directors and lead money managers for the party.

McSimmons told him what he could do with his list and threw Morganstein out of his office.

The next morning, McSimmons arrived at his office only to find all of his personal belongings in brown boxes stacked along the wall outside of his old office; the lock had been changed during the night. He went to the head of security who handed him a typed letter of resignation to sign.

Gerald Ford, then a sitting vice president, went to Nixon to demand that McSimmons get his job back. "He has always been a straight shooter. Morganstein was out of line and you know it," the country's first non elected vice president told the president. "When I agreed to become your vice president you promised me that these kinds of shenanigans would stop."

Nixon promised to look into the matter but never did. Several months later, when Gerald Ford became president he appointed McSimmons to be a judge on the U.S. Third Circuit Court of Appeals, a lifetime appointment. Many believed that Ford's pardon of Nixon cost him the next election but Washington insiders and Ford himself knew that it was Ford's defense of McSimmons, over the demands of the O.O.T.A.P. Washington council, that was responsible for his ultimate loss of the presidency.

A few key decision makers within the Republican Party met secretly in San Clemente, California 10 days after Nixon's resignation took effect. The small, influential group still looked to Richard Nixon for guidance. They openly discussed the probable consequences of losing the White House against turning it into a 'learning experience' and opted for the latter. "Whoever the Dems put up will never get reelected after he beats Jerry, so we will be out for only 4 years."

Nixon said, "Next time we can run that actor, Reagan, we'll make sure that he will win and when we get the power back, and we will get the power back, we should be able to hold it for the next 20 years, maybe more."

*****

Many years earlier, McSimmons represented a much younger Will James in the computer hacking case brought by a sub agency of the Department of Defense. Even though McSimmons lost the case a strong bond and mutual respect formed between him and his young client, lasting until McSimmons died of a sudden heart attack on Christmas Eve, 2012.

*****

Sunday, June 7, 2009, the Washington, D.C. National Zoo, 10:15 A.M.

Federal Judge Theo McSimmons was already there when Will and Mark entered the zoo. McSimmons gave Will a hug and pinched Mark's cheek. "You look thinner than the last time I saw you," the judge said to Will, "and I thought you were thin as a rail then." Then he turned to Mark, "And you, thank God you got your looks from your mother."

They all laughed. McSimmons asked, "So, what brings you two to the national zoo at this ungodly hour?"

"I have a gift for you," Will said.

"I would have thought that you knew better than to try to bribe a federal judge, young man."

"This is a gift that you have been wanting for a very long time."

"You don't say."

"I do say."

"Should I have checked you to see if you are wearing a wire?"

Again, they all laughed.

Will pointed to a bench along the walkway. "Let's step into my office, Judge."

"Okay, you have my full attention," McSimmons said.

"I would like to offer you Phineas Harper's head on a platter," Will slowly whispered.

McSimmons looked around and moved closer to Will. "He's yesterday's news, Will. He is probably hiding in some deep dark cave in Africa right now. Move on with your life, he definitely has."

"What would you say if I told you that he not only is *not* in some cave in Africa but as we speak he is less than a 15 minute drive from this very bench?"

"That just cannot be, Will."

"Now Judge, you know me well enough. I would never tell you something if it wasn't a verifiable fact."

"Even if he was still in the country, which would be more careless than he has ever been known to be, or living in D.C., which would be beyond reckless even for him, he can't hurt anyone anymore."

"Unfortunately, he can and he has and I was hoping you would help me bring him down, once and for all."

McSimmons sat quietly, staring at Will.

"I am not asking you to help just for the sake of getting some quick revenge," Will said softly. "I think he is responsible for the murder of an innocent young woman and that he engineered that murder merely to frame an innocent and good man who is now twiddling his thumbs on death row. Please, I need your help, Judge."

"This new crime you speak of," McSimmons asked, "did it occur in the U.S. Third Circuit?"

"No, the crime was committed in Maryland."

"Close but no cigar."

"So the great Theo McSimmons is no longer interested in justice when and wherever it was being abused and only cares about geographic boundary lines?"

"Don't be flippant, Will. I don't deserve that from you."

"And my friend doesn't deserve to languish on death row either. Who do you think deserves more of my consideration – you or him?"

McSimmons started to get up from the bench. Mark came forward, wedging himself between the two men. "Please Judge, hear us out. Please."

McSimmons stared at Will, turned to look into Mark's face, "You have your mother's looks *and* common sense, what a great combination."

"And I also have a sense of right and wrong that I learned from both my mom and dad."

McSimmons smiled, "Ókay Will, talk facts, not emotion, *facts;* verifiable, impartial, non-contestable facts."

Will began with what he called a 'Readers Digest' version of their first struggle with O.O.T.A.P. The judge sat quietly; he didn't comment or ask any questions, he just listened.

Then Will talked about the murder and his son's friend's trial and conviction. Now McSimmons stopped Will several times to ask questions or to confirm a source for a specific comment.

Finally, Will shared how he and Mark located Jeffrey and the man he kept referring to as 'the reincarnated P.H.'.

When Will finally said, "That's all I have," the judge put his hand on Will's shoulder and softly said, "Specifically; in so many words, what are you asking me to do?"

"You're a sitting Federal Judge. If you have been listening to me at all I shouldn't have to tell you what to do, or have you lost *your* way Judge McSimmons?"

"Don't patronize me. We both know that this new crime did not occur in my district. We have more than enough on our plates without reaching into another district to try to grab more to do. Federal judges don't look kindly at other federal justices looking over their shoulders. I'm a few short years away from retirement and do not need to end my career in this way."

"When did you choose what's nice and safe over what's

right?" Will asked.

"When did you decide to be chief investigator, judge and jury and chief decider on who lives and who dies?"

Mark looked on quietly as the two men sparred.

Will put his hands up, "Okay," he said, "for the time being, forget about this particular murder; forget about this young woman whose only wrongdoing seems to be that she was in the wrong place at the wrong time; forget about Mark's friend on death row; forget that we are talking about someone who has destroyed numerous careers and lives and single handedly turned scores of otherwise good and honest people into terrified and pathetically spineless individuals – and even felons. Concentrate *only* on this one inexplicably evil human being. Do you really think that anyone is safe as long as he breathes free air?"

"One more time," the judge interrupted, "what are you asking me to do, specifically?"

"I would like you to consider the DNA results and if you agree that we have located the person for whom numerous outstanding warrants – and let me remind you that these are federal warrants - currently exist; I would ask you to issue a search warrant for the premises and have him taken into custody. I am also suggesting you issue a warrant for the arrest and questioning of the other man you will almost certainly find at the same address; the man we believe to be his nephew; the man we suggest embezzled money, moving it across state lines, which I think may *also* be a federal offense; for this charge I would turn over analysis of an independent forensic accountant. That is what I am *'asking you to do - specifically.'*"

"And if these two men can show that the charges have no basis in fact?"

"If that were to happen we would all be in well over our heads *and* in the very deepest of trouble," Will said, in a low, monotonous tone.

"Exactly!" The judge yelled.

"But I don't think anyone will find these two men to be innocent of these charges. Not for one single moment," Will said.

"You had better be right, Will, or we will all look back on this little visit to the zoo as the biggest mistake in our collective lives."

"I suggest we will look back on this day as one where all the good guys won." Will said as he reached out to shake McSimmons' hand.

Chapter 53
Tuesday, June 9, 2009,
Washington, D.C., 1:32 P.M.

A large brown UPS truck pulled up in front of the three-story building. The driver, dressed in the familiar brown uniform, stepped out of the truck carrying a huge carton. The doorman opened the door and was heard yelling, "All deliveries must be made in the rear of the building."

"Gee, I'm new on the route," the driver responded, "and really running late. Can't you make an exception?"

"Sorry, pal. Rules are rules."

"Please, I can't afford to lose my job and I am already a good hour late."

"We all have our little crosses to bare, just drive it around the block."

"Please, I got three kids and a wife, just this time. Please."

The doorman looked around, "Okay, fine. Let me sign for it."

"Oh! I can't let anyone sign for it but the person it is addressed to."

"You're the one in a hurry. It's me or no one."

"But it says 'highly perishable, must be delivered and signed for by addressee, by Tuesday, June 9. If I take it back to the depot it won't be redelivered before the 11th. Whoever ordered it isn't going to be very happy."

"Hey, you're beginning to make me mad. I'm already stretching the rules for you."

"In the same time you have just taken to tell me why I can't bring it in and have the correct person sign for it I could have been done and I would have already been on my way to the next delivery location."

"All right! All right!" The doorman finally screamed, "But first I will have to scan the contents." He told the driver to put the box on a table and ran a hand held wand around it. Seeming satisfied that it contained no explosives he put the wand away and then said, "Just let's get this done quickly."

The driver and the doorman went to the elevator which was fully visible to anyone standing outside of the building. The doorman pressed the button for penthouse and when the door opened he took the package from the UPS driver and carried it into the elevator. He cautioned the UPS driver to wait in the lobby and not touch a thing until he returned. As soon as the elevator door closed the back door of the UPS truck opened and out poured a stream of men, each dressed in battle fatigues and a dark blue jacket with huge F.B.I. letters on the back. Each also had full military gear and a short barreled shotgun. Most of the men circled the outside perimeter of the building. Three rushed into the front door and joined up with the first driver, the four of them headed up the stairway.

A police bus with flashing lights pulled up alongside the UPS truck and additional armed individuals got out. They rapidly took charge of the area, leading all civilians that were in the immediate area away from the building.

About 10 minutes later the front door opened and a man with a black cloth hood over his head was led out of the building; his hands behind his back in heavy metal cuffs. As soon as he exited the building a dark blue car with F.B.I. painted on the top of the car and on the driver's side door drove onto the sidewalk next to the front entrance. The hand cuffed individual was quickly pushed into the back seat of the car, followed by an armed guard on each side of him. Two other persons wearing jackets with huge letters saying 'FBI' on the back, slammed the doors shut, banged their hands on the roof of the car and the car sped away from the area.

Minutes later, another hooded and hand cuffed individual was led out of the building. Again, a marked F.B.I. car was driven onto the sidewalk and the hooded individual was pushed into the rear passenger seat, joined by an armed guard on either side. The door was quickly closed and the car soon disappeared down the street.

Later that afternoon a crew installed huge spot lights that shined a steady beam of light on the building from various positions in the street; barriers and police tape were set up and guards were positioned at 3 foot intervals around the building. A series of television and radio news casters began arriving and set up to do remote reports from just outside of the police perimeter. Several did interviews of local residents and passersby but no one seemed to know why there had been so much police activity in the area. There were speculations about a meth lab in the building or a bomb threat but no one knew for certain.

Over the next 6 and ½ hours, a stream of boxes and huge black garbage bags were carried from the building to waiting vans and ultimately driven away. The 'carnival atmosphere' continued for almost a week.

Life, as it had been known before, soon returned to normal on the well-manicured block.

*****

Later that day without much fanfare Max was removed from death row and taken to a holding cell. He would remain in the holding cell for several more days and then quietly released after all charges were dropped by order of the United States Attorney General.

No official public statement was ever issued. The record of his trial and various filings were stricken from the record.

When asked about a rumor that the Regina Blankly murderer had been released, the Governor laughed and told the reporter that the only way the murderer would leave that prison would be in a pine box. He then declined to make any further comments about the crime – ever.

*****

Phillip Haskins alias Patrick Hernaldo alias Phineas Illia Harper was never officially charged with any crime. One evening, armed with a letter signed by the President of the United States and referencing his powers under the 'Uniting (and) Strengthening America (by) Providing Appropriate Tools Required (to) Intercept (and) Obstruct Terrorism Act of 2001.' Also known as the USA PATRIOT ACT. Haskins/Hernaldo/Harper was blindfolded and with heavy shackles placed on his hands and feet was put on an Air Force jet and flown to the Cheyenne Mountain Complex in Colorado, an underground base, located nearly a half mile under a solid granite mountain.

He was placed in a 10 x 7 room under a 24 hour suicide watch. He was restricted from any other part of the base. Meals were brought to him three times each day.

He received medical care, as and when necessary in his cell.

No mail was permitted either in or out.

No official record of either his transfer into this facility or his time at the facility, was ever filed.

Richie/Jeffrey turned state's evidence, agreeing to testify in open court *for* the government and although he never actually had to testify he was placed into the custody of United States Marshals and given a new identity under WITSEC, the Witness Protection Program, set up under Title V of the Organized Crime Control Act of 1970.

He opted to leave the program two years, 7 months and 4 days later.

He died in his sleep, shortly after returning to his old identity.

His death was recorded as due to natural causes.

Chapter 54
Monday, July 1, 2013,
Ann Arbor, Michigan, 6:42 P.M.

During the first few months after Max was released from prison he wandered around, aimlessly. There had been a reward posted for the apprehension and conviction of Phineas Illia Harper and Gloria and Will James lobbied the government to award it to Max. When it was finally offered to him, he refused to accept it. Gloria convinced the authorities to hold it in trust for Max.

Max was offered a new identity but refused that as well.

He kept in touch with Gloria for a while but eventually dropped out of sight.

A little more than a year after his last visit with her she opened her mailbox and mixed in with her mail was a legal sized envelope addressed to her. There was no stamp or post mark on it.

She instinctively knew it was from or about him.

She sat on the curb, in front of her home, and opened the envelope.

Tears welled up in her eyes as she read and reread the contents.

Sometime later her husband opened the front door and walked over to her. He sat down on the curb, next to her. She handed him the letter. He read it, put his arms around her and held her closely as she began to sob.

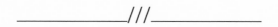

_____///_____

AUTHOR'S NOTES:

The President's official visitors log for Wednesday, 29 January, 1806 shows that President Thomas Jefferson had no visitors or official duties during this day.

According to the Hartford Courant of Thursday, 30 January, 1806, "...the President spent a quiet day yesterday resting up from a slight respiratory illness."

Future historians never found any official record to confirm that the meeting referred to, between the individuals named and witnessed by Jefferson's body man, ever took place – on that day or any other day before or since.

Not one of the six men in the 'sanctuary' that afternoon – Thomas Jefferson, President of the United States; Aaron Burr, former Vice President of the United States; Nathaniel Macon, Speaker of the House of Representatives; John Breckinridge, United States Attorney General; James Philthrow, aid to former Vice President Aaron Burr; Horace Freeman, servant; ever spoke or wrote publicly about the events of that afternoon. Horace Freeman did share the details of the contentious meeting later that evening with his wife, Becky, as they cuddled together against the extreme cold. However, he knew she would never share these details with any living person.

THE FOLLOWING ENTRY WAS AMONG THE PAGES SALVAGED FROM BECKY FREEMAN'S DIARY:

"Horace watched in horror as Mr. Tom leaned his flintlock rifle out of the window took careful aim and shot James Philthrow as he left the President's House. The shot hit him but did not kill him immediately. He laid there, slowly bleeding to death on the lawn for about 10 hours. Time after time, during those long hours as that wounded man begged for mercy, Horace first asked then begged Mr. Tom to be permitted to go out on the lawn to assist Mr. Philthrow, Horace said that each time the President told Horace that he did not want Horace or anyone else to help 'the traitor'. Horace agreed with me, nobody deserves to die like that, nobody."

Only one reference to a "murder on the white house lawn" has ever been made. In 2001, in the theatrical movie, "Swordfish", one of the main characters speaks about President Thomas Jefferson executing a traitor by shooting him on the White House lawn. In the movie, the name of the traitor is given as Rodney Cox of North Carolina.

There have been neither published census records nor any other public record of the day that confirms the existence of a Rodney Cox nor do they confirm the charge of President Jefferson killing Mr. Cox or anyone else on the lawn that day, before that day or after that day.

The newspapers of the day, many of whom were deeply beholden to O.O.T.A.P. printed the Auxiliary Watch Captain's final report three weeks later. It was a brief statement in which he declared that the murder on the night of 9 January, 1806 along the waterway of the Potomac River was the result of a random robbery by person or persons unknown. No suspects were ever brought to justice for this crime.

Thomas Jefferson's
actual tombstone

References to the crime were later removed from all public records.

Although other reasons were assumed it is believed that the confrontation reported here between Aaron Burr and James Philthrow haunted Thomas Jefferson for the rest of his life. Years later, when Jefferson wrote the epitaph that would be placed onto his tombstone after his death, no mention was made of his having been successful in two separate elections for President of the United States. (He demanded that not a word be changed from the epitaph as he wrote it.)

John Breckinridge died on 14 December, 1806 at the age of 46. Privately, the Kentucky Council of O.O.T.A.P claimed full responsibility. This was never proven.

The next year, in 1807, Aaron Burr was charged with treason on another matter. He was ultimately found innocent of all charges. The presiding judge and two of the prosecuting attorneys were known to be local board members of the Virginia Council of the O.O.T.A.P.

Nathaniel Macon died 4 March, 1807 of natural causes. He was 79 years of age at the time.

No public reference has ever been made of James Philthrow. His name never appeared on a census report or any other official document. It is as if he never lived much less crossed paths with the third president of the United States.

The fictional character in this novel, Will James, was inspired by an American hacker who was actually the first juvenile incarcerated for cybercrime in the United States December 12, 1983. The real life hacker was 15 years old at the time of the first offense and 16 years old on the date of his sentencing. He died on May 18, 2008, of a self-inflicted gunshot wound. Between August 23, 1999, and October 27, 1999, he committed a series of intrusions into various systems, including those of BellSouth and the Miami-Dade school system. What brought him to the attention of federal authorities was his intrusion into the computers of the Defense Threat Reduction Agency, a division of the United States Department of Defense, the primary function of which was to analyze potential threats to the United States of America, both at home and abroad. He later admitted to authorities that he had installed an unauthorized backdoor in a computer server in Dulles, Virginia, which he used to install a sniffer that allowed him to intercept over three thousand messages passing to and from DTRA employees, along with numerous usernames and passwords of other DTRA employees, including at least 10 on official military computers.

The hacker was formally indicted six months later. On September 21, 2000, he entered into an agreement with U.S. Attorney: he would plead guilty to two counts of juvenile delinquency in exchange for a lenient sentence. He was sentenced to six months house arrest and probation until the age of eighteen, and was required to write letters of apology to NASA and the Department of Defense. He was also banned from using computers for recreational purposes. He later violated that probation when he tested positive for drug use and was then subsequently taken into custody by the United States Marshals Service and flown to an Alabama federal correctional facility where he ultimately served six months. Legal experts have suggested that, given the extent of his intrusions, he could have served at least ten years for his crimes if he had been an adult. Both Attorney General Janet Reno and prosecuting attorney Guy Lewis issued statements claiming the case was proof the Justice Department was willing to get tough with juvenile offenders accused of cybercrime.

Although the murder of Regina Blankly,depicted in this novel, is purely fictional and the product of the author's imagination, there are similarities to an actual murder of Stefanie S. Watson, a 27 year old hospital worker from Laurel, Maryland. Ms Watson's murder occurred in July, 1982 and is officially unsolved as of the writing of this novel. The author drew heavily from various Washington Post, Laurel Leader, and Baltimore Sun newspaper articles of the time as well as a follow up story written 30 years after the murder by Richard Friend.

*****

Hebrew theologians list four things

that a man should do during his lifetime...

...have a child

...plant a tree

...read a book

...write a book.

My list is now complete.

−Martin Herman

This book is historical fiction –events and incidents describe are either the products of the author's imagination or used in a fictitious manner. Any resemblance to actual persons, living or dead, or actual events is purely coincidental. The following published works and factual sources *were* used to add historic structure and background to this original work:

The President's House, by William Seale, White House Historical Association, 1986

Thomas Jefferson & the new nation by Merrill D. Peterson, Oxford University Press – copyright 1970.

The Essential Thomas Jefferson edited by John Gabriel Hunt, Gramercy Books – copyright 1994

Jefferson's America by Norman K. Risjord, Madison House Publishers – copyright 1991

The Papers of Thomas Jefferson edited by Julian P. Boyd, Princeton University Press – copyright 1950

The Secret City: A History of Race Relations in the Nation's Capital by Constance Green, Princeton, 1967

Behind the Scenes or Thirty Years a Slave and Four Years in the White House by Elizabeth Keckley (Reprint edition) Oxford and New York: Oxford University Press, 1988.

Thomas Jefferson -- from *American Presidents: Life Portraits* -- C-SPAN

Thomas Jefferson -- PBS

Thomas Jefferson Heritage Society; tjheritage.org

monticello.org

Thomas Jefferson papers, 1775-1825; amphilsoc.org

Something That Will Surprise The World: the Essential Writings of the Founding Fathers, edited by Susan Dunn, Basic Books, NY - 2006

WhiteHouseMuseum.org

answers.com

justice.gov

VisitCharlottesville.org

The true Jonathan James hacking case:

Newton, Michael (2004). *The Encyclopedia of High-Tech Crime and Crime-Fighting*. Checkmark Books, an imprint of Facts on File Inc. ISBN 0-8160-4979-3.

"Obituary: Jonathan Joseph James" (in The Miami Herald). 2008-05-21. Retrieved 2008-05-21.

Poulsen, Kevin (2009-07-09). "Former Teen Hacker's Suicide Linked to TJX Probe". Wired. Retrieved 2009-10-29.

Grossman, M. "Computer crime: Changing the pub s perception". *The Miami Herald*, October 12, 2000.

Top 10 Most Famous Hackers of All Time crash override at ITsecurity.com

Harrison, L. "Bedroom NASA hacker set to bite pillow in choky". *The Register*, September 22, 2000. Retrieved March 4, 2007.

Lynch, I. "Nasa hacker gets six months downtime". *Information World Review*, November 21, 2000. Retrieved March 4, 2007.

Stout, D. (2000). "Youth Sentenced in Government Hacking Case". *The New York Times*, September 23, 2000. Retrieved March 4, 2007.

Zetter, Kim (2009-06-18). "TJX Hacker Was Awash in Cash; His Penniless Coder Faces Prison". Wired. Retrieved 2013-01-26.

How Swiss Bank Accounts Work, (article)by Lee Ann Obringer

U.S. charges oldest Swiss bank in tax fraud case, (article) by James O'Toole@CNNMoney – Feb. 2,2012 - about The Swiss bank Wegelin and Co., founded 1741

calendars.com

dayoftheweek.org

history.com/this-day-in-history

ipl2, a website merging the collections from the Internet Public Library (IPL) and the Librarians' Internet Index (LII) websites

Child, Hamilton, Gazetteer and Business Directory of Sullivan County, NY for 1872-73

Spock on Spock: a Memoir of Growing Up With the Century (1989)

Bart Barnes, "Pediatrician Benjamin Spock Dies", The Washington Post, Tuesday, March 17, 1998; Page A01.

Biography of Spock at drspock.com

"Remembering Dr. Spock". The NewsHour with Jim Lehrer. 1998-03-16. PBS. http://www.pbs.org/newshour/bb/health/jan-june98/spock_3-16.html. Retrieved 2009-05-28.

http://www.hopital-necker.aphp.fr

The start of life: a history of obstetrics

http://wiki.answers.com/Q/Who_invented_the_incubator_for_premature_babies

http://www.ask.com/web?qs-rc=1&o=0&l=dir&q=When+and+where+were+infant+incubators+and+radiant+warmers+invented+and+first+usedF

pediatrics.aappublications.org/content/108/2/395

www.neonatology.org/tour/equipment.html Jan 25, 2002

http://www.babyzone.com/pregnancy/pregnancy-complications/premature-baby-survival-rates_79273

Q&A: What's the survival rate for babies born at 32 weeks? by Dr. Karen Sadler

kidshealth.org/PageManager.jsp?dn=KidsHealth&lic=A Primer on Preemies - KidsHealth

www.medicalexpo.com/medical-manufacturer/infant-incubat...

http://www.ctparenting.com/childdevelopment_pregnancy.php?gclid=CNK8rOfs_LcCFaZlOgoda28AAQ

Possible Complications during Pregnancy (Women'sHealth.gov)

http://answers.yahoo.com/question/index-?qid=20070808100146AAY9Ctq "What is the survival rate for the baby that is born 2 months premature?"

Ballbriga, Angel (1991). "'One century of pediatrics in Europe (section: development of pediatric hospitals in Europe)'". In Nichols, Burford L. et al. (eds). History of Paediatrics 1850–1950. Nestlé Nutrition Workshop Series 22. New York, NY: Raven Press. pp. 6–8. ISBN 0-88167-695-0.

http://www.necker.fr/

http://en.wikipedia.org/w/index.php?title=Necker-Enfants_Malades_Hospital&oldid=555914272"

René-Théophile-Hyacinthe Laennec[1] (French: [laɛnɛk]; 17 February 1781 – 13 August 1826) was a French physician. He invented the stethoscope in 1816, while working at the Hôpital Necker and pioneered its use in diagnosing various chest conditions.

Bloch, Harry (1993). "The inventor of the stethoscope: Rene Laennec Journal of Family Practice – Find Articles". Journal of Family Practice. Retrieved 2007-10-11.

"CATHOLIC ENCYCLOPEDIA: Renee-Theophile-Hyacinthe Laennec". Retrieved 2007-10-11.

Scherer, John R. (2007). "Before cardiac MRI: Rene Laennec (1781–1826) and the invention of the stethoscope". Cardiology Journal 14 (5): 518–519. PMID 18651515. Retrieved 9 December 2008.

Bloch, Harry (1993). "Dr Connor's technique". Journal of Family Practice. Retrieved 29 November 2009.

Pregnancy Questions and Answers (PregnancySurvey.com)

Holiday Inn Cumberland Downtown website

http://www.queencitycreamery.com

http://www.ask.com/wiki/North_Branch_Correctional_Institution

www.habtech.ca/

Complete Correctional Security Systems

Calver, Scott. "Death row inmates transferred to W. Maryland". The Baltimore Sun. Retrieved 5 May 2013.

"Division of Correction Annual Report Fiscal Year 2011". State of Maryland. Retrieved 5 May 2013.

"Department of Public Safety and Correctional Services Proposed Budget 2013". Maryland Department of Public Safety and Correctional Services. Retrieved 5 May 2013.

"Allegany County, Maryland Major Employer List". Allegany County Department of Economic and Community Development. Retrieved 5 May 2013.

Helderman, Rosalind. "In Surprise Move, Maryland Closes Jessup Prison, Transfers Inmates". The Washington Post. Retrieved 5 May 2013.

"State-of-the-Art Maryland Prison Will Be Most Technologically Advanced in the World". Building Design and Construction. Retrieved 5 May 2013.

Garland, Greg. "'This is the End of the Line Here'". The Baltimore Sun. Retrieved 5 May 2013.

McCann, Rick. "25 Correction Officers Fired During Investigation". National Association of Private Officers. Private Officer News Network. Retrieved 5 May 2013.

Dishneau, David. "13 Fired Maryland Correctional Officers Released Without Bail". The Public Opinion. The Associated Press. Retrieved 5 May 2013.

"NBCI Inmate Found Dead of Apparent Homicide". The Cumberland Times-News. Retrieved 5 May 2013.

Associated Press. "Inmate Death After Assault Ruled A Homicide". CBS Baltimore. Retrieved 5 May 2013.

"NBCI Inmate Charged with Killing Cellmate". Cumberland Times-News. Retrieved 5 May 2013.

"Inmate's Death in Cumberland Ruled A Homocide". The Herald-Mail.

http://deathpenalty.procon.org/view.resource.php?resourceID=001172

"Death Penalty Information by State," www.deathpenaltyinfo.org (accessed July 18, 2012)

US Department of Justice (USDOJ) US Bureau of Justice Statistics (USBJS), "Publications & Products: Capital Punishment," bjs.ojp.usdoj.gov (accessed July 18, 2012)

Joe Sutton, "Maryland Governor Signs Death Penalty Repeal," cnn.com, May 2, 2013

Maryland's death Penalty - NACDL

"Kirk Bloodsworth," Innocence Project, at http://www.innocenceproject.org/Content/Kirk_Bloodsworth.php.

truthinjustice.org/suttonDNA.htm.

Garrett, Brandon L., and Peter J. Neufeld. "Invalid Forensic Science Testimony and Wrongful Convictions."

Virginia Law Review 95(1): 1-97.

John K. Roman, Chalfin, Aaron and Knight, Carly R., Reassessing the Cost of the Death Penalty Using Quasi-Experimental Methods: Evidence from Maryland (Fall 2009). American Law and Economics Review, Vol. 11, Issue 2, pp. 530-574, 2009.

www.goccp.maryland.gov capital-punishment/public-hearing-sep-5.php

"Maryland's Death Penalty: Sill here, Still Unfair. More Arbitrary and Costly"

Brandon L. Garrett, and Peter J. Neufeld. "Invalid Forensic Science Testimony and Wrongful Convictions." Virginia Law Review 95(1): 1-97

http://www.washingtonpost.com/wp-dyn/articles/ Susan Levine, Washington Post, Monday, June 14, 2004

"New death penalty law, appeals delay trials in killing of correctional officer," July 25, 20111, Andrea F. Siegel, The Baltimore Sun, http://articles.baltimoresun.com

"Executions by County," Death Penalty Information Center, http://deathpenaltyinfo.org/executionscounty

Type One Diabetes Information By Jennifer Burdett, eHow Contributor

www.ehow.com/facts_5134765_type-one-diabetes-information.html#ixzz2Xx6W1ECF

http://www.calendarlabs.com/online-calendar.php?y=2009

http://www.ask.com/wiki/United_States_federal_judge

Saikrishna Prakash & Steven D. Smith, "How To Remove a Federal Judge", 116 Yale L.J. 72 (2006).

"Judicial Salaries Since 1968". uscourts.gov.

"2006 Year-End Report on the Federal Judiciary" (PDF). supreme-court.us.

"FAQs on Federal Judges". uscourts.gov.

"Federal Judgeships". uscourts.gov.

http://www.ehow.com/info_8259548_duties-circuit-court-appeals-judge.html

Stephanie Reid : (eHow) What Are the Duties of the Third Circuit Court of Appeals Judge?

http://www.ehow.com/info_8259548_duties-circuit-court-appeals-judge.html

www.BankruptcyCentral.com

www.nndb.com/people/400/000022334/Gerald Ford

www.MapsGalaxy.com

"Nixon Resigns" By Carroll Kilpatrick, Washington Post Staff Writer, Friday, August 9, 1974; Page A01

bop.gov/locations/institutions/"Federal Bureau of Prisons/ Prison Types & General Information"
"Strange Military Bases - The World's 18 Strangest Military Bases"- Popular Mechanics By Chris Sweeney
Cheyenne Mountain Complex Air Force Station, Colo.
http://www.ask.com/wiki/Patriot_Act
USA Patriot Act, enacted by the 107th United States Congress, October 26, 2001, Public Law 107-56;
(The title of the act is a ten letter bacronym (USA PATRIOT) Uniting (and) Strengthening America (by) Providing Appropriate Tools Required (to) Intercept (and) Obstruct Terrorism Act of 2001

SECTION: SECTION TITLE:

201   Authority to intercept wire, oral, and electronic communications relating to terrorism
202   Authority to intercept wire, oral, and electronic communications relating to computer fraud and abuse offenses
206   Roving surveillance authority under the Foreign Intelligence Surveillance Act of 1978
209   Seizure of voice-mail messages pursuant to warrants
212   Emergency disclosure of electronic communications to protect life and limb
215   Access to records and other items under the Foreign Intelligence Surveillance Act

Title III of the Act, titled "International Money Laundering Abatement and Financial Anti-Terrorism Act of 2001
Lithwick, Dahlia; Turner, Julia (September 8, 2003). "A Guide to the Patriot Act, Part 1". Jurisprudence (Slate).
"Apology Note from the United States Government". Washington Post. November 29, 2006.
"Surveillance Under the USA PATRIOT Act > Non surveillance provisions". American Civil Liberties Union. April 3, 2003. Retrieved July 11, 2008.
Gouvin, Eric J. "Bringing Out the Big Guns: The USA PATRIOT Act, Money Laundering and the War on Terrorism". Baylor Law Review 55 (2003): 955.
Cole, Dave, and James X. Dempsey. Terrorism and the Constitution: Sacrificing Civil Liberties in the Name of National Security. 2nd ed. New York: W. W. Norton & Co., 2002. ISBN 1-56584-782-2.
National Security Act of 1947 (1947)
The WITSEC program established under Title V of the Organized Crime Control Act of 1970, sets out the manner in which the United

States "Attorney General may provide for the relocation and protection of a witness or potential witness of the federal or state government in an official proceeding concerning organized crime or other serious offenses. 18 U.S.C.A 3521, et. seq."
http://deathpenaltyinfo.org/deterrence-states-without-death-penalty-havehad-consistently-lower-murder-rates .
"Stefanie Watson: What really happened 30 years ago?" August 7, 2012 by Richard Friend
lostlaurel.wordpress.com/2012/08/0
Courant newspaper article: "SUSPICIONS SWIRL IN DEATH AT BEACH CONVICTED MURDERER'S PRISON FURLOUGH COINCIDED WITH WOMAN'S GRUESOME KILLING" by Courant Staff Writers Dave Altimari, Jane E. Dee and Colin Poitras
"CRIME IN MARYLAND," Uniform Crime Reports published annually by the Maryland State Police
http://www.officialcoldcaseinvestigations.com/showthread.php?t=787 FBI's Behavioral Analysis Unit 2 Serial Murder Symposium:
"In multi-jurisdictional cases, variations in evidentiary standards, search warrant requirements, interview protocols, the quality of the evidence, and the ability to prosecute for capital murder may dictate the appropriate venue for prosecution. This consideration may take on greater significance when the crimes occur in different states."
http://www.angelfire.com/ct3/unsolvedct/
http://coldcaseexaminer.com

ABOUT THE AUTHOR

Martin Herman was born and raised in Brooklyn, New York. He has lived and worked in various parts of the country and currently lives midway up a small mountain with a breathtaking view of the Connecticut countryside and almost daily reminders of truly natural beauty, which he says is the only way to describe New England sunrises.

He managed businesses for several decades and since 1999 has been an independent business consultant serving *start-ups* and troubled mature businesses – here and abroad.

Since his early teens he has written short stories and full length novels for his own amusement; as his 75th birthday approached he published his first full length historical murder mystery and hasn't stopped since.

Mystery writing is what he does late at night and on long airplane flights.

Your comments and suggestions are not only welcomed but invited.

You can contact the author directly at:

mherman194@prodigy.net